PRAISE FOR THE ANNA STRONG, V

W9-BTT-252

"Urban fantasy with true depth and flair!"
—*Romantic Times* (4½ stars)

"As riveting as the rest . . . one of my favorite urban fantasy series."
—*Darque Reviews*

THE WATCHER

"Action fills every page, making this a novel that flies by . . . Dynamic relationships blend [with] complex mysteries in this thriller."
—*Huntress Book Reviews*

"An exciting, fast-paced novel . . . first-rate plotting."
—*LoveVampires*

"Dazzles readers with action-packed paranormal adventure, love and friendship. With many wonderfully executed twists and turns, this author's suspenseful writing will hold readers spellbound until the very end."
—*Darque Reviews*

"Snappy action and plot twists that will hold readers' interest to the last page."
—*Monsters and Critics*

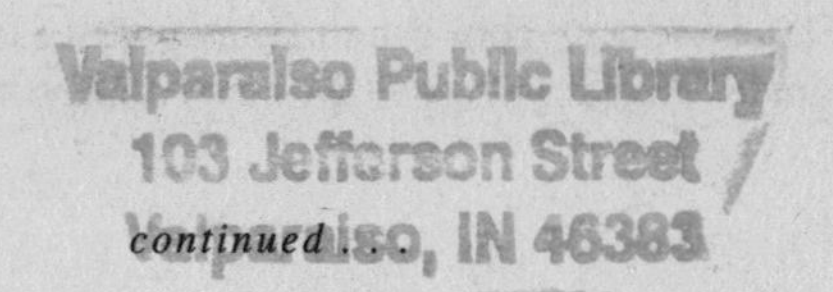
Valparaiso Public Library
103 Jefferson Street
Valparaiso, IN 46383

continued . . .

BLOOD DRIVE

"A terrific tale of supernatural sleuthing . . . provides edge-of-your-seat thrills and a high-octane emotional punch."

—*Romantic Times*

"Once again Jeanne C. Stein delivers a jam-packed story full of mystery and intrigue that will keep you glued to the edge of your seat! Just like [with] the first book in the Anna Strong series, *The Becoming*, I could not put this book down even for a second. You will find yourself cheering Anna on as she goes after the bad guys. Jeanne C. Stein has given us a wonderful tough-as-nails heroine everyone will love!"

—*Night Owl Romance*

"I loved this book . . . hugely enjoyable . . . an exciting read and everything any vampire-fantasy fan could hope for."

—*LoveVampires*

"Jeanne C. Stein takes on the vampire mythos in her own unique manner that makes for an enthralling vampire thriller. Readers of Laurell K. Hamilton, Tanya Huff and Charlaine Harris will thoroughly enjoy this fast-paced novel filled with several action scenes that come one after the other, making it hard for the readers to catch a breather."

—*Midwest Book Review*

"A really great series. Anna's strengths and weaknesses make for a very compelling character. Stein really puts you in [Anna's] head as she fumbles her way through a new life and the heartbreaking choices she will have to make. [Stein] also introduces new supernatural characters and gives a glimpse into a secret underground organization. This is a pretty cool urban fantasy series that will appeal to fans of Patricia Briggs's Mercy Thompson series."

—*Vampire Genre*

THE BECOMING

"This is a really, really good book. Anna is a great character, Stein's plotting is adventurous and original, and I think most of my readers would have a great time with *The Becoming*."

—Charlaine Harris, #1 *New York Times* bestselling author of the Sookie Stackhouse novels

"A cross between MaryJanice Davidson's Undead series, starring Betsy Taylor, and Laurell K. Hamilton's Anita Blake series. [Anna's] a kick-butt bounty hunter—but vampires are a complete surprise to her. Full of interesting twists and turns that will leave readers guessing. *The Becoming* is a great addition to the TBR pile." —*Romance Reviews Today*

"With plot twists, engaging characters and smart writing, this first installment in a new supernatural series has all the marks of a hit. Anna Strong lives up to her name: equally tenacious and vulnerable, she's a heroine with the charm, savvy and intelligence that fans of Laurell K. Hamilton and Kim Harrison will be happy to root for . . . If this debut novel is any indication, Stein has a fine career ahead of her." —*Publishers Weekly*

"In an almost Hitchcockian way, this story keeps you guessing, with new twists and turns coming almost every page. Anna is well named, strong in ways she does not even know. There is a strong element of surprise to it . . . Even if you don't like vampire novels, you ought to give this one a shot." —*Huntress Book Reviews*

"A wonderful new vampire book . . . that will keep you on the edge of your seat." —*Fallen Angel Reviews*

Ace Books by Jeanne C. Stein

THE BECOMING
BLOOD DRIVE
THE WATCHER
LEGACY
RETRIBUTION
CHOSEN

CHOSEN

PORTER COUNTY LIBRARY

JEANNE C. STEIN

Valparaiso Public Library
103 Jefferson Street
Valparaiso, IN 46383

PB FIC STE VAL
Stein, Jeanne C.
Chosen
33410011190719
JUN 27 2011

ACE BOOKS, NEW YORK

THE BERKLEY PUBLISHING GROUP
Published by the Penguin Group
Penguin Group (USA) Inc.
375 Hudson Street, New York, New York 10014, USA
Penguin Group (Canada), 90 Eglinton Avenue East, Suite 700, Toronto, Ontario M4P 2Y3, Canada
(a division of Pearson Penguin Canada Inc.)
Penguin Books Ltd., 80 Strand, London WC2R 0RL, England
Penguin Group Ireland, 25 St. Stephen's Green, Dublin 2, Ireland (a division of Penguin Books Ltd.)
Penguin Group (Australia), 250 Camberwell Road, Camberwell, Victoria 3124, Australia
(a division of Pearson Australia Group Pty. Ltd.)
Penguin Books India Pvt. Ltd., 11 Community Centre, Panchsheel Park, New Delhi—110 017, India
Penguin Group (NZ), 67 Apollo Drive, Rosedale, North Shore 0632, New Zealand
(a division of Pearson New Zealand Ltd.)
Penguin Books (South Africa) (Pty.) Ltd., 24 Sturdee Avenue, Rosebank, Johannesburg 2196,
South Africa

Penguin Books Ltd., Registered Offices: 80 Strand, London WC2R 0RL, England

This is a work of fiction. Names, characters, places, and incidents either are the product of the author's imagination or are used fictitiously, and any resemblance to actual persons, living or dead, business establishments, events, or locales is entirely coincidental. The publisher does not have any control over and does not assume any responsibility for author or third-party websites or their content.

CHOSEN

An Ace Book / published by arrangement with the author

PRINTING HISTORY
Ace mass-market edition / September 2010

Copyright © 2010 by Jeanne C. Stein.
Cover art by Cliff Nielsen.
Cover design by Judith Lagerman.
Interior text design by Kristin del Rosario.

All rights reserved.
No part of this book may be reproduced, scanned, or distributed in any printed or electronic form without permission. Please do not participate in or encourage piracy of copyrighted materials in violation of the author's rights. Purchase only authorized editions.
For information, address: The Berkley Publishing Group,
a division of Penguin Group (USA) Inc.,
375 Hudson Street, New York, New York 10014.

ISBN: 978-0-441-01917-5

ACE
Ace Books are published by The Berkley Publishing Group,
a division of Penguin Group (USA) Inc.,
375 Hudson Street, New York, New York 10014.
ACE and the "A" design are trademarks of Penguin Group (USA) Inc.

PRINTED IN THE UNITED STATES OF AMERICA

10 9 8 7 6 5 4 3 2 1

If you purchased this book without a cover, you should be aware that this book is stolen property. It was reported as "unsold and destroyed" to the publisher, and neither the author nor the publisher has received any payment for this "stripped book."

To Charlaine Harris,
who offered encouragement when I was starting out
and friendship now that I'm on the path.
You are my hero.

To Barbara Seranella,
who—along with her alter ego, Munch Mancini—
was taken from us much too soon.

And to Robert B. Parker.
I never knew him personally,
but I fell in love with Spenser the first moment
I opened The Godwulf Manuscript.
RIP.

ACKNOWLEDGMENTS

As is the case for most authors, there are more people to acknowledge than space to acknowledge them. A few, though, really deserve mention:

My excellent editor, Jessica Wade, and my hard-working agent, Scott Miller. Rosanne Romanello over at Penguin and MacKenzie Fraser-Bub at Trident Media.

My critique group: Mario Acevedo, Terry Wright, Warren Hammond, Tamra Monahan, Margie and Tom Lawson and members emeriti Jeff Shelby and Sandy Maren.

The splendid organization Rocky Mountain Fiction Writers. My Palm Springs guide, Clay Courter.

Readers, each and every one of you whether you love or hate Anna Strong. You keep me motivated.

Finally, my daughter, Jeanette, and my husband, Phil. You two are the best.

CHAPTER 1

IT'S SWEAT.

I wasn't sure at first. I haven't been vampire that long, but I sure as hell don't remember sweating since becoming one.

Drops of moisture pool between my shoulder blades, soak my underarms, collect between my breasts, making a soggy mess of the blouse underneath my jacket.

A new blouse.

It's sweat, no doubt about it.

I can't take my jacket off. I've got a .38 clipped to my belt.

Might make the natives restless. Or excited.

Shit.

I glance over at my partner. He hasn't broken a sweat, so it's not the room. Even if I didn't have a constitution that is impervious to ambient temperature, the air conditioner in this dump is cranked up to ice age.

I start to squirm on the barstool, impatient to get out into the air. Impatient to escape.

Escape?

What?

What the hell is happening?

My temple throbs, like my head is in a vise. A vise that's being slowly tightened.

Great.

I swipe a hand across my forehead. It comes away wet. I sneak a look across at David to see if he's noticed.

He hasn't.

He's busy watching for the skip, Curly Tom, the reason we're stuck in this dive.

I look around, too.

But not for the skip. Something is wrong. I don't know what.

David takes a break from skip alert and peers at me over the rim of his beer bottle. I feel his eyes on me like an irritating swarm of gnats buzzing around my head.

I look up at him and bark, "What?"

"You're squirming like a worm in shit. You not happy to be here?"

Like I should be? I'm burning up and my insides are quivering like a Jell-O shooter. Then there's Lance, tall, blond and sexy, waiting for me at home. No, I don't want to be *here*. I frown at David. "You said we'd be done by ten thirty. And yet, here we are"—I glance at my watch—"at eleven, in a place reeking of stale beer and ripe biker. Bumfuckville, David."

He drains the bottle and motions to the barkeep for another. "Eyes on the prize, Anna. Twenty thou."

"So where is he?"

David swivels on the barstool, takes a slow, lazy look around. "Don't worry. He's coming."

"So's Christmas. I want to go home."

It's my turn to read David's expression. Aggravation mingled with frustration.

"We've only been here an hour. What's your goddamned

rush?" He leans back, his elbows on the bar, facing the door. "Let me guess. That scrawny model boyfriend of yours is waiting for you at the cottage. Am I right?"

"Lance is not scrawny."

"What's he weigh? One-seventy soaking wet? I don't know what you see in him. In a fight, he'd snap like a matchstick."

Oh, David. Would you be surprised. Lance is a vampire, like me, and if it came to a fight, he'd be the one doing the snapping. I force a smile. "He's lean, David, not scrawny." Comes from not consuming a carb in the last fifty years. "Not every man is a pituitary case like you."

A flash of irritation tightens the corners of his mouth. I immediately regret my snarky remark. David is big, true, but a former football player who's kept in shape. He's my partner and friend, and he didn't deserve the crack.

I rub at my eyes with the palms of my hands. It's this damned headache.

I have a headache now?

How can a vampire get a headache?

David swivels his stool away from me and focuses his attention back to the door—a deliberate cold shoulder. Not that I blame him. I don't try to mitigate his snit. Instead I focus on whatever the hell is going on in my body. The head *ache* has turned into an annoying hum and the stomach quiver into a clenched fist. Granted, I've been a vampire for less than a year, but I'm pretty sure we don't get the flu.

Which is what this feels like.

I rub at my eyes again and look around, trying to focus. This is a biker bar—a *real* biker bar—on the outskirts of Lakeside in east San Diego County. Run-down, no flashing neon beer signs in the windows to attract customers. No windows at all. No back door. Probably be in violation of a hundred fire codes if it wasn't classified as a "private club." Sawdust crunches underfoot, absorbing spilled beer and the occasional body fluid. Some wise guy has tacked a Health Department rating code of "F" above the bar.

Members wearing the colors of the local Angels' chapter slouch at the bar or shoot pool under the glare of a green-shaded light. The only reason David and I have been left unmolested and unchallenged is because we know the president of the club. We did him a favor a few years back and he's repaying the debt.

He was only too happy to oblige. The guy we're after isn't a biker. He's a pain-in-the-ass wannabe who robbed and shot a dealer in L.A. and skipped bail. He's been hanging around the bar, bragging about his score, thinking it might gain him access to the club. Trouble is, the prez knows it's only a matter of time before the cops trace him here. He'd rather we get him first. Saves the club the trouble of dealing with Curly Tom.

Good for us. Better for Curly Tom.

With us, it's a payday and he'll end up in jail. With the club, it's self-preservation and he'll most likely end up in a shallow grave in the Anza-Borrego desert.

I let my gaze sweep the room. No one seems to be paying us the slightest bit of attention. Most know why we're here. But I feel—*something*. Anxiety. Apprehension. Dread.

Why? Over this jerk, Curly Tom?

Makes no sense.

David and I are bounty hunters. We've done jobs like this a hundred times. We've faced tougher guys than this joker. And that was before I became vampire. Having superhuman strength and speed tends to boost one's confidence.

So if I'm not experiencing this foreboding over Curly Tom, what is it?

The humming in my head grows stronger.

That's when it hits me.

The last time I felt anything like this, a witch was behind it.

A witch.

The thought propels me off the barstool. The abrupt movement brings David to his feet, too. He looks around, right hand moving instinctively to touch the gun under his jacket.

"Is he here? Do you see him?"

I shake my head. "No. He's not here."

I look around.

But something is.

CHAPTER 2

DAVID GLANCES AROUND TO SEE HOW MUCH ATtention we've attracted with my vault off the barstool. The noise level remains the same, and except for the biker next to David who got bumped when he leapt up, no one seems to have noticed.

That guy is not happy. Beer drips off the elbow of his leather jacket. "Hey, asshole."

David mumbles, "Sorry, man," and signals the barkeep for another round.

The guy shoots off his stool, but when he's standing next to David, who is six inches taller and built like a tank, he shrugs and accepts the beer with a grudging nod.

David waits for him to sit down, then turns his frown on me, "What's the matter with you?"

I settle my butt back on the stool. If I told him what was the matter—that I think a witch might be trying to put a spell on me—I imagine the reaction would be the same if I told him his partner was a vampire. And had been for almost a year.

Not an option.

What is an option is for me to get the hell out of here and find out who, or what, is after me.

Time to go on the offensive. "Ten minutes, David. I'll give it ten more minutes. Then I'm gone."

He opens his mouth to object but snaps it closed again, his eyes on the guy who just pushed his way through the door. "There he is."

Curly Tom isn't curly. He's bald and short and fat, about two hundred forty pounds on a five-ten frame. He's dressed in leathers that bear no markings. At least he's smart enough to know wearing Angels' colors uninitiated is a death sentence. He looks around the bar, a goofy smile on his face, as if waiting for an invitation to join one of the groups clustered at the bar or in the back by the pool table.

No invitation is forthcoming. The barkeep leans over to David and whispers, "Get him and get the fuck out of here."

With bikers, gratitude only gets you so far.

David slides off the stool and motions to the right. I go that way and he goes to the left. Before Curly Tom realizes what's happening, we've got him flanked.

David takes his arm in a steel grip that makes the biker flinch. "Let's take a walk," David says.

Curly Tom's eyes widen, the smile falls from his face. He struggles to break David's hold but in a flash, I've got his other arm. When my fingers close around his forearm in a grip even stronger than David's, he yelps.

"Who the fuck are you?"

That makes the bikers closest to us look around. But they know what's going on. They tighten ranks, their backs to Curly Tom, and in an instant, he sees he's on his own. He starts to dance around, trying to shake us loose. When that fails, he unleashes a shit storm of invective that's as creative as it is ineffective.

David and I hustle him outside.

While Curly Tom continues his diatribe, David and I have a conversation of our own.

"Told you he'd show up," David says.

"Yeah, yeah. Can you get him downtown on your own?"

"Why? You going back inside?"

When I don't answer, he says, "See if you get lucky?"

"Funny."

I push Curly Tom's head down and shove him into the backseat of the Ford Crown Vic we use for work. David snaps his cuffed wrist around a steel bar in the door and straightens to peer at me in the dim light of the parking lot.

"How will you get home?"

"I'll call Lance."

"You'll call Lance. And he'll have to drive all the way out here from Mission Beach to pick you up. Doesn't make sense, Anna, even for you."

His tone makes the thudding in my head worse and the knot in my stomach tighten. Whatever is wreaking havoc with my nervous system is here in this place, and I need to find out what it is. But David is not giving up without a fight.

I slam the car door so hard, Curly Tom bounces in the backseat. "I don't ask you to explain every thing you do. If I did, I might start with why you and that booking clerk from jail pick my side of the desk to fuck on when you sneak back to the office in the middle of the night."

He turns startled eyes toward me. "How—?"

"How do I know?" I smell it. Not the answer I can give. I shake a finger. "I just know, okay. And since she's on duty tonight, I imagine you'll be heading there after you drop this dirtbag off."

He puts a finger to his lips and jerks his head in Curly Tom's direction. "Are you crazy? What if he hears you?"

"Your problem. Now, are you finished grilling me?"

David snatches the car keys from my outstretched hand. It wasn't fair bringing up his affair—he has a steady girlfriend that I'm sure knows nothing about his on-again, off-again fling with the chick from jail—but lately, nothing much is. He stomps around to the driver's side of the car, drops into the seat and peels out of the parking lot.

I release a pent-up sigh.

Finally.

The night closes around me. Moonless. Dead quiet. Mid-July hot. Even so, I start to shiver. I turn my face toward the bar. Whoever—whatever—is affecting me is inside.

The realization makes the feeling grow stronger. Something is there—just out of sight. Something evil. It draws me back. If this is a spell, it's like nothing I've felt before. The witch Belinda Burke's black magic drained her victims of physical strength and left their bodies ill and dying. This is attacking my brain at a primeval level. A warning of danger that's repulsing and magnetic at the same time. I can no more leave it unexplained or unanswered than I could convince David to leave me here alone at a biker bar without resorting to blackmail.

I'll apologize for that later.

A car pulls into the parking lot.

A dark Ford sedan.

Followed by a second.

Nothing says "cop" like identical Ford sedans.

I step back into the shadows and watch.

When one of the drivers steps out, I recognize him.

Detective Harris, SDPD Homicide.

Three more cars, patrol cars this time, pull up around the perimeter of the lot, effectively sealing it off. Harris directs the cops with hand signals, stationing them by the door and around the row of Harleys parked in front. One he sends around back, but the cop returns almost immediately. As David and I discovered earlier, there's no exit in the back, just one small window near the ceiling of the women's bathroom.

When Harris is ready, he unclips his gun, holds it out of sight at his side and disappears through the door.

Hell breaks loose.

Shouting. Swearing. Scuffling and running feet. Bikers pour out the door and straight into a line of cops, all waiting with guns drawn.

At the same time, I hear a sound from behind the building. A small sound, a window sliding open. Too soft for the cops out front to hear but not for a vampire.

Besides, the cops are occupied with corralling stampeding bikers. I make my way unnoticed to the back.

There's a man trying to wriggle through that one tiny bathroom window. His head is down, his hands flailing for purchase against the wood siding. He's stuck.

He raises his head, spies me. "Hey, bitch." He's whispering, but his voice is hard, commanding. "Help me out of here."

The sick feeling in my gut grows stronger.

I stare at the face. Dark skin, eyes filled with hate, mouth twisted in a sneer.

I step back.

"Didn't you hear me, bitch?" He's trying to prop himself up.

This time when he raises his head, I'm ready. I steel myself for the wave of nausea his gaze unleashes.

The headache, the sense of evil, the foreboding twisting my gut. It's all emanating from an asshole stuck like a fat toad in a bathroom window.

I swallow down disgust. "What are you?"

He pauses in his struggles to shoot me a look that's part astonishment, part rage. "What do you mean, *what* am I? Are you nuts?"

All my vamp senses have sprung to alert. I try to get inside his head. *Are you a vamp? A shape-shifter? A witch?*

Nothing.

All I get is a black void, a deep well of malevolence.

And the certain knowledge that he's human.

Human?

How could that be? How can he be affecting my senses like this if he's human?

We stare at each other. He's got my mind locked in a steel vise. Every instinct screams I should rip out his throat, now, before he frees himself, before he gets loose and—

And what?

He's human.

He rouses himself first, face reddening. "You stupid cunt. When I get out of here, I'll kill you." He resumes his wild thrashing, pushing against the wall with the palms of his hands, trying to get his lard ass through an opening barely bigger than his head.

I'm stupid?

I have two choices. Yell for Harris or let the guy do it himself when he realizes he's wedged so tight in the window, he'll likely starve to death if no one finds him.

No. There's another choice.

A voice inside my head.

Kill him.

CHAPTER 3

KILL HIM?

Where did that come from?

There's a stirring in my gut. With it comes a startling realization. Whatever instinct is telling me to take this guy's life is right. Human or not, he's evil. He's a threat.

I pause, sniff the wind. He smells of borax soap and bleach.

Not road dirt and sweat like the rest of his biker buddies.

And underneath the soap—the pungent, familiar odor of blood.

Not his.

He spilled blood tonight.

Whose? Is that why Harris is here?

No matter. This is something I can take care of. My head clears in an instant. The headache is gone. A calmness descends.

Something I *need* to take care of.

I grind my teeth together in anticipation behind lips locked tight. A growl escapes my throat.

When he looks up again, he sees me. The real me. The vampire.

"What's wrong with your eyes?"

No intimidation in his voice this time. Only confusion and fear. I know why. I know what a vampire's eyes look like—yellow, glowing, slit pupils. Cat eyes.

The human Anna tries to intervene. She whispers, "Stop. You can't kill him. He's human. He's done you no harm."

Doesn't matter. My fists are clenched, the bloodlust runs high. I crouch, approach, slowly, deliberately, as a predator stalks its prey. I enjoy his fear. Taste it on the wind, smell it in the sweat that runs down his face. He's mesmerized. Can't look away. A rat and a cobra.

Power runs through me, sweeping away the trepidation and anxiety of before. In its place, eagerness and startling clarity.

The reason I'm here is *to kill him.*

The reason I sent David away is *to kill him.*

CHAPTER 4

"WELL, WELL. LOOK WHO WE HAVE HERE. ANNA Strong."

Harris.

No. Don't look around. Don't stop. Kill him. He's a murderer.

I take another step forward.

"Anna? What's wrong with you?"

The guy in the window finds his voice. "Help me. The bitch is nuts. Look at her eyes."

I sense Harris come closer. He can't know. It stops me. I straighten. Close my eyes. Calm the wild beating of my heart. Jaw relaxes, fists unclench.

When Harris touches my arm, the human Anna is back in control.

"What are you doing here?" He jabs a thumb toward the guy in the window. "I know it's not him. He hasn't been charged with anything. Yet."

"David and I—" I let the explanation hang, drag my

eyes toward the window where the guy is being pulled back inside by a couple of cops.

He isn't protesting.

"Who is he? What's he done?"

Harris waits until the cops inside yell that they've got him before answering. "His name is Joe Black. A couple of hours ago, he murdered his wife and her boyfriend. We got a tip that he rides with the Angels. Took a chance we'd find him here."

He turns and motions for me to follow. I do, reluctantly, processing the fact that I *knew* Black had spilled blood before Harris' words confirmed it.

When we're back in front of the bar, I ask, "Why are you here, Harris? Out of your jurisdiction, isn't it?"

He shrugs without answering, instead issuing instructions to the cops holding Black. They cuff him, read him his rights and shove him into a waiting patrol car. The rest of the cops still have their guns trained on the Angels, all facedown on the dirt.

Harris snaps an order and the cops withdraw to their waiting cars.

I watch as the bikers climb silently to their feet and shuffle back into the bar. No one so much as glances in Harris' direction. They've danced this dance before. They know how cops operate. If they'd done anything less than cooperate, the cops would have torn the bar apart. They'd have searched every biker. Guns, dope, illegal contraband. They know what's at stake. Better to take a little shit from the cops than let things go too far. Unwritten biker code: the good of the many outweighs the good of the one.

In a minute, the music is back on, so loud the building shakes.

The patrol cars pull out. The Ford with Black follows. Harris and I are left alone in the parking lot. He turns his attention to me.

"You didn't answer my question. What are you doing here?"

Harris is about five feet ten inches of bulldog. Past experience has shown that there's no way to blow him off. I don't bother to mention that I'd asked him the same question a minute before. And that he'd ignored it. Instead I reply, "David and I had a job. He's on his way downtown with the guy now."

He looks around. "I don't see your car."

"What are you, a detective? I was just about to call for a ride."

He shakes his head. "Your partner left you here? I know you're a pain in the butt, but I can't see that overgrown Boy Scout dumping your ass in a biker bar even if you deserved it. Which I have no doubt you did. So what's the story? Why'd you stay behind?"

There's no way to explain why I stayed—especially to a human. I'm not sure I can explain it to myself. "Look, you got me. I pissed David off and he left."

Harris looks surprised at the answer. And aggravated. Which aggravates me. "David knows I can take care of myself. I don't need anyone to protect me."

The cynical twist of Harris' mouth takes a downturn. "I'll take you back to town. Get in the car."

His condescending tone sparks a maelstrom of indignation. The instinct to show him just how well I can protect myself is drowned by the more rational desire to get home. I need to think through what happened tonight. I need to talk about it with Lance and see if he has an explanation for a human exerting such influence over me. I might have killed Black if Harris hadn't appeared. I wanted to. Why? Because I knew he was a killer?

How did I know?

How could I have known? The smell of blood could have meant he was a victim not a killer. And yet, I had no doubt which he was.

Harris is at the car, holding open the door, tapping his foot and frowning like an annoyed parent who caught his kid out after curfew.

It takes all my willpower to resist the desire to grab his foot and dump him on his impatient ass.

I shrug off the impulse.

He's a human. A cop, no less.

And I can use the ride.

"Okay, okay. Let's go."

CHAPTER 5

HARRIS DROPS ME OFF AT THE OFFICE. OUR ENtire conversation on the thirty-five-minute ride consisted of Harris asking me if I wanted to go to the office or if he should take me home.

It was a long thirty-five minutes.

At last I'm in the Jag and on the way to the cottage, away from Black's strange influence and Harris' annoying air of disapproval. I can think rationally about the night's events.

The *rationality* is slow to come.

How could I have been so strongly affected by Black? He was human. Not that humans aren't capable of evil—I've certainly met a few. But he *projected* evil. So strongly it caused a physical reaction. That's a disturbing new twist.

Evil. A primitive word.

Why did I pick up on it? Why did I know he had *spilled* blood? What compelled me to want to kill him on sight?

Maybe Lance can help me figure it out. He's been a vampire a lot longer than me—seventy years. He's helped me through other troubling times. The last three months, we've gotten closer. Especially after what happened with Williams.

It's been three months since Williams and I had a confrontation over the death of Ortiz, a vampire he loved like a son. Three months since his wife threatened me because I chose the well-being of another over her husband's. I've stayed away from them both, withdrawn from the supernatural community and kept to myself. My only tie has been to Lance. And Culebra, to feed.

I've been living as a human. Going to work every day with David. Going to movies with Lance. Simple things. A couple of weeks ago, I even flew to France for my mother's birthday. A feat made possible by the fact that I own a private jet—the one part of Avery's legacy I've accepted for myself. Selfishly. Avery was the first vamp I met as a newly turned. Even though he ended up trying to kill me and I'd vowed to accept none of the estate he'd left me, having a jet makes travel too convenient to pass up. Especially with family in Europe. No worries about someone noticing the lack of a reflection in a dark window or why on such a long flight I didn't eat or drink or have to go to the bathroom.

It was only a three-day visit—I didn't want to push my luck—but it was wonderful.

I enjoy the illusion of being human.

Maybe that's what has me upset. Tonight, Black shattered the illusion.

I pull the Jag into the garage, next to Lance's silver Aston Martin DB9. The top is down. I run a finger over butter-soft leather when I walk past. Such a boy's toy. Warmth still radiates off the hood—Lance must have arrived just minutes before. I slip out of the garage and hit the remote on my keychain.

The door is sliding shut when a blur catches the corner of my eye. From inside the garage, something propels itself toward me. Too fast. I'm hit broadside, thrown back. I recover, regain my balance, but not quickly enough. I feel the blade enter, just below the sternum, slash upward, scrape against bone. No pain at first. Just surprise.

Then rage.

The human Anna is gone. The vampire grabs the knife before it can strike again. I don't know what I'm fighting. I can't see a face, can't get inside the head. No time to figure it out. It doesn't matter. I turn the knife on the attacker—plunge it where it will do the most damage, yank it down. The abdomen rips apart, spilling intestines in a spray of blood.

An animal scream.

It tries to turn away.

It's not human.

Finally, a flash of recognition. Vampire.

I grab it, pull it back. *Why?*

No response. My blood is on fire. Self-preservation and fury swamp restraint. I raise the knife and slash at the throat. Blood arcs, splashes across my face before my mouth closes over the wound.

I drink until I feel the last flutter of life.

I let the body fall. Watch as it shrivels into the image of an old man.

Vampire.

Lance is suddenly beside me—teeth bared and claws extended. He sees the body on the ground.

Then he looks at me. My hands clutch at my chest. Blood flows over my fingers. He *knows*. My blood.

He pulls me to him, rips the torn fabric of my shirt. He places his own mouth over the wound and begins to suck at it.

I groan with the pain and pleasure. Healing starts from the inside, organs repair themselves, cells regenerate. Lance's arms are steel around me. His concentration shifts once he knows I'm all right. Blood—mine, the attacker's—

its smell and texture, a siren song. Lust replaces alarm. Need replaces concern. He lowers me to the ground.

We fumble with our clothes. We're both in jeans. It takes too long to try to wriggle free. Zippers are ripped apart, denim shredded. When he mounts me, it's with relief and joy.

No shared thoughts. No shared desires.

Joy.

A primal celebration. Acknowledgment that I escaped the death from which no vampire returns.

After, he raises himself up on his elbows. "What just happened?"

I run my nails down his back. "I don't know. Right now, I don't care." I raise my hips and clench my thighs to push him deeper inside. "We can figure it out later. I'm not finished with you yet."

He moans and pushes back. "I hope not."

A WHILE LATER, CALMER, SATED, REASON RETURNS.

Lance sits up, looks around. "Maybe we'd better go inside."

We're on the driveway, in the shadow of the garage, but he's right. A glance at my watch. We've been out here forty minutes. We can't have made too much noise since I've sensed no neighbors approach to have a look. Still, we do have a body to dispose of.

We scramble up, clutching ruined clothing, air cool against bare skin.

Lance points to the mummified corpse. "What are we going to do about him?"

The knife is where I dropped it. Blood and intestines are a rusty smudge on the driveway. Lance smears dirt over the spot and picks up the knife. I grab the corpse by a desiccated arm and drag him through the gate into the backyard. When a vampire is killed by stake or fire, he turns to ash. When he's drained, his corpse reverts to what his human age would be. If it's twenty, he looks like a twenty-year-old, if it's fifty, a fifty-year-old. Judging by the looks of this guy, he must have been well over one hundred.

Which adds another piece to the puzzle.

I close and lock the gate. Why would an old-soul vampire attack me?

Lance and I take time to shower, soaping off blood and dirt, losing ourselves for a few minutes longer in pleasure rather than the problem lying in the grass outside the back door. But reality can't be shut out forever, and reluctantly, we leave the warm cocoon of the bath to get dressed and face the corpse.

Soon we're in the backyard, steaming mugs of coffee clutched in cold hands, looking down at what's left of my attacker. I hand my mug to Lance and bend down to riffle the guy's clothing. Cotton long-sleeved T-shirt, black hoodie, cotton slacks, tennis shoes.

No jacket. No wallet. No ID.

"Any idea who he was?" Lance asks.

I straighten and shake my head. "Not a clue. I haven't pissed anybody off lately. At least, not that I know of." I glance toward the garage. "He came from inside the garage. Maybe he wanted your car?"

Lance snorts. "He's not very smart if he was after my car. That thing has so many anti-theft devices, it does everything but blow itself up if it's tampered with. Besides, if he was already in the garage, and you didn't see him, why wouldn't he just wait for you to leave?"

"Not only didn't I see him, I didn't sense him. Not then, not during the attack, not after, when I bled him."

"He was shielding himself from you," Lance says. He holds out my mug.

"Right to the end," I reply, taking it.

Lance releases a breath. "You and David have any jobs lined up the next couple of days?"

I shake my head.

The sun is beginning to tint the sky. He squints up at it.

"Let's take a drive," he says.

"Where?"

"To my place in Palm Springs. We can bury the mummy in the desert along the way. We'll spend the weekend."

"I'll get a sheet."

Lance follows me inside. "And we're taking your car."

When I raise a questioning eyebrow, he replies, "The Jag has a bigger trunk."

But his thoughts say, *No way am I putting a rotting corpse in the Aston Martin.*

THE RIDE THROUGH THE DESERT ON AN EARLY JULY morning is lonely and quiet. Not many souls willing to brave temperatures already into the eighties. Having a vampire's constitution, however, allows Lance and me to put the top down on the Jag and let the warmth of the sun bake our bones.

I'm driving. We take the 15 to 74—the scenic route on a road that hairpins back and forth as it gains elevation through the Santa Rosa Mountains. This is rattlesnake and coyote terrain. Desolate in a beautiful way.

We choose a place to turn off at a junction between the highway and an unmarked dirt road. In the fall and winter, this is a popular ATV playground. In the summer, the only visitors slither or scurry away at the sound of the car's approach.

We drive miles into the desert, the road so well traveled the Jag has no trouble on the hardscrabble surface. Ten miles from the highway, we park. We'll have to go on foot from this point if we want to bury our mummy friend where he's not likely to be found when the change of season turns the desert back into a four-wheeling playground.

Lance hoists the sheet-shrouded body over his shoulder. I grab a pick and shovel, and we start toward an outcropping of rock in the distance. Up until this time, we've traveled in silence, enjoying the sound of the desert wind, the feel and smell of it in our faces, the guttural purr of the Jag's engine. But after a few minutes, I feel Lance's gentle intrusion into my head.

What should we do about this guy?

I frown. *Besides bury him? I don't know. What do you think? After all, we can't be sure he wasn't after your car. Maybe he's just a thief.*

A snort. *If he's been watching the house at all, he knows we're vampire. Not too smart to try to steal from one of your own.*

Maybe he was down on his luck. Saw this as an opportunity to make some real money.

Lance shakes his head. *He was an old soul. Even if he hadn't understood the concept of compound interest, he would never have gotten so desperate he'd resort to stealing. He'd seduce a human into supporting him first.*

I've run out of excuses. Lance doesn't follow with the logical conclusion, just lets the idea drop between us where it lays until I pick it up and put into words what we're both thinking.

"Which means, he wasn't a car thief at all. He was after me."

CHAPTER 6

SAYING THE WORDS OUT LOUD PLUNGES ME RIGHT back into the nightmare of Ortiz' death and Williams' threat. Williams is the only one I know who hates me enough to want me dead. Was this an attempt to make good on that threat?

Lance reads my thoughts. *Why now? It's been three months since the fire. And why would he send someone to do a job he'd want to do himself?*

Both good questions, and ones to which I have no answers. I shrug them off and look around for a gravesite. We're at least ten miles from the car. The wind whistles in my ears and whips my hair into my face. I want to get this over with.

"Let's bury him here."

Lance drops the body onto the ground and reaches for the pick.

Despite vampire strength, the rock beneath our feet doesn't yield easily. It takes Lance and me fifteen minutes to gouge out a hole long enough and deep enough to make sure this vampire jerky treat doesn't become some scavenger's late night snack. No wonder the bikers wanted David and me to take care of Curly Tom. They knew it's not easy to dispose of a body in the desert.

The effort is enough, however, to distract us from the puzzle of why I was the target.

When we've finished filling the hole, we top it with rocks, a subtle pyramid for our mummy. We're covered in dust. We brush ourselves off the best we can and jog back to the car. I'd thrown a towel and a couple of bottles of water in the trunk. We sponge most of the dust off our faces and hands.

Then Lance holds his hand out for the keys. "Want me to drive?"

I toss them to him and he slips behind the wheel. "We'll be at the house in about an hour."

I rest my head against the seat and take in the view. It's been three hours since we left Mission Beach. We're about halfway to Palm Springs, winding our way through the San Bernardino National Forest. The sun is high in the sky and its heat is a salve to my spirit. I realize the attack took my mind off the subject I intended to bring up with Lance last night—the curious reaction I had to Black.

I glance over at Lance, gently probe to see what's on his mind. He's thinking of where he wants to take me tonight. A bar he thinks I'll find interesting. And of friends he wants to introduce me to.

Pleasant, everyday, normal things.

I decide to wait.

IN THE SHORT TIME I'VE KNOWN LANCE, I'VE TAKEN some things for granted. How he made his money, for instance. He's a model. Those cheekbones and a hard body make him a natural for both print and runway work, and since the advent of the digital camera, no worries about a distorted (or nonexistent) vampire film image. He's constantly flying off somewhere for a shoot or a show. I know enough about the fashion world to know a top model makes big bucks. Hence, the house in Malibu and this, a second home he's often talked about but one that I've never seen.

We've taken the turn off Highway 74 onto 111—known to the locals as East Palm Canyon Drive. It's the long, well-traveled artery that connects the various communities that make up the Palm Springs area. High-end boutiques, restaurants, resorts and country clubs pass in a seamless array on a wide highway lined with palms and oaks. A stark mountain range known as the Little San Bernardino Mountains forms a backdrop.

Even under the shimmer of a brilliant summer sun, there's an exotic beauty to the place.

Ours is the only car we pass with the top down. Most people hunker down behind windows rolled tight and air conditioners on high, protection from the blast-oven desert heat.

Lance slows the Jag at the entrance to a gated community with a simple brick sign. Thunderbird Cove. A uniformed guard steps from his air-conditioned perch inside a stone gatehouse and approaches the Jag. He tips his hat and smiles when he recognizes Lance, and the gates swing open like the parting of the seas.

The road sign says Evening Star Drive.

This is when I begin to think there is more to Lance's story than a good life forged by great cheekbones.

Evening Star Drive meanders back toward the mountains. Only the discreet signs on mailboxes identify private residences the size of hotels. I count twelve homes before we stop at the last—a castle that looks like it might have been transported from medieval Europe brick by brick. It climbs four stories into the sky, is topped with turrets and a widow's walk. The only thing missing is the moat.

Lance pulls up into the driveway, fishes keys from his

pocket and hits a remote. One section of a wall slides up to reveal a garage. He pulls the Jag inside and kills the engine.

"Honey," he says, "we're home."

Lance leads the way toward a door at the end of a three-car bay. Beside my Jag, there's a small vintage MG convertible in the garage. It gleams under a dust cover made of gauzy muslin.

Another boy toy.

And a lime green Prius. A hybrid? Not exactly Lance's typical mode of transportation.

The door to the house opens before we get to it. A woman no bigger than a minute bursts through. She's dressed in long paisley skirt and white cotton blouse knotted at the waist. Her honey-colored hair is tied back from her face with a comb. She's barefoot and gives off a serious earth-mother vibe.

The Prius.

She squeals and envelops Lance in a hug, dancing on tiptoes to do it. "It's so good to see you, Rick. I've missed you."

Rick?

Lance is laughing and hugging back. "I've missed you, too, Adele." He pushes her gently away and reaches for me. "This is Anna, my houseguest for the next few days. Anna, this is Adele. My very good friend."

Adele blushes. Physically, she looks like she might be fortysomething. Laugh lines crinkle her eyes and frame her mouth. The vibe she gives off, however, is *older.* I scan but detect no otherworldly presence. Doesn't mean she's human, though. My senses automatically spring to alert.

"Rick is too kind," she says. "I'm the housekeeper. Anything I can do to make your stay more pleasurable, don't hesitate to ask."

She's looking at me with keen eyes. Before I can react,

she's raised a hand to touch my face. "Very good bone structure. Are you a model, too?"

"She could be," Lance answers, putting an arm around my shoulder. "But what she does is much more exciting. She's a bounty hunter."

Adele's eyes widen. "Like Dog? I watch his program all the time on TV."

Lance moves us toward the door. "Yep. She catches the bad guys just like Dog."

"Uh—not exactly." The image of Adele thinking me a female Dog spouting Jesus and counseling skips on clean living is too bizarre. And what would that make David? His tart-tongued, bleach-blond wife?

Now *that's* an image.

The current passing between Lance (or is it Rick?) and this tiny woman has my head swimming. She's emitting a fiercely protective air toward him. There's a story here, and I can't wait to hear it.

Lance smiles down at me. *You will.*

Adele shepherds us through the entryway and into a kitchen the size of Rhode Island. We keep walking—through a dining room bigger than the entire first floor of my cottage and a living room with glass walls that look out over a swimming pool, and finally, she opens another door and gestures us inside.

"I know you must be tired from the drive. I have drinks waiting for you on the side bar. Rick, you have several messages on the desk. The boys are in town for the weekend. They're having a party tonight at Melvyn's." She cocks her head to the side and looks me up and down. "I do hope you brought evening clothes, Anna."

Another abrupt change of subject that knocks me off-kilter. She's like a train leaving a station and I have to run alongside to keep up. "Evening clothes?" Except for the jeans I have on, all I brought were two pairs of shorts and a couple of T-shirts.

Adele plunges ahead with an airy wave of a hand. "No matter. You're what—a size four? I'll call Stephen. Luckily, you look like an Armani type—nice shoulders, narrow waist. I'll have him bring some things for you to try. Now, what's your shoe size? Seven and a half? Eight? I'll have him bring an assortment of Jimmy Choos—or would you prefer Blahnik?"

Lance moves to Adele's side, taking her arm and turning her toward the door. "You choose. Anna and I are going to wash the road dust out of our throats and relax a while before I return any calls. See that we're not disturbed, will you?"

Adele smiles and nods and leaves us with a bemused parting glance. Lance closes the door, turns an imaginary lock and nails an imaginary board over it before turning to me, swiping a hand across his forehead. "Whew. Alone at last."

I hardly know which question to ask first. I settle on, "Who the hell is Rick?"

Lance smiles and moves to stand in front of a mahogany-framed fireplace. He looks at me, arms crossed over his chest. With hurricane Adele gone, I have my first opportunity to look around the room. It's dark-paneled, full of heavy, overstuffed leather furniture, one huge desk and a fireplace with a coat of arms over the mantel.

Lance hasn't moved. Since he seems to be making a point of *something*, and that something must be near or on the fireplace, I step forward for a closer look. He glances over and up.

The coat of arms?

I'm about to remind him how much I hate games when I'm rewarded with a thumb jab.

Okay, the coat of arms.

It's a huge crest, a gryphon or phoenix in the center surrounded by three arrows and a Latin inscription. The only word I recognize is a name—DeFontaine.

"I don't understand. Whose house is this?"

"It's mine."

"DeFontaine? That's not your name." I frown. "Is it?"

Lance laughs. "You didn't really think my name was Lance Turner, did you?"

His laughter ignites a spark of irritation. "Why the hell wouldn't I believe your name was Lance Turner?"

The tone of my voice squelches his amusement. He backtracks with a quick, "That was stupid. You wouldn't have any way of knowing Lance is a professional name. I'm sorry. I should have told you before." He winces. "My real name is Broderick Phillipe DeFontaine. Any doubt now why I don't use it professionally?"

He lets his voice drop, waiting for the recognition to hit.

It does. It would to anyone who has been around for the last hundred years or so. "DeFontaine? The South African diamond people?"

A nod.

"You're a member of the DeFontaine family." Now I'm not only startled, I'm shocked.

Another nod.

I take a closer look around the room—at the sumptuous appointments, the art in gilded frames, the leather-bound books lining the walls. Even the smell of the room is subtle but rich. A blend of citrus potpourri and old money.

Jesus. Did I know this guy at all?

I turn my gaze back on Lance. I feel as if I'm seeing him—Lance or Rick, short for Broderick, I assume—for the first time.

I know a lot of rich people—and rich vampires. *Rich*, however, doesn't begin to describe the net worth of a family that, until recently, controlled the diamond business. And had for hundreds of years.

"I don't know how to feel about this."

Lance is smart enough to remain silent. He shows that

he knows me a hell of a lot better than I do him. He's reading the confusion that could easily shift to anger with the wrong prompting, the wrong word, so he does nothing. He stands very still and waits for me to come to my own conclusions.

Part of me feels he should have told me who he was sooner. Part of me wonders truthfully if it makes a difference. Lance or Rick, this is the man who healed me, then trekked across ten miles of desert to help me bury the vampire who attacked me.

"Jesus." This time I say it out loud. "I can't wait to see what you get me for my birthday."

Lance's laugh is a mixture of relief and delight. In two steps, he's across the room and at my side.

I hold up my hands and gently push at his chest. "Whoa, there, cowboy. Not so fast. I have a shitload of questions."

He takes a step back. "Ask away."

Adele mentioned drinks on the sideboard. A glance around and I spy a bar set up. A cooler, a bottle of white wine in an ice bucket, red wine and glasses. "Any beer in that cooler?"

He's there and back faster than my eyes can follow with two open bottles of Corona and a plate of lime slices. He holds one of the bottles out to me and waves me toward the couch.

I take the beer, squeeze a lime slice through the neck of the bottle and take a swig, debating which existence to question first—past or present, human or vampire. I sink into plush couch cushions, arrange myself so I can see Lance, watch him, read his expressions, and jump in.

CHAPTER 7

I DECIDE TO START WITH SOMETHING EASY, SOMEthing mundane to gauge his reaction. "How did Adele know we were coming?"

Lance is surprised. He expected something more Anna-ish. Like, "What the fuck is going on?" I can tell because his mouth turns down and his eyebrows jump up. He recovers quickly and replies, "I called her from the house this morning. When you went inside to get the sheet."

"How?"

Understanding sparks his eyes. "On the telephone. No magic involved."

"Who is she? She seems to know you pretty well. Does she know what you are?"

He shakes his head. "That I'm vampire? No. But she knows I'm—not normal. She's never asked what I am, and I've never offered. She is the granddaughter of an old family friend. Her parents worked for us in South Africa. I used to keep up with the family and when I came to the States forty-five years ago, she was just a baby. She attended college in the East. We saw each other once or twice. After graduation, she came to California for a job. It didn't work out. I had inherited this place, so I asked if she'd like to live here, manage the house when I was away, take charge of the staff when I was in residence. It was supposed to be a temporary thing. She stayed on."

"And this was when?"

"Twenty years ago."

"So she's fortysomething. She knows you're eighty. And she looks her age and you look like you could be her grandson. She's never questioned it? What is she? Witch? Shape-shifter?"

Lance waves the question away. "She's a good friend and a good administrator. That's all I need to know. She has a home here as long as she wants it."

"That's not what I meant and you know it." His answer brings my animal instinct for self-preservation to the surface. "She's human and you have this cavalier attitude that she doesn't wonder what *you* are. You aren't afraid she'll make the connection and stake you in your sleep?"

He frowns. "I wasn't before now."

I look around the room. The house in Malibu is filled with funky furniture, Warhols on the walls, bright splashes of color. Its best feature is the ocean, a few steps away from the wall of glass that frames it, capturing a sun-soaked ever-changing landscape. The feel of this place is dark, heavy, full of old things and older memories.

I wave a hand to take it in. "This isn't you."

"I agree," he replies without hesitation. "It's pretty much the way I inherited it. I don't spend much time here, you know. A weekend here and there. It's become more Adele's house than mine."

"But you have friends here. She mentioned 'the boys.'"

Suddenly, Lance's expression mirrors more concern than curiosity. We've been talking out loud, but now, he answers with a quiet, *Not friends exactly. The man who sired me also has a place here. He and his entourage, others he's turned, travel together. I don't enjoy seeing him. But it's the price I pay for my freedom.*

It's the first time Lance has mentioned the circumstances of his becoming. Something in his tone triggers an alarm. I know what it's like to be under the control of a powerful vampire. My anger burns through. *Does he threaten you?*

He smiles at the tone of my response. He reaches out a hand and touches my cheek. *No. We've made our peace. I am allowed to live my own life. But I am expected to pay my respects when we're in town together. This party tonight. We'll go, he'll show me off as his famous protégé, we'll leave. It's not important. The rest of the weekend will be ours.*

His tone betrays more than his casual words, however. A little nervousness, a bit of agitation. It's there though he's trying to hide it. My protective instincts spring to the fore. I want to know more—the story of how he became vampire. But I don't press. Not now.

I smooth the concern from my thoughts. *What about your human family? Is there anyone you're still close to?*

A shrug. *My parents are dead. I have two brothers who manage the business. For obvious reasons, I don't see them. They live a world away. I'm not interested in the business, never was. We communicate through lawyers, mostly, though I've divested myself of most of my family's holdings. This house and a trust fund is all that's left. When I move on, the house and trust fund will go to Adele.*

A smile. *So you see, like you, I have to work for a living. I'll have to buy those expensive birthday presents just like anybody else.*

The old Lance, the one I've come to know and depend on, is back. The fact that he had a past he didn't share has no bearing on the man he is now, the man who has been nothing but good to me. I put the beer bottle on the coffee table in front of me. His smile warms me, ignites a familiar hunger. "How long before Adele and her couturier blow in?"

He places his bottle on the table beside mine. "She won't disturb us until we're ready. What did you have in mind?"

My roaming hands discover that he knows *exactly* what I have in mind. It's obviously on his mind, too.

"Where's the shower?"

CHAPTER 8

I'VE ALWAYS KNOWN THAT WHEN IT COMES TO SEX, my attitude is, well, different. I've never had any illusions about sex and love being either interchangeable or interdependent. I had my first sexual encounter at sixteen. I chose the guy carefully—he was older (a friend of my brother's) and rumor had it he'd been involved with a married woman (a teacher, no less). I figured that meant he was (a) adventurous and (b) skilled. I hadn't read *Penthouse Forum* and Krafft-Ebing for nothing.

Turned out he was neither, much to my chagrin. But he was eager to please. We spent a few wonderful weeks educating each other. Would have gone on longer if my brother hadn't found out. Still, I figure that guy owes me any future success he had with women.

My point is, I have loved sex—the act, the smells, the pure joy of it—since that time, since that boy. As a human, I thought sex enjoyable. As a vampire, it is liberating, sublime.

The pleasure of sex is the only part of being a vampire that comes close to justifying the existence.

A cosmic joke. Vampires cannot procreate—not like humans. Perhaps as consolation, they're given bodies that respond to sex in an extraordinary way. Bodies that are aroused with a look, a thought. Bodies that warm, become vibrant, alive during the act. Sex overwhelms the senses, wipes the mind clean of all worry, concerns, fears. Sex without consequence. Sex that reminds us of how it felt to be *human*.

Lance is not human. I am not human. But for a few minutes, we make love as if we were. No biting. No blood. Nothing but the feel of his body, on top of me, inside me. We move together, slowly, locked in the most intimate embrace, wanting to prolong the moment until we can hold back no longer. When he comes, it's to the pulse of my own orgasm, and when it's over, he whispers in my ear.

I bury my face in his shoulder, afraid to acknowledge that I heard what he said.

Afraid that I might be feeling the same way.

Afraid of what it means if I do.

ADELE'S DISCREET KNOCK ON THE DOOR COMES MINutes after Lance calls to let her know we're ready to rejoin the world of the living. He doesn't use those words, of course, but there's a reason the French call the orgasm "*la petite mort*."

We're in the bedroom—another huge room with huge furniture. Lance said his parents decorated the place seventy years ago. It's obvious that their taste ran to Old World castles and provincial country chateaux. Lance never cared enough to invest either time or money to change it, and Adele doesn't seem to mind.

I've showered and traded dusty jeans for a clean pair of shorts, tugged and smoothed my T-shirt, run fingers through wet hair. I can only imagine what it looks like. Times like these, not having a reflection is a blessing.

Lance hasn't mentioned what he whispered in my ear.

I won't.

We sit side by side on the edge of the bed, comfortable with each other again despite the few moments before when I know Lance was disappointed. He expected a response. He probably deserved one. I can't verbalize why I'm not ready to echo his sentiment. I just know that I'm not.

Lance has changed into board shorts and a T-shirt. He's running a brush through his own wet hair when Adele swoops in, her arms loaded with garment bags. She hangs them in a closet and comes to stand in front us, her face wreathed in a bright smile.

"Will you need help?" she asks. But her expression says she already knows the answer. She seems pleased that I'm here with Lance, like an indulgent sister who is happy her brother found *someone*.

Lance puts his arm around my waist and gives the reply we both know she is expecting: "I'll help."

"Thank you, but I've been dressing myself for quite a while. I think I can manage on my own."

Adele excuses herself, pausing at the door to look back at us. "Stephen and I are having coffee downstairs. He has shoes with him so when you've decided on the clothes, come down and pick what you'd like."

She pulls the door closed behind her.

I get up and move toward the closet. "So, who is Stephen?"

Lance joins me. "He manages the Armani shop in town."

"And he comes when you call? Must be nice to be a DeFontaine." I look into the closet. "There are a dozen outfits here. How long does Adele think I'm going to stay?"

Lance joins me, reaching past my shoulder to retrieve one of the bags. "Let's see what we have."

He unzips the bag and withdraws a long gown of black silk. "I like this. Try it on."

I pull my T-shirt over my head and shimmy out of my shorts to stand naked while Lance slips the dress over my head. It settles over my body like a warm breeze. It has a V-neck and scoop back and a skirt of soft pleats. I twirl in front of him and the skirt billows around me with a whisper of silk.

"How do I look?"

The glint in his eye and a familiar quirk to the eyebrow makes me take a step away. "Whoa. If we have sex after every wardrobe change, Stephen will be here through dinner."

"And the problem is?"

I laugh. "Let's just see what else he's brought."

We shuffle through a dozen outfits—all beautiful, all exquisitely detailed. Not my usual attire, for sure. But there is something magical about well-made couturier clothes. I choose the Cady gown I first tried on, a sleeveless jersey dress and micro pinstripe trousers with a black V-neck sweater gilded front and back with rhinestone insets.

I'll knock 'em dead in those slacks the next time David and I have a court date.

I sort price tags, adding up the purchases. "Good thing I brought a credit card."

Good thing I have a job.

Lance is gathering the discarded outfits and says offhandedly, "No need to worry about that. It's been taken care of."

My turn to raise an eyebrow. "What's that mean?"

"It means I own the Armani license here in Palm Springs. An investment. I've never had the opportunity to take advantage of it before. Adele prefers more earthy styles. With you, on the other hand, I can."

"Am I dreaming? You own an Armani store?"

A nod. "You can keep everything if you'd like. I wish you would."

"Okay. What's the catch? There's got to be a catch."

He's close again, nuzzling his lips against my neck. "No catch. You want to show your appreciation? Be grateful. Very grateful. I can think of a hundred ways to take advantage of grateful."

I take his face in my hands, press my body against his. "So can I. Do we have time?"

"I'm the boss, remember?" He scoops me up. "We have all the time in the world."

THIRTY MINUTES LATER, WE'RE HEADING DOWNstairs, bodies glowing, skin flushed with the afterglow of sex.

Adele and Stephen rise from a couch in the living room when they see us approach. Stephen is tall, angular, with sharp cheekbones and dark, close-cropped hair. He's a walking advertisement for Armani—cotton slacks, tonal striped shirt, twill dress blazer—right down to the Metro Shield sunglasses tucked into the open neck of his shirt. Must get a great employee discount. He grins as Lance makes the introductions.

Adele is right, Stephen says. *You are beautiful.*

Stephen is also vampire.

It doesn't surprise me that Stephen is vampire. Why should it? We're well integrated into the human community. I take his outstretched hand. *Thank you. For the compliment and for taking the time to bring the clothes.*

Anything for the boss's lady.

Lance folds the garment bags over the back of a chair. "You can return these," he says. "I think Anna should take them all, but she wouldn't hear of it. She is a model of restraint."

Restraint? I think about what we were just doing in the bedroom and wink at him before turning to Stephen. "Will you be at the party tonight?"

He looks over my head to Lance as if surprised that I

know about it. Surprised and—I can't quite interpret the other emotion I see in his expression. My feeling is that he's not entirely pleased with the idea.

He recovers quickly, smoothing any lack of enthusiasm from his face. "Yes." A glance at his watch. "And now I need to get back to the store. Come into the dining room. I have a selection of shoes for you to try."

We leave Adele and Lance in the living room discussing household matters. As soon as the two of us are out of earshot, I ask, *So what was that look?*

He feigns ignorance with a shrug. He's busy sorting shoe boxes. *What look?*

He pulls out a pair of strappy Jimmy Choos and holds them up for my consideration.

I nod, take them from his hand and slip them on. They'll be perfect with the gown.

But I'm not *that* easily distracted. *The look you gave Lance when he said I would be going with him to the party. You seemed surprised that he'd ask me. Is there a reason I shouldn't go?*

Stephen pauses two beats too long before answering. *Of course not. It's just that Lance—Rick—has never brought a date to one of our soirees before. It's . . . interesting.*

A date? It's not like I'm the local prom queen. I'm one of their own. I throw Stephen a sharp-eyed look of curiosity. *Why wouldn't he bring me?*

He's guarding his thoughts, not letting anything but his words through. Finally he says, *Do you like the sandals?*

Yes.

He slips them from my feet and replaces them with a simple open-toed Blahnik pump. I turn my ankle to the right and left, as if examining the shoe, when in reality, I'm trying to probe his mind. I don't know how long he's been a vampire, but it's obviously long enough to know how to block an intrusion.

I take the shoe off and hand it to him. "I'll take this pair, too. I think that's all I'll need for the weekend."

His features soften. With relief? He stands and begins the process of putting the extra shoe boxes into an oversized canvas tote bag.

I move to his side and hand him boxes. *How long have you been vampire?*

Five years. And you?

Not quite one.

He turns and looks at me, eyes wide. *Really? You seem—I don't know—much older.*

If I was a mortal woman, I'd be insulted by that.

He holds up a hand, smiles. *No offense meant. You give off a serious old-soul vibe.*

He's just about finished repacking the boxes. *How do you know . . .* I almost say Lance, then realize I should probably be calling him Rick. It's how he's known here. I start again. *How do you know Rick?*

Stephen hoists the bag to his shoulder. *We have mutual friends. The vampire community in Palm Springs is small but closely knit.* He throws me an ironic smile. *Incestuously so.*

It doesn't take a genius to figure out the meaning in *that* remark. *You have the same sire?*

You'll have all your questions answered tonight. It should be an interesting evening.

It's the second time he's used that word. This time, there's no mistaking it. The subtle inflection he puts on the word "interesting" doesn't necessarily reflect a sense of anticipation or eagerness. I'm not sure whether Stephen is looking forward to tonight or dreading it.

Before I can ask anything else, he's moved into the living room. Lance is gathering up the garment bags. He leans over and kisses the top on my head when we join them. "I'll walk out with Stephen. See you in a minute."

Stephen says his good-byes to Adele, and he and Lance move toward the door.

Adele is clearing away the coffee service when she stops suddenly and looks up at me. "Do you care about Rick?"

It's asked with fierceness I recognize and appreciate. A fierceness that hardens her mouth and tenses her shoulders.

The same fierceness I'd use if I were concerned about the well-being of one I love. It prompts an honest answer. "Yes."

Her shoulders relax, she resumes cleaning up. "Do me a favor tonight, will you?"

"All right."

"Watch out for him."

"Watch out for Lance? That's a strange thing to say."

She picks up the tray. Her eyes are bright with concern that she's trying to mask with a smile. "You're right. I shouldn't have said anything. Ignore me."

"But you did. Adele, is there something I should be on the lookout for? Someone?"

She busies herself folding napkins, rearranging cups and spoons on the tray. She's not looking at me. "It's probably nothing. And besides, you're smart. I can tell. If there's something wrong, you'll figure it out."

Lance is closing the front door. I look up to watch him approach and when I turn around, Adele has made her escape into the kitchen.

CHAPTER 9

LANCE SPENDS THE AFTERNOON GIVING ME A grand tour of the house. Three floors of art, books, antique furniture and family history. A simple, pleasurable, uncomplicated exercise. I don't recognize Lance in much of it, but it's like visiting a museum. You don't have to have a personal connection to what's on exhibit to appreciate interesting *things* that represent the past.

Adele doesn't join us.

While we explore, I watch Lance and listen to his thoughts. There's no anxiousness in his manner, no nervousness about the party. He is neither alarmed nor disturbed at the prospect of attending. If anything, he is looking forward to it. He doesn't hide the fact that he's glad I will be accompanying him. I begin to feel that either Adele and Stephen are misguided in their concern or that my suspicious nature made me misconstrue what could be innocent remarks. Stephen because I'm a stranger being introduced into what is obviously a close-knit "family." Adele because she is afraid *I'll* hurt Rick. Asking me to watch out for him might have been another way to ask me not to hurt him.

We don't see Adele again until just before we're ready to leave the house. She's on her way out, too. She's dressed in black slacks and a fitted white top, a pair of simple flats on her feet. She's knotted a bright silk scarf resplendent in jewel tones at her neckline. She looks me over. "That gown is perfect for you."

Her compliment pleases me. I realize that I *want* her to like me. It's silly and makes no sense, but I want her to like me. I reach out and touch the scarf. "That's beautiful."

She smiles. "It was given to me by my mother. It's always been one of my favorites."

Lance asks, "Adele, would you like to join us for a drink before the party?"

She shakes her head. "No. But thank you for the invitation. It's my bridge night. Can't keep the girls waiting, you know."

She leaves through the front door. Her manner is relaxed, untroubled. No furtive glances my way, no whispered reminders of our conversation earlier. There's a big SUV waiting in the driveway. When the driver sees Lance silhouetted in the doorway, she waves. I make out two other females sitting in the back.

"Do you know Adele's friends?"

Lance closes the door. "Most of them. Sometimes she hosts the game." He touches my arm. "She's right about this gown. I don't think you've ever looked more beautiful."

His hands slide up my arms, his fingers begin to slip the straps off my shoulders.

The passion in his face burns through his fingertips, rages through his thoughts, stirs my own. "Maybe we should skip the party."

His lips are so close. I raise myself up to meet them. His kiss is all the answer I need. I let the gown fall in a silken puddle at my feet. I kick off my shoes and stand before

Lance naked and trembling and in a frenzy to get Lance naked, too.

He's stripping off his jacket when his cell phone rings.

"Don't answer it," I breathe, fumbling with the buttons of his shirt.

But he has the phone in his hand and by his expression, I know he recognizes the number. He pushes me gently away and puts the phone to his ear. He says nothing. In another few seconds, he snaps the phone shut.

"I'm sorry, Anna. We have to go. It's important we're not late."

He stoops to retrieve his jacket.

"We have to go? This minute?"

But he's reaching down for my dress. I snatch it up before he can. "Who was on the phone?"

He doesn't answer the second question, either. I can't get anything from his thoughts. I can forgive a lot of things, like the fact that he's kept his true identity from me, but here I am, standing naked in front of him, and he's pretending not to notice. The first time *that's* happened. Embarrassment yields quickly to anger. I turn my back and yank the dress back up.

Lance makes a noise in his throat. "Talk about coitus interruptus, huh?" He traces a finger across my shoulders. "I am sorry, Anna. We'll pick this up when we get home, okay?"

Something has changed. He's trying to be flippant, but his thoughts are troubled. Irritation tempers to concern.

I face him, slipping into my shoes. "Was that Stephen on the phone?"

Still no answer. Instead, he holds out a hand. "Let's get going."

Now I'm wildly curious. Who could be so important that Lance would drop everything (meaning me) to hustle us out of the house? And why did his mood change so abruptly?

CHAPTER 10

ONCE WE'RE ON THE WAY, I DON'T JUMP RIGHT IN and insist that Lance tell me who called. My instincts tell me to be patient even though patience is not one of my strong suits. I'll go in the back door if I can't get in the front. I try probing, to read his thoughts, but bump up against the steel curtain drawn around them.

Lance senses my concern, shifts into tourist guide mode as if to distract me. He keeps up a steady stream of chatter as we head to the restaurant, calling my attention to points of interest along the highway. He may be doing it for his benefit as well as my own. In any case, it works because by the time we pull into the parking lot, a little of the anxiety has faded from his mind.

But not from mine.

I remember my conversation with Adele and anxiety comes flooding back. I wish now I'd asked more questions. Was it something Lance said that prompted her concern? Or did she pick up on Stephen's reaction to hearing I'd be accompanying Lance to the party? I glance over at Lance, wondering if he's listening to my thoughts. But his attention is on the valet hurrying over to greet us. His mind is closed to me. Whatever worries he's harboring, he's determined to keep them to himself.

The valet comes directly around to the passenger side of the car, but Lance is quicker. He's out of the car and opening my door before the valet or I can do it myself. For once, I don't disparage the old-fashioned act of chivalry. I take his hand and let him help me from the car. He bends over my hand and kisses it. I feel like a schoolgirl on a first date. Come to think of it, maybe that's exactly what I am. I've always been the aggressor in relationships. I'm surprised at how nice it feels to let someone else take the lead.

Perhaps it's the place itself that's inspiring such romanticism. Melvyn's is located on the property of the Ingleside Inn, tucked off the main route so it seems isolated from the bustle of Palm Springs. It's a Spanish style masterpiece, redolent with lush greenery and resplendent with flowers. A riotous array of flowers, the scent of jasmine so potent it makes the senses swim.

Once inside, the maitre d' greets Lance like an old friend. The rest of our party has yet to arrive, so he suggests we wait at the bar.

I throw Lance a pointed look. *We left because you said we shouldn't be late. So where is everyone?*

Lance shrugs, squeezes my shoulders. *I'll make it up to you.*

He orders champagne. He's more relaxed again, his smile easy and confident.

Melvyn's is a great place to people watch. The bar is dark and intimate, the walls lined with pictures of the rich and famous who have visited here. There's even one of Lance—his arm around a gray-haired man.

I point to the picture and raise an eyebrow.

"The owner, Mel Haber."

I'm suitably impressed. Lance whispers names in my

ear as he recognizes locals who stop by our table to say hello. Humans. Mostly geriatrics. I wonder how long it will be before he will have to give up such a public existence in a place where he does not age. For the time being, it doesn't seem to bother him.

The champagne works its magic. By the third glass, I've forgiven him for rushing us out of the house. He's no longer apprehensive. He's laughing. His hand finds its way under the tablecloth to stroke my thigh through the silk of my gown. He inches his chair closer. Soon I feel his touch on my bare skin, his fingers dangerously close to sparking a reaction that is bound to get us thrown out of the restaurant.

He's watching, eyes flashing, feeling my body's rising heat. He's enjoying this.

I lean toward him, my own hand finding its way under the table. *Careful. Two can play—*

The words get choked off. My breath catches. My stomach twists into a knot. I jerk back and away from Lance and my eyes search the crowd.

Something is here. Something threatening. Something evil.

It's happening again. Just like when I was with David in that bar. This time, Lance is the one reacting with shocked alarm. He *feels* it, too, through me.

"Anna, what's wrong?"

I don't know. My heart is pounding. I feel sweat break out on my face. I want to stand up and run, but I can't. I can't even articulate the numbing fear that's bringing the animal so close to the surface.

"We have to get out of here."

Lance is on his feet. "Let's go."

I'm weak with relief at his response. I push back my chair and let him take my arm.

The waiter hurries over to our table. "Is she all right?"

Lance fumbles in his pocket and pulls out a fifty. "For you. Put the champagne on my tab."

The waiter nods that he will and stands aside for us to pass.

The pounding in my head and chest reach a crescendo. The instinct to attack is so strong, I'm not sure I can control it. The problem is, I don't know *what* to attack. As we go, my eyes roam the room, lighting on each face, trying to identify the threat. My gaze is met with startled, fearful, questioning expressions. I must be changing into the vampire and I have no control. I'm exposing myself to a roomful of humans and I have no control.

We're almost at the door. I duck my head, turn into Lance's shoulder, hiding the animal, swallowing back the panic. His arms tighten around me. "Hold on, Anna. We'll be outside in a minute."

He understands.

The door opens in front of us.

A figure in bass relief, a plangent voice.

"Rick. You're not leaving? The party is just about to start."

Something pulls tight within me.

I look into the face. Rugged, timeworn. Eyes cold, black, empty. Hair burnished copper, drawn back in a ponytail. Thin lips curve in a smile. No warmth. No humor.

I pull at Lance. "We have to go."

Lance is staring at me. "Anna. This is Julian Underwood. This is my friend."

No. This creature in his finely tailored suit is not anyone's friend. This creature is not simply a vampire. This creature is evil.

Lance, get away.

But he doesn't move. I know he's staring at me. I know he's confused. I feel it. I don't take my eyes off the monster.

Anna. Please. You don't know what you're doing.

I do know. My fingers flex, curl into fists.

The animal in front of me, this Julian Underwood,

draws himself up. He locks his eyes on mine. He's old. Older than any other vampire I've met. Centuries old. He's in my head, not just reading my fear but tasting it. He's rolling it around like a kid rolling a lollipop around his mouth. He likes it. He wants more.

It's grown quiet in a bubble around us. Humans come and go, passing us like a wake around a ship, not noticing the drama playing out in front of them. They laugh and chatter among themselves. There are five male vampires accompanying Julian, Stephen among them. They alone tense as they watch us. Their eyes are on their sire. They each have a female escort. Human. Young, beautiful. The women continue to talk among themselves, oblivious. They prattle on about hair and makeup and the beautiful gowns and jewels given them by their vampire escorts.

They are here for one purpose, and they are excited, eager. They are impatient for the pleasure that comes with being a blood host.

Only Underwood is alone.

Lance takes my arm. Gives it a gentle shake. "Anna. What's the matter with you?"

Underwood stops him, removing Lance's fingers and thrusting his hand away. *You've done well, tonight, Broderick. You've brought me quite a gift.*

Lance jolts upright. *Gift?*

Underwood is watching me. He feels my anger escalate. Smiles.

I look at Lance, raise my hand. "Don't worry. You and I will be leaving together."

Underwood's rage takes control. *Tell her, Broderick.*

But Lance is shaking his head. *No. I didn't mean—*

Underwood crooks a finger, sending a spear of white-hot pain at Lance. We all feel it, all of us under the influence of his mind. Lance cries out. The others stagger back.

I alone, remain still. The pain is intense, concentrated, a laser knife slicing at the core of my body. I want to fight it but something says no. Something tells me to focus on the pain, draw it in, redirect it.

Send it back.

Underwood closes his eyes. Only a tiny movement in his shoulders, an involuntary gasp, tells me it worked. Instead of debilitating him, though, the way it did Lance, the way it did the others, he welcomes it, absorbs it, lets it permeate his body and mind. After a moment, he licks his lips and smiles down at me.

You have a few tricks of your own, don't you?

He snaps his fingers. Breaks the spell. Turns to Stephen and the others. *Go inside. The private dining room is reserved for us. Tell Brian we're ready.*

As one, the five vampires and their hosts pick up the thread of their conversation as if nothing happened, move through the door, disappear into the interior of the restaurant. They show no reaction to the numbing pain of a moment before. Even Lance stands quietly beside me, his mind reflecting only concern for me. The events of the last five minutes lost.

I want to shake him. Scream. Snap him out of the fugue state he's lost in.

Underwood speaks to me. *And what about you, Anna Strong? Will you be staying?*

That he knows my name does not surprise me. He knew it before Stephen, before Lance. This creature in his Dolce & Gabbana suit and Ferragamo shoes made himself comfortable in my head. *How can you ask? You already know my answer.*

He shakes his head, mouth turned down in a frown of disappointment. *I was hoping for a more adventurous spirit. I'm sorry you feel so threatened.*

Threatened? I want to sink my teeth into his neck, shake him like a wolf with a rattler. Only Lance's presence keeps me from attacking. I don't know what hold he has on Lance, what harm he's capable of inflicting. Best to get away.

He signals to the doorman. "Would you be kind enough to call Ms. Strong a cab?"

I wave the doorman off. "That won't be necessary. Lance brought me, he'll take me home."

Again, a shake of the head. "I'm afraid not. Broderick and I have a lot of catching up to do. If you insist on leaving, it will be alone."

I look up at Lance. He has shut me out of his head.

My stomach contracts at the thought that he would want to stay. When he meets my gaze his expression is resigned and unafraid. What is wrong with him? He can't see this man is evil?

Lance takes my shoulders in his hands. "I won't be long."

No. Lance, he can't force you to stay. If it's a spell—

He kisses me, softly, on the lips. *Spell? Why would you think that? Julian is not forcing me. I want to stay.*

He drops his hands.

Underwood is watching me. Once again, he signals the doorman, who picks up a telephone at the valet desk.

Lance leaves me with a small wave. Underwood and I stare at each other.

"Don't fight it, Anna. Broderick and I are old friends. I'll send him back to you when we've caught up." He drags a finger down the length of my right arm. "He's safe with me."

My skin burns where his finger touched my skin. I jerk back, instantly angry with myself for the reaction. It's just what Underwood expected, his eyes narrowing with satisfaction.

"You fuck."

But Underwood has already turned away from me. I stare at his back.

I don't know what to do. I know I can't stay. When I looked into Underwood's eyes, I was looking into an abyss—empty, threatening, full of horror. I'm afraid if I stay, I'll be drawn into that pit. Even the depth of my disgust isn't enough to protect myself from this kind of evil. How could I imagine I'd be able to protect Lance?

I'll have to trust Lance's instincts. Underwood is his sire. It's too late now to ask the questions I should have asked him earlier. The questions I'll ask him the minute he gets home.

Underwood is more than an old-soul vampire. He possesses more than vampiric powers. He uses sorcery.

What sort of creature does that? What sort of demon?

CHAPTER 11

I'M ALONE IN THE HOUSE.

Restless.

Afraid.

Not for myself. For Lance.

I never should have left him. I let that bastard Underwood get to me. Now he's out there somewhere with Lance, and I'm here making myself crazy with worry. The worst thing? I don't know why. It's not as if Lance isn't capable of taking care of himself.

A clock somewhere chimes the hours. Midnight. Lance has been gone three hours.

I'm not waiting any longer.

I run upstairs, change out of the gown and into jeans and a T-shirt. I grab my keys and head for the garage.

Shit. I realize I don't know where the restaurant is located. I didn't pay attention on the ride over. I plug the name into the Jag's GPS system and the directions flash on the screen.

I'm there in twenty minutes. The parking lot is still full.

Music floats on the air from a lounge somewhere to the right.

The doorman stops me at the door. "I'm sorry, miss. No jeans after nine."

I stare at him. I didn't think places that had dress codes still existed. I fish a twenty out of my wallet. "I won't stay long. I just need to see if my friend is inside."

He waves away the money. "Sorry. Maybe if you tell me your friend's name?"

"Lance Turner. No, wait. He's probably known here as—"

"Rick." The guy grins. "The model, right? Sure. He was here. With Julian Underwood's party. They left about ninety minutes ago."

Ninety minutes? "Do you know where they went?"

He shakes his head. "No. Sorry."

A couple approaches and he moves away to open the door. When he comes back, I add another twenty to the first. "You wouldn't happen to know where Mr. Underwood lives, do you?"

He frowns. "If I started giving out customer's personal information, I wouldn't have a job very long, would I?"

Shit. He continues to glare at me as if I've insulted his integrity. He's a valet at a goddamned restaurant, for Christ's sake. It makes me want to show him what a real insult would be—knocking his ass to the ground in front of all his "customers" and slapping him until he squeals like a girl.

But what good would that do? None, except get me arrested.

I turn my back on the self-righteous jerk, run to the car. Time to move on.

Maybe Adele is back and knows where I can find Underwood. She knows so much about Lance's life, she's bound to know where "the boys" like to party.

I let myself back into the house through the garage. The

MG is still gone. I'm beginning to feel more anger than concern—at Lance, at myself. Why would he stay with Underwood instead of coming home with me? Why did I let him?

I start up the stairs, calling to Adele.

There's no answer.

Then I hear it.

A moan.

It stops me.

I grow still.

Listen.

It comes again. So soft, so low, it takes all my concentration to get a bearing on the sound. A human ear would never pick it up. In the silence that follows, I wonder if I imagined it. Could it be the wind?

No.

When it comes a third time, I *feel* pain behind it.

A spasm of alarm triggers the animal instinct. I feel the pain because I'm *meant* to feel it. I know it as surely as I know whose pain I'm feeling.

Lance.

Somewhere in this house. Not upstairs.

I ignore the frenetic beating of my heart.

Concentrate.

Lance, where are you?

No answer. Another ghostly moan.

From somewhere beneath me.

A basement?

Lance didn't show me a basement today.

Why isn't Adele here? She could tell me—

No time.

I start for the most logical place to find basement access. That cavern of a kitchen. There are no obvious doors that look like they would lead to a set of stairs. What next? There are a dozen sets of cabinets lining the back and one side of the kitchen. I open a half dozen before I hit on the right set. This one conceals not shelves and drawers but stairs.

I run down and into the darkness. It smells musty and dry. Old wine and long-forgotten root vegetables. Dust. Something else.

Blood.

Vampire eyes have no trouble seeing in the dark. They welcome it. Senses become more acute. Instincts sharpen.

I listen and watch. No more sound. No movement. I probe the darkness with my mind. I feel it. Lance is here.

He's here.

Lance.

No response except an unusual one. An instantaneous shutting down of his mind. He's hiding from me.

From me?

But not fast enough.

In two steps, I'm across the floor. I see him, huddled in the corner. He's naked, curled in a fetal position.

My human voice. "Lance. Why didn't you answer me? What's the matter?"

He burrows deeper into the corner. "You have to leave me alone, Anna."

I step closer. "You're hurt. I can see it. What happened?"

Go away. Please. You'll only make it worse.

Make what worse?

I'm at his side now. Close enough to see his face. Close enough to feel his despair. Close enough to see the bloody tracks ripped across his back.

CHAPTER 12

MY HAND FLIES TO MY MOUTH, STIFLING THE gasp. I don't ask who did this to him. I don't have to ask. I know.

I know.

I bend down, take his hand, hold it against my heart. "Let me help you upstairs."

He pulls away. I don't let him. After a moment, he gives in. Rises on shaky legs. I don't know when Adele will be back. I look around to find something to cover his nakedness. There's an old blanket on the floor. I wrap it around his waist. He allows me to lead him upstairs.

In the light, I see what's been done. Whip marks, something jagged, barbed. But something else. A white substance cakes the wounds, keeps them open, bleeding.

The smell tells me. Brine. The sea.

Salt.

Why salt?

Lance turns dull eyes toward me, answers the question

he read in my mind. "Salt keeps a vampire's wounds from healing. Leaves scars."

In a burst of clarity, I understand. Underwood wanted to inflict a punishment that would mark Lance forever. Scars like this would end his modeling career. End that part of him that's connected to the human community.

"Why?"

He turns his face away.

He doesn't need to answer.

It's me. Underwood did this because of me.

I want to howl in anger. All this because I refused to stay with him tonight? There has to be more. It doesn't matter. I swallow the rage. Save it for later to relish while I plot my revenge. Now, I'll get Lance into the shower. Maybe it's not too late to mitigate the damage.

"You can't," Lance says simply.

I turn the rage outward. "What do you mean, I can't? I won't let him do this. You can't let him do this. What's the matter with you?"

Lance's expression is resigned. He's prepared to accept Underwood's punishment.

I'm not.

"You can't fight me. Either you let me help you or I'll do it without your help. I'm stronger than you. You know it."

In spite of his anguish, Lance smiles. "I'm sorry to have gotten you mixed up in this."

He's been leaning on me. Now he straightens as much as his injured back allows. "I suppose truth be told, I'm more afraid of you than Julian anyway."

Humor. A good sign.

"Glad to see you've come to your senses." But my voice is rough with outrage. I put an arm around his waist and we trudge up the stairs to the bedroom.

I guard my thoughts. Lance has been through enough. I'll take care of him. Tonight.

I don't bother to strip. I climb into the shower with him, turn the water on his back. He winces and cries out. Vampires have remarkable healing powers, but we aren't impervious to pain. The salt makes it worse. I'm trembling at his suffering, but unless we get all the salt out of the wounds, the healing can't begin. I use my fingers to gently open the cuts, let the water dissolve the salt, wash it away. The water runs red with blood. It soaks my clothes, splashes on my face. I taste it. It's Lance's blood and—another's.

Lance has fed tonight.

I flash on the women in Underwood's entourage.

They were there for one purpose. It shouldn't surprise me that Lance would partake. We are vampire.

I don't like the unfamiliar stab of jealousy piercing my heart. It's unreasonable.

We are vampire.

I focus on Lance. The cuts, now clean, begin to heal. I think we have stopped the scarring. Any marks left at all will be unnoticeable. Having a fresh infusion of human blood has made the difference. We are revenant creatures, the walking dead who derive sustenance and immortality from what we take from the living.

I should be grateful to the women who provided Lance the gift that is allowing him to heal like this. I should be. I run a hand lightly over his back. The cuts are fading. My own blood would have eased the pain, but only a human's blood could have worked this miracle.

I should be grateful.

Except the jealousy returns. He owes this human a debt. *I* owe this human a debt. The thought stabs at my heart.

Lance has been leaning against the shower wall, propped on one hand, back to me, head down. I put my arms around him. I listen to his heart, feel the cloud of physical discomfort lift from his thoughts only to be replaced by a darker shadow. Despair. The torment is as real as the pain.

"It's all right, Lance," I whisper. "You're safe now."

Only when he begins to shake do I realize he's crying. He won't turn around. Won't let me into his thoughts. I've never felt so helpless. I do the only thing I can think of. I tighten my arms around him and hold him as he cries.

I'VE LOST TRACK OF TIME.

Lance is quiet against me, no longer shaking. I can't tell what he's thinking because he's not letting me in. He still won't face me.

When the water in the shower turns cold, I stir and drop my hands. "We should get out."

At the sound of my voice, he rouses himself and pushes open the shower door. I turn off the tap and step out after him.

He's wrapping a towel around his waist. When he turns, he looks surprised to see I'm dressed. Embarrassment darkens his face. "I didn't realize—"

I put a hand to his lips. "It's all right." I begin to peel off my clothes, let them drop into the sink. When I'm naked, he steps close and wraps me in a towel. His hands are trembling, his fingers icier than usual. If he were a human, I'd say he was in shock. I don't know if vampires experience such frailties.

I take his hand and lead him into the bedroom. I'm not shielding my thoughts. I know Lance is reading them as we crawl exhausted under the bedclothes. Our bodies don't touch, but I've never been more *aware* of a physical presence. We're linked now by something more than mutual attraction or sexual convenience. It happened without my knowing it. It happened without my consent.

But it happened.

The feelings that washed over me when I saw Lance in that basement. The jealousy I experienced when I knew he'd been with a woman—even to feed. The deep rage that burns inside when I think about Underwood. The satisfaction I will experience when I make him pay for what he's done.

All real and powerful, emanating from the one emotion I'd managed to avoid my entire human life. The one emotion I never imagined I'd experience as vampire.

The one emotion I expected to elude me forever.

Lance rolls on his side and looks down at me. The halo of his hair surrounds his beautiful face and glows in the darkness as if backlit. "You still can't say it though, can you?"

I roll toward him. Brush a tangle of hair from his face. Touch his cheek. "You know," I whisper. "Isn't knowing enough?"

CHAPTER 13

LANCE IS ASLEEP BESIDE ME. SO WHY AM I AWAKE? The clock on the nightstand says six a.m. We've been in bed only a few hours.

It's the sun. The fucking desert sun, peeking through a chink in the curtains, sending a laser spear of light directly at my eyes. A cosmic wake-up call.

That's why I'm awake.

I lift my face, sniff.

That and the smell of coffee.

I groan and roll over.

Adele must be awake, too.

Memories of last night flood back. I raise myself on my elbows and lean toward Lance.

He looks peaceful. I doubt he'll remain that way when he wakes up. When I start questioning him.

I need to find out why Underwood attacked him so savagely. I need to find out what part I played in it, because the one thing I'm sure of is that I am at the core of Underwood's cruelty. He wanted something from me last night and when he didn't get it, he took it out on Lance.

Why would Lance allow it to happen? Why wouldn't he fight back? Or did he, and was what happened the result of his resistance?

I scoot carefully away from him, not wanting to disturb him. I start to swing my legs over the edge of the bed.

An arm encircles my waist, pulls me back. "Where are you going?"

Lance wraps his arms around me, cradles me so that his head is on my shoulder. Our bodies fit together like two halves of a whole. It feels right—like this is the way we are supposed to start each morning and this is the way we are supposed to end each night. When he presses his body against mine, his erection nudges the small of my back. An invitation.

I groan a little and try to move away. "Lance, wait. We need to talk about—"

The words die on my lips.

He's smoothing the hair away from my neck, nuzzling my earlobe, tracing his tongue along my chin line. The tremor starts in my core, heating my blood, sending sparks of arousal to every part of my body.

I'm lost. In the rhythm of Lance's heartbeat. In the feel of his lips at my neck. When he opens the vein, starts to drink, the world is reduced to tactile pleasure. His hand slips between my legs, his fingers begin their persuasive and skillful exploration, his penis throbs against my skin.

I don't want him to stop. I moan and push back against him, urging him on, until I can control it no longer.

The first waves of orgasm come quickly. I want him inside me. I push him away, feel the skin on my neck tear as we reverse positions. Blood trickles down my breasts. I don't care. I'm on top, guiding him between my legs, forcing him deep inside, opening his neck. His blood is what I want. Blood that tastes of Malibu and the sun and me and—

The host from last night.

She's there and I want to drink her in. Lance had her. I want to have her, too. She tastes like good wine and expensive perfume. Her blood rolls over my tongue and down my throat but as much as I drink, I can't rid him of her. Not completely.

Anna, stop.

Lance's voice from far away.

No.

I burrow my mouth closer to his neck, continue to drink, impervious to everything except the need to drain him of this woman's blood.

Lance grabs a handful of my hair, yanks hard, pulling my head away from his neck.

I fight it, fight him, lunge again for his neck. She's still there. Still running through his veins. I want her out.

He flings me back on the bed. His hand is at his neck. Blood runs between his fingers, down his chest, soaking sheets and blankets. His eyes are wild, questioning, afraid.

Anna. Heal me.

For an instant I stare at him, uncomprehending. The animal disappears when the human Anna grasps what she's seeing. My stomach lurches.

What have I done?

Lance. I'm sorry.

I reach for him and he hesitates only a second, searching my face, assuring himself that he recognizes the human, before bending near me, allowing me to close my lips around the jagged wound in his neck. This time, I'm not drinking, not taking in blood, but sucking gently to repair the damage. The artery mends, the skin knits closed. The angry flush of my assault fades as I watch.

But Lance is pale, weak. I drained too much blood.

What have I done?

I open a vein in my wrist with my teeth and hold it to his

lips. He grabs my hand and sucks at the dripping blood eagerly. He's like a starved animal. He drinks until the color returns to his flesh.

Then he stops.

He stops.

He wipes his hand across his mouth and without hesitating, brings my hand once more to his lips to close the wound. Then he bends his head to my neck and I feel the rush of cells regenerating, of skin renewing itself.

When he's done, we both sink back on the bed. Instead of the pleasure of coupling, we're drained, exhausted and confused. I feel it in Lance as strongly as in myself.

I had questions for Lance. I imagine now he'll have questions for me. But nothing he asks can be as disturbing as the questions I have for myself.

CHAPTER 14

A SHUDDER OF DISGUST RACKS MY BODY. WE'RE lying close, but not touching. I'm afraid to touch him. Afraid he might pull away.

I've never lost control like that. Never felt the bloodlust so strongly I didn't know when to stop. I'm embarrassed and ashamed, hiding it behind a curtain of carefully guarded thoughts. I want to say it out loud, admit it to Lance, but the truth is too damning to drag into the light. I was jealous. Jealous of a mortal woman. Jealous of the woman who may very well have saved Lance's life.

Lance breaks the silence first.

"I should never have brought you here."

His simple declaration fuels my shame. He blames himself.

Not what I expected. Not what I deserve. My shoulders tense, a second tremor of disgust raises bile in my throat. I open my mouth to object and he puts a finger over my lips.

I didn't know he would be in town. Stupid. I should have asked Adele when I talked to her. I didn't think.

A thousand questions present themselves, but the most important thing I can say now is the truth. *You're here because of me. Because of that thing that attacked me in my garage. You're here because you were helping me. None of this is your fault.*

Lance doesn't answer. His mind is troubled; he is unconvinced. I take his chin in my hand, turn his face toward mine. *We have to talk about Julian. Why did he attack you last night? Why did you let him?*

Lance releases a long breath. He doesn't try to pull away, but he doesn't meet my eyes, either. *Julian is my sire. I owe him.*

Owe him? I think of the animal who sired me—Donaldson—who never planned to turn me, only to rape and kill. Somehow the idea of *owing* a sire anything is as repugnant as it is ludicrous.

I sit up in bed, pull a corner of the bloodstained sheet up and shake it in Lance's face. *Julian is the reason this happened. What the hell is going on? He's more than vampire. He possesses magic. How?*

Lance sits up, too, leans against the headboard. *He claims his mortal mother was a gypsy, his father a warlock. He's been vampire nearly five hundred years.*

A warlock? I flash on Belinda Burke and her sister, Sophie. Both witches, the female equivalent. The black magic witch of the pair, Belinda, I killed with my own hands. Magic is passed along in the genes like bone structure and eye color. That explains the magic, though I didn't know it was possible for a warlock to become vampire. Two incredibly potent creatures combined in one. Leads me to the next question.

How did he become vampire?

This time there is no hesitation. Lance begins to talk as if sharing the story might lessen the burden of his guilt.

He was born in Labourd in Basque in the sixteenth century, during the time of the Spanish Inquisition. His father was burned at the stake as a Sorginak witch. His mother barely escaped to Italy with her own life and the child. But when he was sixteen, plague hit her village. She died within a few days. Julian was left to die, too. That's when he was "rescued" by a mysterious stranger who restored him to life and took him to live in Eastern Europe.

Lance releases a breath, looks away, then back at me. *You're not going to believe who he claims sired him.*

Let me guess. Vlad. Dracula. Who else would such an egomaniac claim as his sire?

Lance's eyebrows shoot up. *How did you know?*

If Lance's expression weren't so serious, I'd be laughing. *You are kidding, right?*

He shakes his head. *No. And he seems to be able to back it up. He has documents that date back to the fourteenth century, given to him, he claims, by Vlad.*

Now I do laugh. *How could you believe that crap? Is that how he seduced you? What was going on in your life that would make you vulnerable enough to fall for such bullshit?*

Lance tenses. Anger shadows his eyes and tightens his mouth. He pushes away from me and swings his legs out of bed.

I'm immediately sorry for the outburst. Truth is I know nothing about the circumstances of Lance's becoming. I was taken without my consent. Perhaps he was, too. I watch him as he disappears into the bathroom. He slams the door shut and I hear the shower. He's back in a few minutes dressed in jeans and a T-shirt. I jump out of bed and step in front of him before he reaches the door.

I'm sorry.

He stops, but only because I'm blocking his way. I can see he's fighting the urge to push me aside. I hold up a hand in apology. *I really am sorry. I had no right to say that.*

His shoulders remain rigid.

Please. I want to hear more. I want to understand what

the connection is between you and this man. It's more than a familial bond. You let Julian whip you like an animal and you were willing to bear the scars of that whipping forever. I need to understand.

Lance takes a tiny step backward. *I can't tell you why it happened. I won't. I can only tell you that by allowing you to help me, I may not have forever. Not after this.*

After what? For Christ's sake, Lance, tell me. If you don't, I swear I'll go after him. I'll make him tell me. I'll kill him if he doesn't.

Lance lets a smile tip the corner of his mouth. *You plan to kill him anyway, don't you?*

Then you lose nothing by telling me, do you?

Jesus, Anna. The sternness has returned to his face. *You may be powerful, but do you really think you can best a five-hundred-year-old vampire? You said it yourself; he's more than vampire, he possesses magic.*

I can tell by the set of his jaw that this argument will get us nowhere. *At least tell me how he turned you. You know my story.*

His expression says he recognizes a diversionary tactic when he hears one. His thoughts confirm the look, but to my surprise, he turns around and takes a seat on the edge of the bed.

Better sit down, too, he says. *This may take a while.*

Then he adds, "Suppose we could ask Adele to bring us coffee first? I smell it brewing."

I nod and he reaches for the phone, makes the request and hangs up. "She'll be right up."

"Then I'd better get dressed."

I'm glad for the chance to gather my thoughts. Instead, as I pull on shorts and a T-shirt, I find gathering my thoughts is the last thing I want to do. Thinking means examining what happened in that bedroom and I can't face it. So instead, I listen. To Adele's knock as it announces her arrival, listen to Lance and her chat about last night—he gives her a highly fictionalized version of our evening—and listen to the clank of a coffee service being set up. I wait until I hear the snick of the door closing behind her before reappearing.

Lance is pouring coffee into two mugs. He's pulled the bedclothes up over the pillows to hide the blood. He looks up when he sees me. "Adele says good morning."

I take the mug from his outstretched hand, avoiding his eyes. Sip.

Kona blend. Good stuff.

We return to our perches on the side of the bed. I don't look at Lance or push him to begin. I know he will when he's ready.

And he does.

He drains his cup, slouches back against the headboard.

"I was born in South Africa in 1925. On my family's estate. You know the business they were in. From the time I was old enough to understand what diamond mining was all about, I hated it. Progress has been made in the last century, sure. But slave labor is still slave labor even if those slaves are now given nicer places to live and better food to eat."

Lance twists the cup in his hand. "My brothers and sister never seemed to mind. Their lives revolved around the next shopping trip to the continent, the next glamorous soiree. They paid more attention to their pampered pets than the people who broke their backs to provide that lifestyle. I couldn't wait to get away."

He sets the cup down on the nightstand. "I shouldn't have been so anxious. I ran away from home when I was seventeen. Went to Cape Town. It was December 1942. A British ship en route to South Africa, the HMS *Ceramic*, was torpedoed by a German submarine west of the Azores. Took the ship three hours to sink and the Germans let it. Saved one man for interrogation, but let the other six hundred fifty-six die. Most aboard were South Africans returning home."

His eyes take on a faraway look. "Like most South Africans, I was outraged. And like most idealistic seventeen-year-olds struggling with private demons I couldn't fight, I wasted no time in joining the battle against demons I could. I enlisted in the South African Third Infantry Division. If I couldn't fight my parent's system, I could sure as hell fight the Germans."

I touch his arm. "What did your parents do when they found out?"

A bitter smile twists the corners of his mouth. "Nothing. My father decided the discipline would be good for me. Even took credit for my enlisting. Ironic. Since I was the only one in the family who exercised any kind of discipline at all. But it didn't matter. Not really. For the first time in my life, I wasn't Broderick DeFontaine. I was Aircraftman Rick DeFontaine, and I had work to do that would benefit all people, not just the self-indulgent rich."

He picks up his cup and crosses the room to the coffeepot. "The Third Division never took part in any battles while I served. We mostly organized and trained the South African home defense services."

He raises the pot in my direction. I nod and hold out my cup to him. He fills it, returns the pot to the warmer and rejoins me on the bed. "I don't know how much you know about Germany's war plans. Early on, Hitler devised what he called the 'Madagascar Plan.' All of Europe's Jews were to be forcibly deported to Madagascar." He shakes his head. "Maybe if it had been allowed to happen, lives would have been saved. But Madagascar was a strategic island and British troops invaded it in mid-1942. The Battle of Madagascar took place before I joined, but following the end of the campaign, I was assigned to a reconnaissance squadron. We flew missions over the countryside, looking for Japanese who had plans of their own for the island. During one of those missions, the engine on our plane failed. We crashed in an isolated area. The pilot died. I didn't."

The tone of his voice suggests he might be thinking the pilot had been the lucky one. His thoughts are black with despair.

I'm glad you didn't die, Lance. My life would be empty if you'd died. You have to know that.

He smiles at me, sadly, then looks away. "I was found by a peasant family. I didn't speak Mâlagasy and they didn't speak English. They tended to me the best they could, but I'd suffered a compound leg fracture in the crash and a couple of nasty cuts, one of which nearly took my right ear. Infection set in pretty quickly. I'll never know why they did what they did next. Maybe they were afraid of what would happen if I was found with them. Maybe they thought they would be blamed for my death. But once it became clear that I wasn't getting better, they took me to an area known as Tsingy. It's a park now, but in 1942 it was nothing more than an isolated forest of limestone, mangrove swamps and lakes. They left me there. With water and a few scraps of food."

Lance is rubbing at his left leg, at a ghostly ache from a long-healed wound. I put my hand on top of his to stop it. "What happened then?"

He shuts his eyes. "I was crazy with fever and delirium. I half crawled, half stumbled for days until I could go no farther. Finally, I just lay down on the ground and waited to die. I had no idea how far I'd gone or how long I'd been alone. The last thing I remembered was staring at a night sky. It was a sliver of a moon and a sky awash with stars. Suddenly, one of those stars became a fireball that moved across the sky. It flew in a rainbow arc with a glittering tail from east to west. A shooting star. Then it stopped. Seemed to hover right over me. I reached out my hand to touch it and a shadow passed between us. A shadow that became a figure, then a face. A shadow that became a man."

Lance rubs his eyes, draws a sharp breath. "He leaned over me and asked one question. 'Do you seek death or immortality?' Simple question. I had no way of knowing how complicated my answer would prove to be."

Lance gives me a rueful smile. "I never told anyone the story before. Not even Stephen or the others. We were brothers but we each kept the secret of how we became. Julian never told us that we had to. Somehow, though, we knew it would make him unhappy if we did."

"What was Underwood doing in a forest in Madagascar?"

He shrugs. "At the time, I was too sick to ask. Later, it didn't seem important. He saved me. Or so I thought."

Lance's mood shifts suddenly. He's anxious, as if realizing that sharing his story with me might make Julian unhappy, too.

I rub his arm, reassure him with a warm smile. "He won't know that you told me. What happened after he found you in Madagascar?"

But he's not reassured by my touch or smile. He frowns, begins once again to twist the cup in his hand, his thoughts turbulent and disjointed. He's frantic with worry that he's done something wrong, that Underwood will *know*, that he's put me in danger.

"Lance." I take him by the shoulders. "Julian won't hurt you anymore. He won't hurt me."

His eyes are wild. "He's too strong. He knows things. He knows about you. What you are. He thought I was bringing you to him last night. *Delivering* you to him. It's why he got so angry. He realized what I felt for you. It's why—"

His voice breaks off. A sob catches in his throat. He is shaking and afraid, and I don't know what to do. I've never been exposed to anything like this before. Even Avery, the vampire who made my life a living hell in the weeks after I was turned, wasn't able to exert this much control. He used the subtle power of seduction and then it only worked when we were together. Underwood is wielding his control like a sledgehammer and seems to be able to reach across time and space.

I realize I have only one way to fight it. Get Lance out of here. Sort through what I've learned and come up with a plan to break Underwood's hold. My first impulse to kill him may be a good start. But Lance is in bad emotional shape. The most important thing now is taking care of him.

"Let's go back to San Diego."

Lance shakes his head. "It won't do any good. He wants you. He won't stop and he won't give up. He needs you. It's so close now. The prophecy will be fulfilled and you're the one who will make it happen."

Lance's words come at me like stones launched from a slingshot. "I don't understand. What are you talking about? When I make what happen? You're not making sense."

This time, when Lance looks at me, the cloud has lifted from his face, his eyes are clear. "You are the one."

Oh god. I shut my eyes. Not Lance, too. I've lived the last year being regaled by those in the vampire community who think of me as some sort of uber-vamp. It's why Avery focused his attention on me and Williams won't leave me alone. I hate it. Until now, Lance was the one vampire who never pressured me to pursue the ridiculous claim.

Until now.

Lance grabs my shoulders, eyes boring into mine. "Underwood knows, Anna. It's the reason he sent me to you."

"*He* sent you to me?" I shake my head. "No, Culebra sent you to me. I remember. It was at that bar, Glory's. You said Culebra sent you."

Something flashes behind Lance's eyes—shame, sorrow, remorse.

And the lie.

He looks away. *It wasn't Culebra. It was Julian. Him and Warren Williams.*

CHAPTER 15

NO.

It can't be true.

I jump up, away from Lance, not wanting to look at him, not trusting myself to be close.

I feel everything he's feeling. A hurricane of conflicting emotions.

It doesn't matter.

Because mingled with the regret, the fear, the love, is everything he's hidden from me.

The lie that it had been Culebra who sent him to me as a *distraction* all those months ago. That Underwood and Williams were working together. They wanted someone to get close to me. Someone supernatural. Someone who could be controlled. Someone I would be attracted to.

They sent me Lance.

Bile burns the back of my throat. I clutch my stomach to keep from gagging.

How could I have been so naive? I think back to conversations I had with Culebra about Lance—I never once broached the subject of how he knew Lance. I never thought to ask. I didn't care. I was gullible and accepted Lance as eagerly as a bitch offered a pork chop.

Oh, and how that fucker Williams played me. He made fun of my relationship with Lance. Made me defend it. Knew if he mocked it, I'd most likely stay with Lance.

And I did.

God.

I want to howl with rage.

How could I have been so stupid?

I have to get out of here.

Where are my car keys?

I dart frantically around the room. My head and stomach—my *blood*—is on fire. I sweep *things* off the nightstand, Lance's mug, a book, a lamp. The sound of breaking pottery doesn't quell the thirst for vengeance. I grab a chest at the end of the bed. Push it with so much force it slams into the wall.

Even the splintering of wood, the rain of broken plaster, is not enough. Fury makes the animal leap to the surface.

I *feel* Lance, moving toward me. I whirl to face him.

He stops. He sees it in my face. Danger. The animal enraged, betrayed. The animal wounded.

He steps back.

Finally. I spy my keys and purse on a chair. Where I'd thrown them after finding Lance last night.

Last night.

I can't think about it now.

I can't think of anything except getting away from here.

Lance tries to reason with me. He holds out his arms. He uses words like danger and risk, caution and threat. Empty words from far away that ricochet around my head like leaves in a whirlwind. He wants to protect me.

I bare my teeth, laugh and snarl. "You can't protect yourself."

He lets his hands fall to his side. He has no answer to rebut the truth.

I'm done.

I don't bother with shoes. I run downstairs, almost smacking into Adele. She jumps out of the way. She has a fresh pot of coffee in her hand. I smell the hot coffee as it spills, see her jerk as it scalds her. She yelps.

I don't stop.

"Anna, what's wrong?"

But I'm past her. Her voice trails behind me as I race through that cavernous house. Too much space that suddenly feels claustrophobic, I'm so anxious to get away.

From far off, I hear Lance pounding down the stairs, too. I have a wide lead. I hit the remote control on my way out the back door and by the time the garage door opens, I've got the Jag in gear and I'm screeching out of the driveway.

I'm at the gate when an explosion shakes the car.

A boom. Deafening. Painful. My hands clasp my ears.

Then silence. Nothing until the security guard is out of the guardhouse and pounding on my window. "Are you all right?"

I look up at him, ears ringing, head reeling, smell of blood in my nose. I open the door, stumble out. "What the hell was that?"

He's looking over my shoulder, back the way I came. "I don't know. Came from the direction of one of the houses."

One of the houses? I follow his gaze. Black smoke roils up against the distant sky. There aren't that many houses on this road. I can see half of them from here.

I can't see Lance's.

Jesus.

I start to run, oblivious to the guard's pleading that I should stay with him, that I'm hurt.

Hurt? It isn't until he says it that I realize the blood I smell is my own. I must have hit my forehead on the steering wheel or the dash. I don't know. I don't care. I wipe the blood out of my eyes with a forearm and keep going. The fastest way is over fences, through yards. Easy for me. Easy for vampire.

Follow the smell, the smoke. Acrid. Metal and rubber.

A car?

No one around. No one peering out windows or spilling from doors to see what happened. Where the hell is everyone? Are these all vacation homes? Are they all empty? No matter. The absence of mortals gives the vampire rein.

Two minutes and I'm at the scene.

The last house at the end of the road. A ball of flame surrounds a red MG.

Lance's car.

CHAPTER 16

A FIGURE MOVES INSIDE THE CAR.

Lance.

A dry heave racks my body as a sickening flashback to another vampire caught by flames propels me back.

Ortiz in a warehouse. A burst of light as his body ignited.

The vampire retreats.

I couldn't save Ortiz.

I can't save Lance.

Can I?

Another flash. Williams face. Distorted. Angry. *You could have saved Ortiz. Flames can't hurt you.*

Lance is pushing at the door, pounding on the window. Neither yields. He can't seem to break free. His strength should be enough. Is it his terror of the fire? Fear that even if he gets out of the car, he has nowhere to go?

The floor of the garage is a sea of flame. Something in the garage exploded, not the car. The flames haven't touched Lance yet. But they're creeping toward the car.

They could ignite the cloth top or the gas tank sitting in the undercarriage.

Adele at my side, screaming.

"Help him!"

Lance claws at the roof of the car, trying to rip it open.

He hears Adele, looks back, sees me. When our eyes meet, he stops fighting. He drops his hands, shakes his head. He resigns himself to death. Like Ortiz. He welcomes it because—

Reparation.

He doesn't want me to risk my life for his. It's there in his thoughts. Sorrow and regret.

No.

I won't lose him.

The need to save him is stronger than the fear. The animal is stronger than the human. I need vampire. She is reluctant to come back. Flames are one of the ways we can die. She remembers Ortiz, too.

I force her to come. We have to try. She relinquishes control with a snarl and a cry.

I crouch, leap through the fire toward the car like a lioness through a burning hoop. I'm at the car. Hands grasp scorched metal, pull. Flames lick at my skin, my clothes. Pain rips into me. I hop on bare feet, first one then the other, to keep from howling with it.

The door is stuck. I gather all my strength, heave and pull it from the hinges. I toss it away, reach in, pull Lance out. I scoop him up, cradle him against me, leap again. One minute we're in hell and the next, we're lying in the grass at the side of the driveway.

Then a whoosh and another burst of light and heat as the gas tank of the MG catches. The car is consumed in a fiery ball.

Too close.

Sirens. From the highway.

I look over at Lance. "Are you all right?"

Adele looming over both of us. "My God, Anna. You saved him." She reaches out a hand, stops herself, pulls it back, blanching.

What's wrong with her?

Lance speaks then. *You came back.*

There is so much gratitude and surprise and puzzled astonishment in those three words that, in spite of the anger I felt—what, two minutes ago?—I now find myself smiling. *I'm still mad at you.*

He reaches out a hand. *I can live with that.*

Adele squats down. "The police are coming. What do you want to do?"

Lance climbs to his feet, reaches down, pulls me up with him.

Gently. For the first time, I see the way he's looking at me, too. With great concern. "What?"

But he's speaking to Adele. "We'll answer their questions. Not much else we can do." He looks at me. "But you. I'm not sure how we can explain . . ." His words trail off, his eyes sweep the length of my body.

I glance down. My clothes are scorched remnants. Tattered shorts and what's left of a T-shirt. But my skin.

My skin.

I hold up a hand. Blackened skin is already flaking and beginning to peel away. My legs. My torso. The healing process has begun. But the realization that I'm burned over most of my body brings with it *consciousness.*

First, pain. The shock of it. Great debilitating waves of pain.

Blinding. Searing. It buckles my knees. Lance catches me, eases me to the ground.

Then. Comprehension.

Lance's eyes, watching, reading.

He understands.

I went through fire.

I went through fire.

Ironically, I think Williams was right. In a way. Flames don't kill me. But *hurt* me? You bet your ass.

Another siren joins the chorus.

"We have to get you away from here."

Lance's voice reaches out, pulls me back.

"If the police see you, they'll insist you go to a hospital."

Adele. "Take her to my room. They'd have no reason to go to the back of the house."

The sirens grow louder. I glance at the garage. The flames burn themselves out. The MG is reduced to a charred metal hulk. But the garage itself, the structure, and the adjoining house are curiously untouched.

Lance picks me up and runs through the front door, Adele at his heels. Where his hands touch my skin, the pain is so great, I have to bite my lip to keep from crying out. He feels it. He trembles at the thought that he's causing me so much agony.

I try to smile. It hurts too much.

Adele's room is off the sunroom in the back. Lance carries me inside, lays me on the bed.

Someone is pounding on the front door.

Adele shoos Lance out with a wave of her hand.

"I'll take care of her. You go speak to the authorities."

Lance leaves quickly. Adele moves to the side of the bed. "What can I do to help you?" she asks.

Open a vein and let me drink, the vampire inside me says.

"Nothing," the human says. "I'll heal. It may take a while. Go help Lance with the cops. Tell him to come when he's finished. By then, maybe I can move up to his room. Give you yours back."

"Don't worry about that," Adele says. "There are plenty of extra bedrooms in this house."

She moves toward the door. "Are you sure I can't get you anything?"

She's having a hard time looking at me. I've seen enough CSI programs to know what a burn victim looks like. If she didn't know I wasn't human before, she sure as hell knows it now. It must be awkward having to talk to a piece of charred meat.

"Maybe some water?" I reply.

She's happy to run any errand that takes her away from me. When she returns with a bottle of water, she holds it out. "Do you need help drinking?"

"No. Thank you. Go see what's going on outside. I'll be fine."

She leaves and I take a long drink. I'm not feeling nearly as confident as I let on. I hold up a hand, flex my arm. I don't seem to have lost bone or muscle mass. Only skin. I touch my face. Not much damage there. At least not that I can feel. My hair? Dry on the ends, but I still have hair. That's got to mean something.

My arms, legs and torso are burned the worst. And the balls of my feet.

The pain isn't as bad.

I let my body relax, let my head drop against Adele's pillow. The scents of lavender and baby powder tickle my nose.

Subtle undertones almost drowned out by the putrid smell of burned flesh.

My burned flesh.

I close my eyes. Weariness washes over me. I fight it. There are so many things I should think about. So many questions to ask. So much uncertainty to puzzle through.

But the need of the body to escape pain is stronger. I can't fight it.

One moment I'm conscious, the next I'm not.

CHAPTER 17

I'M DREAMING. AT LEAST, I *THINK* I'M DREAMING.

I sense Adele standing over me.

"Is she asleep?"

A male voice from out of sight behind her. "Yes. She'll be out for quite a while."

"Is she in pain?"

"We've taken care of it. You can go back downstairs. She shouldn't be disturbed."

ADELE AGAIN. THIS TIME, MY EYES ARE OPEN. HER hair is tied back from her face with her mother's scarf. She raises my head, brings a glass to my lips. "Drink, Anna."

I do. A sip of water.

The same male voice as before, "Be careful. Just a little."

I know that voice. Who is it? I can't turn my head. The effort to raise it is too much. I try to speak.

Adele holds a finger to her lips. "Not yet, Anna. Go back to sleep. It's not time."

As she steps back, I hear him say, "She's not really awake. Her eyes may be open, but believe me, she's still asleep."

He's wrong, I think as I drift back off.

THIS TIME, I STRUGGLE FOR CONSCIOUSNESS, SWIM toward the surface against a strong current, determined to stay awake. Before I open my eyes, I listen.

A clock ticks. A bird sings. A dog barks. Under it all, the faraway hum of traffic.

Something else.

A heartbeat nearby. Soft breathing.

A human. Close.

Blood. I smell it.

Yet, it awakens no hunger.

Why?

I open my eyes.

Above me, tiled fresco.

Familiar. Lance's room.

I turn my head toward the sound of the heartbeat.

A woman sitting on a chair near the bed. She's asleep, I watch her chest rise and fall. I don't recognize her. Why is she here?

I try to sit up. Something stops me. A glance down and I know why. A wide strap across my chest. It allows no movement.

Panic.

I pull at it and start to yell.

The woman jerks awake.

Her movement sends a sharp stab of pain into my right arm.

A flurry of footsteps from outside.

The door flies open.

"Lance?"

He's at my side. He bends over, drapes his upper body over my chest to prevent me from moving. "Shhh," he croons. "It's all right. I'm here. Don't try to move yet. Let me loosen the restraints."

Restraints? Not comforting. I struggle harder.

He's fumbling with something at the side of the bed. Another sharp twinge and my arm is free. Then he pulls at the strap and it falls to the side.

The woman in the chair is watching wide-eyed. Suddenly, Adele is at her side. She pulls something from the woman's arm and slaps a piece of gauze where a small bubble of blood is blossoming.

"Hold your arm straight up for a minute," she tells her. "And then you can go downstairs."

I watch uncomprehending. "Lance, what's happening?"

He is smiling and stroking my hair. "Welcome back, Sleeping Beauty," he says. "How do you feel?"

How do I feel? I don't know. I press my fingers against my eyes. How am I supposed to feel?

Suddenly, the touch of my fingers against my eyelids trips the memory.

My skin. On fire. The pain.

I hold up my hand, turn it back and forth, amazed at what I see.

The ravaged skin is gone. My hand is undamaged. I trail my fingers up my arm. Throw back the covers. I'm wearing a large T-shirt. Under it, the skin of my torso is smooth, flushed. Normal.

I choke out the words. "I'm healed."

He nods. "You're healed. And it only took two days." He laughs. "And a dozen or so hosts."

I glance again toward the woman. She has a Band-Aid at the crook of her elbow. Adele is walking her out.

"How did you do it?"

"Took a page out of a medieval text. You couldn't feed,

but you needed blood to heal. We set up an intravenous line between you and the donors. Worked like a charm, though we had to keep you doped up. Couldn't have you thrashing about and pulling out the needle."

I shake my head. "How did you come up with that idea?"

A voice from behind him, the voice I remember from a dream, spoke up. "It was my idea, actually."

Of course it was. If I thought I could pull it off without falling flat on my face, I'd jump out of bed and hug the guy stepping around to join Lance at the side of the bed. But I can't trust my legs, so I do the only thing I feel capable of. I hold out my arms and beam a smile. "I should have known. Who else would have the guts to tie me to a bed and force-feed me?"

Daniel Frey grins back. "Who else indeed."

CHAPTER 18

TWO HOURS LATER I'VE HAD A SHOWER. WITH Lance's help. A déjà vu moment, only this time, he's supporting me. Two days flat on your back and even a vamp's legs become wobbly. Then, dressed in shorts and one of Lance's tank tops, I'm sitting by the pool on a chaise between Lance and my friend Daniel Frey.

Frey has shorts on, no shirt, no shoes, and is as unaffected by the blistering desert heat as Lance and I. It's late afternoon, but the sun is still strong enough to bounce shimmers of heat off the pool deck in flickering waves. I tip my head back and soak it in. My arms and legs tingle with the kiss of sun on new skin.

Now if I could just get the smell of burned flesh out of my nose.

Adele placed a pitcher of iced tea on the table in front of us before disappearing back into the house. Lance told me she took charge of the women who donated blood to me: fed them, watched until she was sure they were strong enough to leave, and sent them home in a car with money and a certificate to the Armani shop. The hosts seemed pleased with the attention and the gifts. It freed Lance to stay by my bedside.

I don't know how I'm going to repay her kindness—or her discretion. If she didn't know what I was before, there is no doubt she does now.

My thoughts and attention shift to Lance. I reach for his hand. "What made you think to call Frey?"

"He was the obvious choice," Lance answers. "After what happened a few months ago in Mexico. Frey saved Culebra's life. I never thought your life was in danger, but I didn't know what to do to speed the healing process." He raises his glass to Frey. "He not only knew but came here and took charge. I owe him."

"*We* owe him." I raise my glass, too.

Frey gives a modest little smile, returns the toast.

He's a handsome man, fortysomething, dark hair touched on the sides with gray, a terrific build. He's also a shape-shifter and a friend. We were lovers once, it happened not long after I was turned, when he came to my aid in a different way.

He's watching me and the smile broadens, as though he senses what I'm thinking.

Lance *does* pick up on it. He skewers me with a raised eyebrow. *Should I be jealous?*

Frey, who is privy to Lance's thoughts but not mine, answers before I can. "No. That was a while ago. Anna was just learning what it meant to be vampire then. She's come a long way."

Nice that he said that out loud. Shape-shifters and vampires can read each other's thoughts. Unless you do something stupid like I did. Months ago, I bit Frey in a pique of childish frustration and concern over what I perceived as a threat to my niece, Trish. Frey was helping her. At the time, I hadn't been sure. Once a vampire feeds from a shape-shifter, the psychic link between them is broken. It's a wonder Frey still thinks of me as a friend.

A wonder and my very good luck. Which calls to mind the second question. Frey doesn't drive. Something about having feline sight as his other form is panther. Cats see on the blue side of the spectrum. Gives them great night vision, but makes it difficult to distinguish a broad range of colors. Red, yellow and green, for instance.

"How did you get here?"

Another tip of the glass to Lance. "He provided transportation. Sent a helicopter."

I grin at Lance. *Of course you did.*

Lance grins back.

Frey leans toward me, his expression turns serious. "Lance filled me in on what happened. Anna, do you realize the implication of this? You went into a burning garage and came out unscathed."

"Unscathed? Hardly. You saw what I looked like."

He shakes his head. "Okay, not exactly *unscathed*. But you survived when you should have gone up like a Roman candle. Vampires don't walk through flame and live. You know that. You saw what happened to—"

He stops, maybe because he sees my shoulders tense, maybe because he realizes that by saying it, I'll have to face the truth.

"Ortiz," I say it for him. "I saw what happened to Ortiz." I rub my eyes with the heel of my palms, trying to shut out the image and push away the guilt. "So Williams was right when he said I could have saved Ortiz. But how could I have known? Williams certainly didn't tell me, and the bastard had a thousand opportunities."

Frey glances at Lance. "There's something else we think you should know."

The muscles across my shoulders grow even tighter. "What?"

"The garage fire."

"What about it?"

Lance picks up the story. "My first thought was that it was an accident." He reaches out a hand and places it on my arm. "But now, I'm not so sure."

And I'm not sure I understand. I frown. "Then what?"

"I think it was deliberately set. A device rigged to go off ten seconds after the back door closed."

"Wait a minute." I'm remembering Saturday morning. How mad I was at Lance. How all I wanted to do was get away from him. "I went out that door. Why didn't I trip it?"

"You didn't *close* the door," Lance replies. "You left it open. Probably didn't even realize it. I came out after you were already gone, and I did close the door. Ten seconds later, the garage blew. The fire investigators say it was a gas leak from a water heater. Fueled by a spark when the garage door was raised. They're writing it off as an accident. And I'm going to let them."

He looks over at Frey, then back to me. "But that was a new water heater, and you had raised the garage door minutes, not seconds, before. Someone poured propane on the floor of the garage to make sure there would be fire. Lots of it. And set a device to go off when the back door closed."

"So we were both targets?"

Frey and Lance exchange looks.

"What?" Irritation is bunching my shoulders even tighter. "Stop fucking around. Tell me."

Lance says, "We think it was a test."

"A test of what?"

As soon as I ask it, the answer pops into my head. I stare at Lance. "Someone wanted to see if I could survive fire." Doesn't take a genius to figure out who that someone is. Especially knowing that he and Williams were working together. "Julian Underwood."

I'm right. I see confirmation in the eyes looking back at me. That Julian Underwood would risk Lance's life, the life of someone he has known for decades, sparks such rage that I find only one way to express it. I hurl the glass in my hand across the patio with such force it shatters against the far wall, pulverizes, rains bits of glass on the flagstone.

My hands are shaking. I interlock my fingers. When I can at least control the anger in my voice, I raise my eyes to Lance. "He thought you and I would walk out that back door together. The fire would ignite. Either we'd both be dead, or only you'd be. Either way, he didn't care. He didn't care if he killed you. He only wanted to see if he could kill me."

Frey leans forward. "And now he knows," he says. "He knows what Williams has been saying is true. You are indestructible. The Chosen One."

That stupid expression brings simmering anger boiling again to the surface. "Why does everyone always throw that at me? The Chosen One. Sounds like bad Buffy. There's nothing special about me. I'd know if there were."

"Then *think*." Frey's voice is hard, insistent. "How do you explain what you did? How do you explain pulling Lance out of those flames? Vampires can't do that. Williams couldn't do that. From the beginning, he recognized it."

"Recognized what?" The volume of my voice escalates with frustration. "He's done nothing but fuck with me. If he's trying to win me over to some great cause, he sure as hell has a strange way of doing it."

Lance looks at Frey. His expression makes me think they've spent the last two days discussing me. It's pissing me off. "Okay. Will you stop acting like conspirators in a spy movie? What is it you're not telling me?"

This time, Lance takes point. "I told Daniel about what happened in San Diego. How you were attacked. We think there's a connection between that attack and the fire."

"What connection? Williams wouldn't be dumb enough to send a vamp to attack me unless he was damned sure that vamp was strong enough to kill me. He didn't. And after I killed it, how could Williams know I'd bury it in the desert and come here with Lance? He couldn't. No one knew. We made the decision on the spot."

Lance's gaze slides away. A wave of guilt emanates from him making me realize the reason for his remorse and regret. "I can't be sure that Julian didn't know. We have a powerful connection. Remember, Adele said he called the afternoon we arrived. That he was in town, too. It's a pretty big coincidence."

"No." A vehement shake of my head. "I don't believe it."

"Well, there could be a simpler explanation." Frey lifts a shoulder in a half shrug. "You could have been followed."

Lance and I exchange glances. Now that's an explanation I can accept. An explanation so obvious I can't believe we didn't think of it ourselves. "I didn't pay much attention on the drive," I admit. "There wasn't a lot of traffic, but I wasn't looking for a tail."

"Neither was I." Lance is visibly and emotionally relieved at the possibility that he hadn't led Julian to us.

So am I. Until I realize the implication. Williams is here? Lance picks up the thread of my thought.

Williams and Underwood working together.

Again.

His face flushes. "It is my fault."

"Christ, Lance." I grab his arm and give it a shake. "It is not your fault."

Frey looks from Lance to me. "I don't understand."

Lance is reluctant to admit to Frey how we came to be together, so I do. Briefly, unemotionally. Frey's eyes never leave Lance's face as I tell the story of how Lance and I met. Of the lie that it was Culebra who brought us together when in reality, it had been Underwood and Williams.

I wish I could read what Frey is thinking. I can't. I see only a subtle shift in his attitude toward Lance. Not so trusting. A shadow of suspicion in his eyes, a tensed jaw muscle.

"Frey."

He turns to me, eyebrow raised.

"I trust Lance with my life."

Simple words I've never meant more seriously.

Frey is still and quiet. He looks at me for a long moment. Then he nods. "All right. Your instincts have always been good. I respect them." He turns to Lance. "Maybe we should pay this guy a visit. Get some answers."

Lance tries to hide his alarm at the suggestion. He manages to shield his actual thoughts from him, but Frey isn't stupid. He senses Lance's anxiety. Suspicion once again tightens the lines around his mouth. "Unless there's a reason you'd rather not have us meet with him."

Lance's face mirrors his distress. But it's not fear for himself I'm picking up. Frey has no idea how powerful and cruel Lance's sire can be. Lance is afraid for Frey and me.

"No, not yet." I draw Frey's attention with a wave of my hand. "I'll take care of Underwood when the time is right."

"Anna, I don't think you can wait too long." A sense of urgency creeps into Frey's voice. "In a few days, you will have been vampire for a full year. You may not want to accept it, but if what Williams and Julian suspect is true, you will come into your full powers on the anniversary of your becoming. That marks a transitional period for the Chosen One. They've tested you. They know you are the one. They are going to do everything they can to influence you. To channel your power to forward their agenda."

I manage a wry smile, though the grimness of his expression sends an icy finger sliding along my spine. "They're going to try to control me? Is that what you're saying? How the hell are they going to do that? You're being melodramatic, my friend."

"I don't think so." Frey leans forward, his eyes devoid

of all humor. “I have never known a Chosen One,” he says. “But I have known *of* them. They are charged with shaping the destiny of the vampire race. It’s a tremendous responsibility affecting not only vampires but all of mankind. There are likely to be more tests. You will be tried in ways you can’t imagine. But the end result will be the same. The fate of the world is literally in your hands.”

CHAPTER 19

THE FATE OF THE WORLD?

Frey is so solemn, so serious, it takes all my strength not to insult him by replying with a derisive laugh. Instead, I temper it down to a derisive snort.

"Frey, my friend, do you hear yourself? You know me. You've been through some of the worse times of my life with me. What makes you think anyone in his or her right mind would put the fate of the world in my hands?"

He closes his eyes for a moment. Shakes his head slowly. "You constantly denigrate yourself. But I have seen you at some of the worst times of your life and you always choose the right road, the moral path. This time, though, choices may not be so clear. Williams and Underwood are powerful vampires. They will try to influence or coerce you. You need to be on guard now more than ever."

Listen to him, Anna, Lance's own concern burns into my subconscious. *You have to protect yourself.*

"Protect myself? From what?" I look from Lance to Frey. "What do you expect me to do? How do I protect myself? Hide in a cave? Abandon everyone I care about? What?"

Lance and Frey have no answers. I see it in the worry that shadows their eyes, the grim set of mouths drawn tight with concern. I also see that it's up to me to put an end to this nonsense. The Chosen One will have to wait. There is another more pressing problem to take care of first—Underwood has to pay for what he did to Lance.

I push myself away from the table and stand. "I suggest we go home. David is going to be wondering where the hell I am. Lance, will you come with me? Frey?"

The two men exchange looks, probably thoughts, but thoughts they keep from me. Lance gives in with a shrug. "When do you want to go?"

I pause, pretending to think about it when in reality, my path is already set. "Tomorrow morning, first thing. Lance, why don't you take Frey into town for dinner? I'm beat. I think I'll turn in."

They look at me as if I am crazy to suggest they leave me alone.

Gives me a chance to throw the foolishness back at them. "Hey. You don't think I can take care of myself? I walk through fire. The Chosen One, remember?"

Frey's lips tip up. Even Lance's shoulders relax a bit.

"And I'm not alone. Adele is here. It's early. If you leave now, you'll be back before dark. Nothing bad happens before dark. You've seen enough slasher flicks to know that."

There's still too much hesitation in his eyes. "Look, I bet there's not much to eat in the house. Whatever Adele has been feeding the hosts is probably gone. Frey is a meat eater. How long has it been since he's had a good steak?"

Frey's mouth twitches at the word "steak."

"See?" I smile, big and bright. "Go. It's the least you can do, Lance. If I wasn't still a little shaky, I'd come, too."

"Well," Lance says finally. "I can take Frey to a steak house I know in the neighborhood. It's close. We'll be back in less than an hour."

"Good." I rise up on my toes and brush my lips against his. "See you in an hour."

I'm practically dancing with impatience, waiting while the two men go upstairs, change clothes, come back down, issue a hundred directives about door locks and alarm systems and finally, *finally*, head out.

Repairs on the garage haven't been made yet so the Jag, a rental car Lance arranged to have delivered to the house and Adele's little Prius are all lined up in the driveway. The men head for the rental car.

Adele joins me at the door as I'm waving them off. All the hosts have been safely sent home and she looks tired and relieved that the crisis has past. "I think I'm going to my room," she says. "Unless you need something?"

"As a matter of fact, I do," I reply. "Julian Underwood's address."

She throws me a puzzled frown. "Why?"

"I lost an earring Friday night. At Julian's. He called while we were on our way back here and said he'd found it. Since we're leaving early tomorrow morning, this is my only chance to get it."

In spite of my incredible ability to lie on demand, she doesn't look convinced. "Why not wait until Lance gets home? Let him take you?"

"Did you see how tired he is? I'll bet he hasn't slept in forty-eight hours. When he gets back, I'm taking him straight to bed."

I throw a little wink in for good measure.

She gives me a "too much information" look. Still, she hesitates. "Are you sure you're up to driving yourself? I could take you."

I smile, pat her arm. "You are too kind. But I wouldn't dream of imposing."

She gives in with a shrug. "I'll write the address down."

She pulls a small notebook out of a credenza near the front door. She prints the address in neat, precise, block letters. "Do you need directions?"

"No. Thanks. I have GPS in the car."

She starts to turn around and in spite of how anxious I am to get going, I find myself stopping her with a hand on her arm. "Thank you, Adele. For what you did for me."

She nods and pats my hand. "You are good for Lance. I can see that. I'm happy I could help."

We exchange the kind of smile that two people who share a common bond often do—warm, sincere, protective, touched with concern. She loves Lance, too.

I watch as she strides away. If something happens to me tonight, I'm glad she's here.

Not that I expect anything to happen to me. In fact, just the opposite. I expect tonight to resolve the threat against Lance and me once and for all.

With that thought, I run upstairs. Change into jeans and a T-shirt, slip on tennis shoes. Then I'm out the front door.

IT TAKES ME FIFTEEN MINUTES TO FIND UNDERwood's address. I glance at my watch. Doesn't leave too much time to beat Lance and Frey back home. I lose another five minutes because the address turns out to be a sprawling resort called Lake La Quinta. When I locate the lobby and ask for Julian Underwood at the front desk, I'm asked if I want his suite or the suite of one of his guests. Evidently, he has the whole spread.

At my reply, I'm told he's staying in the Lakeside suite and given directions. I hear the clerk telephoning Julian discreetly as I walk away. If not for vampire hearing, I'd never have caught it.

Rolling lawns, lush gardens and views of the Santa Rosa

Mountains as backdrop fade into insignificance at the sight of the "lake" that fronts the property. I don't know if it's man-made or natural, but the amount of water surrounding this desert oasis in drought-plagued Southern California is remarkable.

Underwood must be watching for me because he opens the door before I ring. He looks surprised to see me. Surprised and suspicious. But he cloaks those emotions quickly behind a façade of cordiality.

"Anna. What an unexpected pleasure."

All the way over, I've braced myself for the onslaught of emotion I would likely experience when I once again face this monster. For he is a monster. If I hadn't been convinced of it before, what he did to Lance proves it beyond any doubt. First the beating, then risking Lance's life with the fire. His disregard for life churns the fury in my stomach like acid.

But it's different this time. I was unprepared at the bar, ignorant of the pain he was capable of inflicting. Now I know. Now I'm filled with powerful emotions of my own—rage and the need for revenge.

I have to smother those feelings. Underwood can't know what's really behind this visit. There isn't time.

Not now.

Underwood stands aside and motions me into his suite. His hair is loose today, falling to his shoulders in burnished waves of gold. He's dressed in slacks and an open-neck shirt, Gucci loafers on his feet. In the confined space of a room, his cologne assaults my nose. It's cloying with strong undertones of something flowery and bitter. Makes me want to stand as far away from him as possible.

"I heard there was some trouble at Lance's." He says it like one might comment on gossip heard about a stranger.

I nod. "A gas explosion. The water heater blew up."

"Anyone hurt?"

"Not seriously."

"Good." His smile is gratuitous, rehearsed. "I'm very glad to hear that."

I ignore the platitude, look around. We're standing in a living room with two sets of double doors leading out to a deck that fronts the lake. In front of the lake is a pool. More water. Around that pool lounge the five women who accompanied Underwood and his entourage to Melvyn's. Bikinied, waxed, gorgeous. I wonder which one Lance had that night. My gut clenches at the image the thought triggers. The animal writhes with jealousy.

Swallow it down.

No time for this. Focus. I shift my concentration to the surroundings, the room, to clear my head. Simple furniture. A sofa covered in striped silk damask, a matching chair, an oak credenza. All in muted tones of cream and white. From where I stand, I can see two bedrooms flanking the living room.

"Nice digs."

"Thank you. It's my home away from home."

"You have the whole resort to yourself?"

"I know the owner. We have an understanding."

"I'll bet you do." I'll bet Underwood gets anything he wants. One way or the other.

Like Williams.

He motions to the coffee table, set with two glasses and an open bottle of wine. "Would you join me in a glass of wine?"

Two glasses? I suspect the second wasn't meant for me.

Is he in one of the bedrooms? I probe, discreetly, to see if I detect another vampire presence. But Williams is adept at shielding himself. I pull my thoughts back.

Focus.

I shake my head. "I can't stay. I'm here to make you a deal."

He steeples his fingers and tilts his head, a gesture of polite curiosity. But his expression is tinged with humor, too, as if he finds the thought that I'd come to offer *him* a deal absurd.

But it's why I'm here. To protect Lance and Frey until I find out what they want. Knowledge . . . then revenge.

"Yes. Here it is. From this moment on, you will leave Lance alone. You will never bother him again. Nor will you go after anyone else I care about. Not my family. Not my partner David. Not the attendant at my car wash or the clerk who takes my dry cleaning or the cashier at my corner liquor store. If any one of them so much as breaks a nail, I will make you sorry. I will make you pay. Do we understand each other?"

Underwood's smile is dark and dangerous. "And what do I get in return for agreeing to this *deal*?"

I get in his face.

"What you wanted from the beginning. You get me."

There's a moment of silence. Underwood and I stare at each other, waiting for the other to blink first. Neither of us does. What breaks the stalemate is the sound of clapping.

We both turn.

And there in a bedroom door, like the wizard stepping out from behind the curtain, is Warren Williams.

CHAPTER 20

WILLIAMS CONTINUES TO CLAP AS HE JOINS US in the center of the room. "Well played, Anna," he says. "Well played."

I ignore his entrance, glance at my watch. I've been gone too long. I can't waste time pretending to be shocked or surprised by his appearance. I expected the melodramatic bastard. I look from Underwood to Williams and back again. "Do we have a deal?"

Williams wants to drag this out. He's enjoying the moment. I'm giving him what he's always said he wanted, but he needs to keep me dangling. He looks tanned and relaxed and well fed, much better than the last time I saw him—skewered like a piece of meat on an iron bar. He sees the image in my head and a flash of white-hot anger blazes forth from his eyes.

You have to answer for Ortiz.

His words spark understanding. *Lance. His death was to be your revenge for Ortiz, wasn't it?*

Underwood steps between us. *Knock it off. There will*

be time for recrimination later. When we've accomplished what we must.

Williams takes a mental and physical step back. *You're right.* He lets the tension drain from his shoulders, soften the lines around his mouth. He's smiling again when he looks at me.

"Yes. We have a deal. If you are willing to accept your destiny. Let me guide you. Are you?"

It's as painful as a gut wound, but I nod.

"When are you going back to San Diego?"

"Tomorrow morning."

"Good. I'll be in touch tomorrow afternoon. Expect my call."

Underwood has been silent, his thoughts cloaked, his expression grim. He's the one I'm most worried about. He's the one who has the hold on Lance. Now he turns a frown on Williams. "I don't trust her. We have her here now. How can you let her go?"

Williams lets the corners of his mouth tip up, more leer than smile. "She loses everything if she reneges. She knows that."

Now it's my turn. I jerk a thumb toward Underwood. "Can you control this asshole?" I feel Underwood tense at the slur. He sends a message to Williams that I'm not privy to, but Williams is still focusing on me. *As long as you keep your part of the bargain, Underwood will not bother you or Lance again. You have my word.*

I wish his oath inspired more confidence. But for now, it's all I have.

THE RENTAL CAR IS IN THE DRIVEWAY.

Shit. Shit. Shit.

Lance and Frey beat me back.

The front door flies opens as soon as I pull up. They pounce the moment my feet touch pavement.

Lance gets his shot in first. "Where the fuck did you go? Are you crazy? I told you to stay inside. Do you have any idea how worried we were when we got back and you weren't here?"

He finally runs out of words but not anger. He grabs my shoulders and I brace myself; he looks like he wants to shake me until my teeth rattle. Instead, he crushes me to his chest and hugs me until I squeak in protest.

"Lance," I'm finally able to gasp. "I'm all right." I keep my thoughts carefully neutral. "Nothing happened."

Frey has been standing quietly to the side. "Where did you go?"

"I needed some air, that's all. I took a drive."

Lance has my face in his hands. "Why didn't you wait for us to get back? We would have taken you for a drive. God. I was so worried."

I let the warmth of his sweet concern wash over me. "I didn't mean to be gone so long. I'm sorry I worried you." I glance over to Frey. "Both of you."

Lance is smiling down at me, my reassuring words sending relief flooding through his mind and body. I hug him, burying my face in his shoulder, thoughts concealed.

When I look over at Frey, however, he's frowning. His expression says he knows bullshit when he hears it. For once I'm glad he no longer has access to my head.

LANCE AND I HAVE RETIRED TO HIS BEDROOM, FREY to a guest room down the hall. For whatever reason, Frey didn't challenge me in front of Lance or grill me about that missing hour. Maybe he wanted to wait until we were alone but the opportunity never presented itself. Lucky for me.

Lucky, too, that Adele hadn't joined us to ask about my earring. Since we plan to leave at first light in the morning, I'm hoping she won't get the chance.

Lance is waiting for me in bed. I slide next to him and

he leans over me. His fingers trace the contours of my face, brush my lips.

"Are you too tired?"

I pull him closer, pressing my body against his. "Have you ever known me to be too tired?"

He lets his hands roam my body. He's willing to go slow, coax and tease, do all the work. Find that sweet spot with fingers and lips and bring me to the brink. But my blood is already on fire, my body humming with the need to feel him inside. I guide him into me, urge him with hips and thighs, whisper encouragement until neither of us can hold out any longer. We come together in an explosive flood of release.

Later, lying still and quiet next to him, I know.

No matter what happens, what I did tonight to protect him—to protect everyone—was the right thing to do.

WE'RE ON THE MOVE BY FIRST LIGHT. ADELE APPEARS from her room just when we're heading out the door, but she's still too groggy with sleep to manage more than a quick hug and wave before closing the door behind us.

One disaster avoided.

I throw Lance the keys. Frey takes shotgun.

That leaves me alone in the backseat. Good. The guys can talk about whatever manly things guys talk about and I can rest my head against the back of the seat and be alone with my thoughts. *Cloaked* thoughts, just in case Frey urges Lance to drop in unannounced for a visit. I know he still has questions about last night. It would be like him to send Lance on a spy mission into my head.

Lance. He is so good. So trusting. He hasn't known me as long as Frey. Do I feel bad about misleading him? No. I suspect I should be more concerned about this pact I made with Williams and Underwood than hiding it from Lance. I try to dredge up anxiety but honestly, I keep coming back to the old adage: the devil you know is better than the devil you don't. Or in this case, the *two* devils. It won't be easy working with Williams, but the sooner I let him make his pitch, the sooner I can turn him down. And take him down. Along with Underwood.

First, though, I get the answers I need. The answers Williams has been dancing around for the last year.

I can't pretend to be unaffected by Frey's reaction about this "chosen" thing. A Chosen One is usually the destroyer of . . . something. One of the first things I learned after becoming vampire was that a person's character doesn't change. If he is good as a human, he will remain good as a vamp. There is no amount of money or power that could tempt me to ignore what I've held dear my entire life—family, friends and now, Lance. Frey knows all this. How can he think I could be influenced any other way?

I watch Lance and Frey bantering back and forth in the front seat. Yesterday, Frey was being melodramatic and overly protective. Lance bought into it because he cares for me. As I do for him.

But there is another piece to the puzzle that has yet to be solved.

How was it that Underwood affected me so powerfully at our first meeting? It couldn't be simply the magic—I had the same reaction with that biker, Black. No magic there. He was purely human. No, it couldn't be *who* they were; it was *what* they were. Malevolent. Malicious. Mean.

Jesus. Is this going to happen to me every time I come across a nasty piece of work? I'm going to have to learn to either handle the effects or suppress them, or I won't have much choice except to spend the rest of my vampire existence hidden away in a cave.

The effort to keep my thoughts private is taxing. Frey and Lance are blathering on about baseball—a subject I can't believe either of them really finds interesting. Acronyms like ERAs and RBIs punctuate the conversation. It makes me smile.

I tune in for a while, the sound of their voices relaxing me. It would be easy to drift off. I shouldn't try to fight it. Truth is, I'm not feeling up to full strength yet. I'm going to need all my energy to face the coming battle.

It will be a battle. Of that I'm certain. Just not the one Frey envisions. This will be a very personal battle with Williams and Underwood on one side, me on the other.

But a battle for what purpose?

I've never thought of Williams as evil. Just misguided and as focused on his own objectives as I am. He's working with Underwood, though, so I can't trust those objectives. Underwood is the older, more powerful vampire, and he is without scruples. His influence on Williams can't be good. I wish I'd known about their alliance earlier.

I close my eyes. I wish Lance had trusted me enough to tell me the truth about the way we met.

Well, too late to obsess about that now. I'm tired. I'm cocooned in soft, warm leather. Two of my favorite men are close. I feel safe, protected.

I let go, let the soft monotone of voices from the front seat lull me into a gentle sleep.

CHAPTER 21

I AWAKEN TO THE SOUND OF A SLAMMING CAR door. Frey's smiling face peers down at me as he opens the rear passenger door.

"About time you woke up."

We've arrived at Frey's condo complex. He holds the door open so I can climb out. "Would you like to come in?"

"Is Layla around?" It's an automatic response. Layla is his girlfriend. She doesn't like me. Maybe because she knows Frey and I have had sex. Maybe because I always seem to be calling Frey away from her for one crisis or another. Or maybe (and most likely) it's because he always comes.

Frey can't read my thoughts, but he may as well be able to. "I don't know what is between you two," he says, shaking his head as I climb out. "But yes, Layla is most likely home."

I give him a peck on the cheek. "Then some other time." I grab his hand as he turns. "Thank you."

He returns the squeeze and lets himself in through the security gate. Lance and I watch until he disappears down the walk.

I scoot in beside Lance and we head for the cottage. For the first time, it dawns on me that I've been gone four days. Four days. That makes today Tuesday.

Shit.

I grab for my cell phone, only to discover that the battery is dead.

Lance glances at me. "What's up?"

I'm rummaging in the glove compartment for the charger. "I think David and I had a job yesterday. He's going to be pissed."

I pull out the cord and plug it into the dashboard. When the power comes up, I wince to see I have six messages from my partner. Each message is worse than the one before. David starts out mildly curious that he can't reach me, veers to concerned when my phone goes right to voice mail, borders on irritated when he goes by the cottage and finds me gone and develops into full-blown anger when Monday comes and I haven't bothered to get in touch. His last message is a brief, "Goddamn it, Anna. Where the hell are you?"

"Bad news?" Lance asks.

"I may be out of a job."

Lance grins and puts his own cell phone to his ear. His smile melts away, though, as he listens to *his* messages. In fact, I'd be willing to bet his expression now mirrors the one on my face a few moments before.

"Uh-oh," I say. "What did you forget?"

He glances at his watch, which makes me do the same thing. It's a little before nine.

"Jesus," he says. "I'm supposed to be in L.A. for a catalog shoot in thirty minutes. How about dropping me off at the airport? I'll catch a shuttle." He doesn't wait for a reply but punches in a number and tells whoever is on the other end that he's been delayed and will be a couple of hours late. Then he rings off.

He steers the car onto the road, a frown puckering his brow, until a sudden thought makes him shake his head and sit up straight in the seat. "I'm not going to L.A. What the hell am I thinking? I'm staying here with you."

He starts to reach for his cell phone again. I stop him. "Of course you're going to L.A. I'll be fine. If something happens, Frey is a phone call away."

And nothing is going to happen. After all, Williams and Underwood think I'm working with them now. Of course, Lance doesn't know that.

Lance's expression tells me I haven't convinced him. "What if there's another attack? What if Williams tries again? You need someone around to watch your back. I can't do that from L.A."

He can't do it here, either. Right now, the best thing he can do for *me* is to get *himself* out of harm's way.

"Lance, trust me. I can take care of anything Williams throws my way. How long will you be gone?"

"I can be back tomorrow night."

"Then it's settled. I'll be with David the rest of the day and probably most of tomorrow. No need for you to give up a paying gig to babysit me. Serious groveling takes time."

He actually manages a grin at that. "Will you go right to the office?"

"May as well get the ass chewing over with."

We're pulling into the commuter terminal at Lindbergh Field. Lance's expression morphs again to pinched and anxious. He stops at the curb but doesn't jump out. "I think this is a bad idea. I shouldn't leave you."

I give him a little push. "Go. You can't spend the rest of your life tailing me. Besides, I have to face David. I have more to fear from him right now than either Williams or Underwood. And what's the worse that can happen? He shoots me? I can handle bullets. Now go."

* * *

IN SPITE OF WHAT I TOLD LANCE, I DON'T GO RIGHT to the office. I need to change clothes. I do take the precaution of parking on Mission, though, instead of pulling into my driveway. No sense taking the chance that Williams hasn't planned another surprise. It would be just like him—a "don't fuck with me" gesture.

But I don't see or sense anything out of the ordinary when I approach the cottage. In thirty minutes, I'm back on the road.

Now, during the drive to the office, all I can think about is the reception I'm likely to get from David. We've been partners for several years, but it's only been the last year, since I became vampire, that our relationship has been tested. I disappear for days at a time (this weekend a case in point), can't do many of the things we used to do like eating out (can't ingest food) or going to the gym (large mirrors *everywhere*) and can't seem to tolerate any female he's attracted to (is it my fault that I am a better judge of character than he is?)

We've almost called it quits before, and truth is, maybe we should now. It's not fair to him. But the other truth is, I like him. I like the job we do. A lot. And I need the money. I don't have a trust fund to fall back on. I refuse to tap into Avery's legacy.

The other logical alternative for me would be to go back to teaching. Frey teaches. And it works for him.

Just the thought of being back in a classroom turns my cold blood even colder. Criminals, otherworldly villains, monsters. I can handle them with one hand tied behind my back. Hormonal teenagers, though, are something else.

No. As self-serving as it is, I need to ease David over this latest bump. I can do it. I've had practice.

Still, anxiety tightens my shoulders as I approach the office. David's Hummer squats like an obscene yellow beetle in its designated parking space so I know he's inside. The irony is not lost on me that here I am, a vampire, nervous about facing a mere mortal.

I blow out a breath, run my hands through my hair, tug at the bottom of my sweater and peek into the office.

David is at the desk. He doesn't notice me at the door. He doesn't notice me because he's focused on the woman sitting in *my* chair opposite him. He doesn't notice me because he's thrown his head back and is laughing.

Laughing.

It pisses me off. He's supposed to be brooding. He's supposed to be concerned. He's supposed to be on the telephone trying to reach me again.

He is not supposed to be laughing.

I shove through the door, startling him. He recovers and beams a smile at me. The woman turns, smiling, too.

"Hey, Anna," David says. "I'd like you to meet our new partner."

Partner?

My back stiffens. What the fuck does that mean?

I can't think of anything to say to that startling revelation. So I stare—at them both.

She's gotten to her feet. She's wearing jeans and a white cotton shirt tucked and cinched with a broad leather belt. She's taller than me—probably five-nine or so—and sinewy thin. She has auburn hair drawn straight back from her face in a ponytail. She's one of the lucky females who can pull that off. Probably because of those big green eyes and a full-lipped smile that show off a set of too-perfect teeth. She has come away from the chair to stand in front of me, hand outstretched.

"Hi, Anna. I'm Tracey Banker. Pleased to meet you."

I take her hand, give it a perfunctory shake. Let it drop. She's wearing perfume—too much of it—something woodsy with undertones of burned sugar and bitter almonds. It makes my nose twitch.

Tracey glances back at David. "Well, I'm sure you two have things to discuss. I'll leave you to it. I'll check with you tomorrow morning?"

David nods, and she brushes past me. He watches her as she leaves, then turns his gaze on me. "Well? Aren't you going to yell at me? Ask me what the fuck I was thinking? Tell me I had no right to take on a new partner without your okay?"

He's glaring, muscles tense, jaw tight, ready to launch a counterattack.

"No."

The answer startles me as much as it does David. I ignore the comically puzzled expression on his face and sink into my chair. "Where did you find her?"

He looks at me out of the corners of his eyes, as if he can't trust my reaction, and takes his own seat across from me. "Remember the kickboxing classes we used to take?"

His emphasis is on the "we used to take." I don't comment, just nod.

"She's the new instructor at the gym now. Ex-cop, wounded in the line of duty. Took an early retirement and has been looking for something to occupy her time besides teaching. We went for coffee after a class last week, I told her what we do. She said she'd be interested in filling in if we needed it. Yesterday, I needed it. You weren't around. I called her. She came. We made the collar."

He says it matter-of-factly, no subtle undertones, no recrimination, no opening for rebuttal.

Makes me feel guiltier.

"What business arrangement have you made with her?"

"Fifty-fifty split if it's just her and me. If the three of us work a job, she gets twenty-five percent, you and I split the rest. She ponies up twenty percent of the monthly office expenses regardless of the number of jobs she works. We cover her insurance, reimburse car expenses."

"You got that in writing?"

He picks up a contract from the middle of his desk. "Just needs your signature."

He holds it out, still looking as if he expects me to start ranting. No one is more surprised than me that I'm not. I pick up a pen, take the paper from his hand and sign my name on the dotted line.

David slips the signed contract into a folder on his desk. "So. Do you want to tell me where you were yesterday?"

Battling monsters.

"Lance and I went to Palm Springs for the weekend. He got—sick. I stayed to take care of him. I am sorry. Really."

"You lost your cell phone?"

I wince, smile deprecatingly. "Battery went dead. I forgot to pack the charger."

He's weighing my words, assessing my expression, calculating the sincerity of my apology. I don't blame him. He's heard the same story more than once. Only the circumstances of *why* I let him down ever change.

I expect him to respond the way I would—with something snarky. I knew we had a job on Monday so where were we that I couldn't get to a phone? The dark side of the moon?

Instead, he surprises me by asking, "Is Lance all right?"

"Yeah. Thanks for asking."

He pushes away from the desk, folder in hand, and crosses the room to a filing cabinet against the far wall. He places the folder in a drawer and closes it. When he comes back to the desk, he slips a jacket off the back of his chair and drapes it over his arm.

"Well, we don't have anything on the docket for the next few days. Think you can cover the office? I'm going to San Francisco to look at some property with Miranda."

Miranda is a real estate developer who has become more

than an investment advisor to David. They are lovers. The lover he sometimes cheats on with that booking clerk at the jail. Which leads me to think it's not a serious relationship, not that he's shared any details with me. I don't have such a good track record with his girlfriends.

"Sure," I respond quickly. "It will give me a chance to get to know our new partner."

He shakes his head. His expression says he's still suspicious, still skeptical of how easily I accepted Tracey into our fold. "You aren't going to scare her off while I'm gone are you?"

I hope my laugh doesn't sound as forced as it feels. "Of course not. Have fun in San Francisco."

He looks not at all reassured by my words. But he does leave.

Which is good.

As soon as he's gone, I put in a call to Warren Williams.

I know he said he'd be in touch with me, but I want to get the ball rolling. Show him I'm serious about our agreement.

The phone rings five times, then goes to voice mail.

Voice mail? Where is he? He's supposed to be sitting by the phone waiting for my call.

Abruptly, I click off.

Damn it. The expression "revenge is a dish best served cold" has never been a favorite of mine. I don't want to wait for the rage to cool. What he and Underwood did to Lance—did to me—is unforgivable, and I want to strike while my blood still boils.

CHAPTER 22

WAITING HAS NEVER BEEN EASY FOR ME.

Waiting makes me peckish.

Waiting reduces me to finding ways to distract myself, reduces me to tackling distasteful *chores*.

So, when I've caught up on email, balanced my checkbook, filed an accumulation of piled-up shit (mea culpa to David), read through the stack of law enforcement bulletins on top of the filing cabinet and drained the last bottle of beer in the fridge and Williams *still* hasn't called, I'm irritated and antsy enough to bite the head off a chicken.

Tossing the last empty bottle into the trash, I trudge on out to the deck that borders the back of our office. It's a still, clear and quiet afternoon, the skyline mirror-imaged on the water. I watch sailboats play motor tag on the bay while they wait for the wind. When I was human, it was the kind of afternoon David and I would spend at the Green Flash, a bar down the street from my cottage, drinking beer and eating nachos and watching humanity parade past on the boardwalk.

Nostalgia sweeps over me. I took those days for granted. It's a stupid human flaw—not appreciating the simple pleasures because they are simple and routine and will always be a part of your life.

Or so you believe.

I plop down in a deck chair and tip it back, hoisting my feet to rest on the railing. So much has happened in the last year. So much has changed. You hear the cliché "not the person she once was" all the time. In my case, it's not an exaggeration. Last July my biggest concern was when I'd next see my DEA boyfriend, Max. I wasn't in love with him, but the sex was great and our casual relationship suited us.

Next thing you know, I'm attacked and turned by a vampire. Even though the sex was even better, Max couldn't get away fast enough when he learned the truth. I saved his life—hell, I've saved a lot of lives in the last twelve months—but to the world at large, I'm still a bloodsucker. A monster.

I can't reveal myself to my family, to David, to any mortal outside of the few who know and safeguard the secret . . . that there are supernatural creatures living side by side with them. It's the reason I sent my family halfway around the world. I couldn't bear to see the horror in their eyes should they discover my secret. It's also the reason I'm glad they have my niece, Trish, to care for. She will fill the void when circumstances force me to move on.

Perhaps subconsciously I've already accepted Tracey because she might be the one to fill the void for David, too.

A breeze springs up over the bay. The sailboats hoist their sails to capture it, cutting engines as they forge straight, sure paths out to sea.

I wish my path was as clear.

I hold up my right hand. The palm looks the same. The skin on the back of my hand is smooth and cold as alabaster. I let it drop back into my lap. Three days ago I was a walking charcoal briquette. Today, there isn't a trace of damage.

I close my eyes. Listen. I can hear and feel everything going on inside my body. Blood pulsing, heart pumping. Muscles, sinew and bone flex and contract on command. Nerves vibrate with energy.

I'm dead.

Yet I've never felt more alive.

CHAPTER 23

I'M STILL IN A FUGUE STATE WHEN THE OFFICE DOOR opens.

I don't have to turn from my perch to know who's come in. Her perfume precedes her. If we're going to work together on a regular basis, David better tell Tracey to go easy on the stuff.

She's his recruit, after all.

She walks straight through the office and joins me on the deck, pointing to a second deck chair. "Mind if I join you?"

I scoot around so I'm upwind and nod my head. "Have a seat."

I notice then that she has a brown grocery bag in her hand. She sits down, opens the bag and pulls a couple of bottles of Corona from inside. She offers me one.

I take it.

She might work out after all.

We open our beers and drink.

Tracey wipes foam off her lips with the back of her

hand. A simple, unaffected gesture. For some reason, it tips the scales from finding reasons *not* to like her to reserving judgment. Maybe even being willing to give her a chance.

She did come bearing beer.

We drink in silence for a few minutes before she says, "Detective Harris sends his regards."

I choke on that. "Really? He sent his *regards*?"

A grin. "Well, not so much *regards* as a word of caution. To me. To be on my guard. He thinks you're . . . How shall I put this?"

At the pause, I jump in. "A lunatic? Crazy?"

She laughs. Nods. "Pretty much." She eyes me over the bottle. "He thinks you had something to do with Warren Williams being run out of the police chief's job. Care to comment?"

"You sound like a reporter."

"Just a curious ex-cop who thought Williams did a good job. And I don't believe you were responsible for his troubles, by the way. As I understand it, he used you as bait to catch the hit man who shot David. You did nothing wrong."

I look away from her. No. I did nothing wrong. Did I? A cop lost his life, David got shot, and a father and daughter were put in danger because I got into a fight with my partner. I was mad at David so I reacted like a spoiled teenager—ran away and got drunk. Set a chain of events in motion that . . .

Ancient history.

I guzzle another mouthful of beer, keep tilting the bottle until I've drained it.

Yeah, Williams used me. But we both knew I was in no danger. The hit man was human. I'm not. Trouble was, no one else could know. And when it was all over, Williams ended up paying the price because he couldn't expose the truth.

Williams. Where the hell is he?

"Anna?"

Tracey is leaning toward me. "Are you all right?"

I hoist the empty bottle. "I will be if you've got any more of these in that bag."

She fishes inside, pulls out two more. Hands me one, takes the other for herself. We clink the bottles together and drink.

After a long pull, I shift in the chair so I'm facing her. "Why did you come back this afternoon? You said when you left you'd be back tomorrow."

She jabs a thumb behind her. "Left my jacket."

I look. A black Windbreaker hangs from a coat hook near the door. "And you brought beer because?"

A shrug. "I thought maybe David might still be here and we'd . . ." She lets her voice drop.

"Ah. You're smitten. I should warn you, he's been seeing someone. He's on a trip with her now. Probably won't be back until Friday."

She sighs and settles back in the chair. "Well, I've never shied away from a challenge. And in a way, I'm glad you and I had a chance to get acquainted."

I hide the smirk by taking another pull.

Get acquainted? Oh, Tracey. You don't have a clue.

TRACEY LEAVES AT FIVE WITH AN OFFER TO TAKE ME to dinner. An offer I, of course, decline. I tell her I have a boyfriend waiting for me at home and that she doesn't have to come in tomorrow since we have nothing on the docket and David won't be in.

We part ways with a wave and a "see you on Friday."

I'm relieved when she's gone. This girl talk thing is hard. But I can report to David that I behaved myself and that our new partner and I had a chance to bond.

The other good thing was that it distracted me from pacing the floor, wondering why I haven't yet heard from Williams.

At six, I lock up and head for the cottage. Lance calls while I'm driving home. He asks if I'm all right, if I've heard from Williams or Underwood, if I want him to come home tonight. I answer yes, no, no. He says he'll call again later and that he misses me.

I miss him, too. I miss his smile and his laugh and the way our bodies fit together. I miss having him around during the day. I don't want to sleep alone tonight. I don't think I want to sleep alone ever again. There's a hole my life that only he can fill. I miss him so much I ache.

"Anna?" he asks when a long moment has past. "Are you there?"

I blink and rouse myself. "Yes. I miss you, too."

IT'S AFTER MIDNIGHT.

Williams still hasn't called.

Trepidation replaces the irritation I felt most of the day. Something is wrong. There's no way in hell Williams would let me dangle like this. He's waited too long to have me under his thumb.

I pick up the phone and call his cell. Again.

Same result. Again.

Five rings, then voice mail.

I toss the phone on the bed.

Should I try calling him at home?

I shuffle downstairs. His home number is programmed in my landline. He's only called here once or twice from that number and never from a cell. I scroll for the number, press send.

The call is picked up so quickly, I don't hear it ring.

"Warren?"

A woman's voice. One I recognize.

The knot in my gut grows tighter. "No. Sorry, Mrs. Williams. It's Anna Strong."

There's a long moment of silence. I'm sure she's processing the same emotions I am. The last time we saw each other was at Ortiz's funeral. She made it clear how she felt about me—that I'd betrayed my own kind, left her husband near death to save a witch. She accused me of unleashing a war against innocents, something I understand less now than I did at the time.

One of the questions I'd hoped this *alliance* I'd forged with Williams would answer.

I wait another moment before asking, "You haven't heard from him?"

She makes a noise, a small choking sound, as if her breath is caught in her throat. "No. If you know something—if you know where he is . . ."

There's desperation in her voice, fear. When I don't respond, it veers to anger. "Damn you, Anna. What did you do, change your mind?"

Again, she doesn't give me a chance to answer.

"He told me he talked to you. He said you'd come to an understanding. He was optimistic that you were ready to cooperate. If it was a trick, if you've done something to hurt him, I swear I'll come after you."

I doubt it would make a difference if I told her Williams and I *had* come to an agreement. She has no reason to trust me. Better for her to be angry than afraid. Fear is debilitating. Let her nurse the anger. Anger gives you focus. Anger gives you strength. Anger keeps the inner demons at bay.

"I'm sorry to have disturbed you, Mrs. Williams. I did see your husband in Palm Springs yesterday. I'm sure he'll be home soon. Try not to worry."

Stupid. Empty sentiment.

She makes that sound in her throat again—half gasp, half stifled hiccup. It's only when she breaks the connection without another word that I realize what she was doing.

Crying.

CHAPTER 24

I DON'T LIE DOWN, DON'T TRY TO SLEEP.

Instead, I spend the night pacing. Something has gone terribly wrong. What it is, I can't say. I only know it involves Williams and Underwood.

And that is not good.

Lance thinks I've lost my mind. I've called him three times in the early morning hours. I tell him I just want to hear his voice. In reality, I'm terrified he won't pick up. Irrational, maybe, but I don't stop until he tells me he's on the way out the door to the last photo shoot and that he'll be headed for the airport by noon. He'll call me when he lands in San Diego and I'll pick him up.

I'm making yet another pot of coffee when the doorbell rings.

It's seven a.m. Too early for visitors. Not that I ever get visitors. Not the drop-in kind. To get visitors you have to have friends.

I can count my friends on three fingers.

Frey will be getting ready to go to school.

David is out of town.

Lance, ditto.

My stomach twists. Not vampire senses, but human gut reaction tells me whoever is on the other side of the front door is not here to deliver flowers.

I flip the coffeemaker on, cross the room to the front door.

I realize how anxious I am when my shaking hand slips off the doorknob at my first bungling attempt to open the door. I take a firmer grip, literally and figuratively, and pull the door open.

Detective Harris nods in greeting. Behind him, a uniformed policewoman stands off to the side.

Harris and I stare at each other a moment before he says, "Sorry for the hour. I have some news. Do you mind if I come in?"

I open the door wider, the only invitation I'm capable of extending. My throat has gone tight and dry. Harris comes inside, the policewoman doesn't. She moves to stand beside the door as I push it closed.

My first thought, Harris is human. It must be human circumstances that bring him here. "God. It's not David, is it? Has there been an accident?"

He shakes his head. "No. Not David." He pulls a small notebook from a pocket in his jacket, opens it, glances down at the page, then up at me. "You were in Palm Springs recently?"

Now I know how wrong I was. Whatever happened, it has nothing to do with the mortal world.

I nod. Wait.

"Did you see former police chief Warren Williams while you were there?"

"Yes."

"Under what circumstances?"

"He was staying at the home of a mutual acquaintance."

"And who would that be?"

"Julian Underwood."

Harris already knows the answers to these questions. I know because he doesn't once consult his notebook or jot anything down. I wait for the question he *doesn't* know the answer to.

"How did Williams seem to you when you saw him at Julian Underwood's?"

I frown. "How did he seem? He seemed fine."

"Not depressed? Anxious?"

Hardly. He'd just secured the pact we'd spent the last year battling over. Can't bring that up. "What's this about? Has something happened to Williams?"

Harris flips his little notebook closed, focuses on my face. "We found his car in the desert. Burned. We found a gun and a spent cartridge. His wedding ring. His watch. It looks as if he armed an incendiary device to torch the car, got back inside, set it off, and shot himself."

There is so much wrong with that scenario that my head swims with the enormity of it. I can only stare at Harris, objections ricocheting around my brain like buckshot against metal. He, in turn, stares back at me. Watching. Waiting. Wondering. Patience personified.

Irritating as hell.

I blow out a puff of air. "Does Mrs. Williams think her husband was suicidal?"

In my head I'm screaming, of course not. He was a vampire. A two-hundred-year-old vampire. His mortal wife would know more than anyone that a vampire that old doesn't commit suicide. He'd outlive any problem he's likely to encounter—or do away with it.

I'm hoping my face doesn't betray my thoughts. Hoping I've scrubbed away all emotion except concerned curiosity.

Harris sidesteps the question. "Mrs. Williams thinks you

may have been the last person to see her husband. Which is why I'm here. When did you return to San Diego?"

"Yesterday. Around nine in the morning."

"Did you come back alone?"

"No. I was with my boyfriend, Lance Turner, and another friend, Daniel Frey."

"And they'll corroborate this?"

"I can give you their phone numbers."

"What did you do after you got home?"

"Went to the office. David was there and our new partner. You know her. Tracey Banker."

"You were there the rest of the day?"

"Until five or so. Then I went home." I hold up a hand. "And no, I have no one to corroborate that I stayed home last night. I was alone."

Harris shakes his head. "Doesn't matter. Forensics puts the time of death at around mid-morning yesterday. I'll take those numbers now, if you don't mind."

Forensics? An immolated vampire would leave nothing but ash. A stopped watch maybe? The clock in the car?

Harris has the notebook open again and a pencil poised. He's looking at me, waiting for me to move. I reach for my cell phone, call up the numbers for Lance and Frey, recite them.

Harris copies the numbers but I can tell from his expression, he's only going through the motions. He doesn't consider me a suspect in spite of what Mrs. Williams might have implied.

And I'm sure she implied a lot.

He starts toward the door, pauses, turns back around. "Warren Williams may have been relieved of his post, but he was a good chief and a good cop. Mrs. Williams doesn't believe her husband committed suicide. I get the impression you don't, either. I know he considered you a friend so I'll tell you, we're not closing the books on his death until we're sure one way or the other. If you think of anything to help in the investigation, I hope you'll call."

I watch Harris stride down the walk to a waiting car, my thoughts and emotions so jumbled, I'm having trouble making sense of either. I close the door, walk zombielike to the couch and sit. Long after Harris leaves, I remain there, head back, legs outstretched, too shocked to do more than stare at the ceiling.

I can't wrap my head around the idea that Warren Williams is gone. He's been a constant source of irritation and I keep waiting for a sense of relief to overtake the sense of shock.

It's not happening.

What is happening is a strong sense of doubt.

Is he gone?

Or is this a trick? It's not entirely inconceivable that Williams concocted some elaborate ruse to disappear off the radar. Maybe he got tired of his mortal existence, his mortal wife, and set up an escape route. It's what a vampire would do if he wanted to start over.

But the timing is wrong.

I can see Williams bailing on his career, even his wife, but not on me. As long as I've known him, he's played up this destiny thing. He has made it crystal clear that he considers it not just mine, but his destiny, too, to shape and direct. Even his wife said so, at Ortiz' funeral. Williams obviously shared with her his vision for the future—my future, our future—and there's no fucking way he'd kill himself before he saw it through.

Unless he didn't kill himself.

Unless he's out there somewhere, waiting for the right time to contact me.

Unless this is part of a grand plan to isolate the two of us.

He might even have some idiotic idea that I'll fake my own death, too, and give myself over to him. He's egocentric enough to consider it. And it certainly sounds like a plan Underwood would agree to.

Underwood.

I should have thought about Underwood sooner.

Dread twines in my gut like a strand of thorns.

Why didn't I think about Underwood sooner?

Williams wouldn't have faked his own death. He'd have no need to. Just as Underwood had no need for Williams once I'd agreed to trade my family and friends' safety in exchange for cooperation.

Jesus. It's so clear.

Williams *is* dead.

Underwood killed him.

It would make perfect sense in Underwood's twisted head.

Underwood and Williams might have been working together to get my cooperation but once they had it, what use was Williams to Underwood? He saw that there was no love lost between the two of us. Maybe he even planned to kill Williams as a show of faith.

I can hear him saying it: *Here, Anna, I've slain the dragon that has hounded you and yours for the last year. You are free of his badgering, his interference. It's my gift to you.*

Underwood has been vampire for five hundred years. He must know more about the Chosen One than Williams ever did. Perhaps he and Williams didn't see eye to eye on how best to indoctrinate me.

He didn't seem pleased that Williams accepted my terms so easily—my cooperation in return for Lance's safety and that of my family and friends. Could that have been what caused the falling out? Was Underwood so distrustful that I'd honor our agreement that he decided to renegotiate on his own?

Oh my god.

The thought makes me lunge for the telephone on the

side table. The first call I make is to my family in France. My niece, Trish, picks up, her voice full of cheerful surprise. Yes, she assures me, everything is fine. My mother is in the garden picking herbs for dinner and my father is in the living room reading the paper. Do I want to talk with them?

I tell her no, that I just wanted to say hello. I ring off with the promise to call again soon for a real chat.

Next I call David. His sleepy voice reminds me that it's only a little after seven and why am I calling so early? In the background, an equally sleepy female voice asks who it is. Except I realize it's not sleep I'm hearing in her voice. When David asks again in a husky, slightly winded tone why I'm calling, it dawns on me that it's not sleep I interrupted.

Mumbling an apology and a stupid excuse about needing an address I'll track down at the office, I disconnect.

My family is fine.

David is fine.

David is more than fine, actually.

Lance will be on his way home in a few hours.

If Underwood doesn't intend on using them for leverage against me, what does he intend to use?

CHAPTER 25

IT'S A LITTLE AFTER NINE WHEN THE DOORBELL rings again.

It catches me as I come downstairs, having finally roused myself off the couch to shower and change from the sweats and T-shirt I sleep in when I'm alone to the jeans and T-shirt I live in when I'm awake.

As usual, I don't think to check to see who is outside before swinging the door open. I wish I had.

Mrs. Williams' unexpected presence catches me totally off guard.

She registers the shock on my face while her own betrays nothing. After a moment, she says, "May I come in?"

Numbly, I nod and step aside.

What am I supposed to say to her?

She crosses the living room and slumps onto the couch. Her eyes sweep the room, appraising, assessing, taking measure of how I live. Her expression remains detached. Even when she feels my eyes on her, she does not react except to meet my gaze with her own.

It's then I see it. The subtle changes.

She's about forty-five, slender, attractive. She's dressed in designer widow—tailored black crepe slacks, charcoal blouse, fitted black blazer. She always had a patrician air about her, the look of one used to being pampered. Her face now is drawn with grief, but the lines are softer, her skin more youthful, her eyes brighter than I remember.

I sense something, too.

A vibe coming off her. Powerful. Intrusive.

She looks away from me. Her shoulders bunch. She knows I'm studying her.

She's wishing she hadn't come. Realizes now it was a mistake.

I know what she's feeling. I know what she's thinking.

I know because I'm in her head.

She's been turned. She's vampire.

CHAPTER 26

HOW? WHEN?

My questions are met with confusion. Mrs. Williams looks at me with panic in her eyes.

I recognize the signs. It was only a year ago I felt the same confusion, the same panic when Avery made his first attempt to connect with me telepathically.

She has not been vampire long.

I sit down on the coffee table in front of her, our knees touching. I want her to look at me.

When did Warren turn you?

She shakes her head, not understanding what's happening. She doesn't realize you have to learn to cloak your thoughts. I'm sure it's something her husband would not have taught her. His need to control would have prevented it.

So, I take the information I need. The story is there. He turned her after Ortiz' funeral, while Warren was still weak and in need of human blood. He sent her out to bring back hosts, telling her what to say and what to offer. He used his background as a cop to teach her what to look for—runaways, vagrants—and how to approach them so they wouldn't be frightened. They were offered money and food (laced with drugs) and after, they'd remember nothing and she'd drive them back to where she found them.

It was easy. She was never afraid. She was proud of how strong she'd become. Warren was proud of her, too. He promised her a new life. Promised her the world once he and Anna achieved what was meant to be, once Anna finally accepted her destiny.

A new world. Where he would be king and his wife would be queen.

I pull myself back from the tangle of thought and emotion emanating from her mind.

New world? I ask, hoping she had something more.

She looks at me with that same panic. She doesn't understand how she can hear me.

It strikes me that not only did Williams never explain that he could read her thoughts, he never explained that she could project hers as well. Another way to keep her under his control. He could cloak his thoughts so she had no idea he was reading hers.

Clever. Manipulative.

Predictable.

I get up and move away.

What do I do now? What do I do with her?

She's watching me. Knowing how she feels about me, it must have been desperation that brought her here. She's a vampire with no idea what it means or how to take care of herself. Williams turned her months ago but left her ignorant of basic survival skills. I'm sure he thought he'd be around. Sure he planned to provide her with hosts and to instruct her in vampire ways.

His own ways, of course.

What to do now?

This time when I sit down, I take a seat in a chair across the room. Put some space between us. Her head is bowed, her hands knotted in her lap. I realize she's crying when I see tears splash onto her hands. She doesn't move, doesn't make any attempt to wipe them away.

"Mrs. Williams?"

After a long moment, she looks up.

"Why did you come to me?"

Her expression shifts, from sadness to despair. She wipes at the tears with the back of a hand.

"Where else could I go? Ortiz is dead. You are the only other vampire Warren ever talked about. Warren was supposed to take care of me. He *said* he'd take care of me. Now he's gone, and I'm alone. I'm frightened."

She clutches at her stomach. "There's an ache—here—that's growing stronger. I'm so *hungry*. I was going to go back to those places I went for Warren but I didn't want to go alone. He never told me what drugs he used on them. I thought you'd know. You need to feed, too, right? You can come with me. Show me what I need to do on my own."

Her desperation is growing stronger. It's in her voice, shadowing her face. When she speaks again, anger is there, too. The lines around her jaw tighten, her eyes become hard.

"And you owe me, Anna. You owe Warren, too. He's gone because of you. Oh, don't try to deny it. Everything that's happened in the last year is because of you. I don't know how. I don't know why. I only know it's true."

There's no sense in mouthing any kind of denial. She wouldn't hear it. Right now she's overcome with grief and more important, the hunger. I remember those first weeks. Avery kept me fed. I didn't know it at the time, but he was feeding me David's blood. The memory still triggers a shiver of revulsion—toward him, toward myself for being such a gullible fool.

I see the same susceptibility in the woman sitting across the room. It may be even worse for her because Williams was her husband long before he turned her. She loved and trusted him. Enough to let him make her vampire to save his life. A selfless act on her part, pure selfishness on his.

When I stand up, she does, too. I wave her back down. "I'm going to make a telephone call. Stay here."

She doesn't argue, lowers herself back onto the couch. For the first time, a glimmer of hope shimmers in her eyes.

I cross to the kitchen, close the door behind me. I dial a number so well known to me I should have it on speed dial.

As luck would have it, Frey picks up. Not Layla. I swipe an imaginary hand across my forehead, a cartoon gesture of relief. "It's Anna."

He doesn't say anything right away. I imagine he's having the opposite reaction at hearing *my* voice. Then he says, "I heard about Williams."

That catches me off guard. "How?"

"He was the police chief. It's everywhere. The newspaper, the TV. Even made national news. That *is* why you're calling, right?" The timbre of his voice changes. "Nothing's wrong is it?"

I wish it were that simple. I tell him about Harris' visit. About Mrs. Williams sitting, as we speak, in my living room. Leave the best part for last. "He turned her."

I hear Frey take a breath. "God. Did she attack you?"

"No. She is inexperienced as a vampire. Williams put her on a short leash. She doesn't know her strength, her powers. She didn't even realize vampires have a psychic connection. It gets worse. She doesn't know how to feed on her own. She's hungry. She's going to need blood soon or instinct will take over. She'll attack innocents. She'll have no choice."

I pause, wishing I didn't have to ask another favor of him so soon. I have no choice. "Will you take her to Beso de la Muerte? To Culebra?"

Frey is quiet. In my mind's eye, I see him weighing options.

He would have every right to say no. He's already missed two days of summer school because of me. And there's the driving thing. I didn't even think of that when I called him. How would he get her there? It was a stupid idea.

I open my mouth to tell him to forget it when he breaks in.

"I can be there in thirty minutes. I'll have Layla drive us. She's always said she wants to meet Culebra. Here's her chance."

"Layla?" Her other form is lion. "She doesn't have trouble driving?"

"She just had these glasses made—with a filtering lens she designed. Moderates the blue spectrum so we can distinguish colors. Seems to work."

For the first time, I'm glad that Layla is a supernatural and, though it pains me to admit it, a clever one at that. "Thank you. Again. And thank, Layla." Those are words I thought I'd never utter. I swallow the bitter taste, continue. "I'll call Culebra. Make sure he knows what's going on and to have a host ready."

We ring off. I call Culebra. Explain the situation. He hadn't heard about Williams. His shock turns to bitterness when I explain about his wife and her predicament. He never liked or trusted Williams, feelings now justified in his mind. Still, he says he'll be ready for Mrs. Williams when she gets there.

When I rejoin Mrs. Williams in the living room, the tears are gone, she's sitting up straighter on the couch. She's regained some of the poise I remember from my first glimpse of her almost a year ago. It was at a party in Avery's home, a mix of vampires and their mortal spouses. He was chief of police, she the wife of a man with power in both human and supernatural communities. She was aware of and comfortable with her position as his consort. She wore the crown well.

She's remembering that now. It's there in her thoughts.

She's berating herself for showing weakness in front of me. In front of her husband's nemesis. She's gathering courage from a misconception that we are equals. She's unsheathing vampire claws.

If I weren't feeling sympathetic toward her, I'd show her how *un*equal we are.

She has a lot to learn.

But not from me. I have neither the time nor temperament to tutor her in vampire ways.

When she sees me at the doorway, she stands. "Can we go now?"

I shake my head. "No. I can't help you today."

Her mouth hardens in a tight-lipped sneer. "What do you mean? I need you to show me what to do. I've never fed on my own. You have to do this."

She's ramping up for a full-blown tirade, I feel it. Before she starts haranguing me, I hold up a hand. "I have someone coming who will help you."

Her face brightens. "A host?"

"No. A shape-shifter who will take you to a place where you can safely feed."

The frown is back again. "You won't come with me?"

"I can't. I have things to attend to." Things your husband is responsible for, I'm tempted to add.

She's not happy with the response. Her body is rigid with protest. I don't care. We stare at each other a few seconds before she looks away. Her need for blood is stronger than her need to argue. She's afraid if she pushes me, I'll throw her out to manage on her own. She's not ready to attempt it.

She looks back at me.

She's convinced she soon will be.

The urge to smile at her is strong. She doesn't realize I'm reading her like a first-grade primer. I understand now why a man like Williams would hide his ability to impose himself into his wife's head. What better way to exert authority than to know what she is thinking and feeling? And to weigh it against what she might *tell* him she's thinking and feeling.

It's a powerful tool for control.

And Williams was all about control.

CHAPTER 27

MRS. WILLIAMS AND I WAIT IN SILENCE FOR FREY to arrive. I keep my thoughts hidden, just in case she's figured out that she heard me *in her head*. She's not a stupid woman. Her husband kept her in the dark about the telepathic connection between vampires and other supernaturals. Once she spends time with Frey and Culebra, though, I have no doubt she'll pick up the trick quickly.

I wonder how she'll react to the realization that Williams was reading her every thought? I know how I'd react.

It's the equivalent of mental rape. No matter how much I loved the guy, it would alter the grieving process considerably.

When Frey and Layla arrive, I'm subjected to the same hypercritical appraisal of my home by Layla as I was by Mrs. Williams. It's even more intense with Layla, since she happens to be an interior designer. Before she even says hello, or acknowledges Mrs. Williams, she says, "Not bad, Anna. Could use a professional's touch—your furniture is a little dykish. And you could use some artwork on the walls." She turns my way with a condescending smile. "I'd be happy to help."

Ire rises along with the hair on the back of my neck. Frey intervenes. I don't know what he says to her, but she turns green cat eyes on him wide with innocence. *I am being nice. I offered my services.*

He closes his eyes a moment in what looks like an attempt to control his exasperation and pushes past her. He extends a hand to Mrs. Williams. "I'm Daniel Frey. I'm sorry for your loss."

She takes his hand, her expression once again riddled with confusion. She must have heard the exchange between Frey and Layla and still can't comprehend why. "You are vampire?"

"No." Frey's voice is soft with understanding and compassion, the same voice he'd use with a troubled student. "I am a shape-shifter. So is Layla. We can communicate with you telepathically. Vampires and shape-shifters have that ability. You'll get used to it soon, I promise."

An appreciation of *why* she wasn't aware of her telepathic powers is blossoming in Mrs. Williams mind. We all feel it. The beginning of doubt as to her husband's motives. Curiosity about what other powers she might have that he neglected to tell her about. A spark of anger.

Still, she summons the strength to temper those thoughts. She hasn't learned to cloak them. Yet. But she is wise enough to know the three beings in the room with her are privy to what's going on in her head. Instead, she concentrates on where Frey and his Barbie doll girlfriend are about to take her.

Layla's mouth turns down in consternation at being classified a "Barbie" doll. She doesn't have an exaggerated hourglass figure; she's thin as a reed. But she does have pouty good looks, and with that long hair cascading down her back, it's easy to make the comparison.

Layla sees the smile that quirks the corner of my mouth.

She shoots me a venomous look. *Watch it. We're here to do you a favor.*

Mrs. Williams looks flustered when she catches Layla's remark to me. She clears her throat in a nervous attempt to draw attention away from her gaffe. "Where are we going? Anna never told me."

Frey, too, is suddenly anxious to put distance between Layla and me. "We're taking you to a place where you can safely feed." He ushers her toward the door with a hand at her elbow, crooking a finger at Layla. Layla follows with another black look in my direction. Once he has them both started for the car, Frey turns back to me.

"Are you going to be all right by yourself?"

"Yes." After this morning, by myself is a welcome relief. "Lance will be home by noon."

Frey doesn't question or argue. The basis of his concern is that Williams was a threat as long as I refused to cooperate with him. It follows then that with Williams gone, the threat should be, too. Frey has no way of knowing my suspicions about the part Underwood played in William's death. With Mrs. Williams here, there was never an opportunity to discuss it and now, what purpose would it serve except to add yet another reason for him to worry about me? I wave him off and watch until the car pulls from the curb. Mrs. Williams' determined face stares out at me from the backseat.

Once they are gone, my thoughts turn to what I should do next. I know of only one way to contact Underwood—at his place in La Quinta. It takes me a moment to get the number and another moment to be connected.

I should have known it would not be this easy. The receptionist tells me Underwood checked out yesterday afternoon.

Of course he did.

Not getting his cell number was a stupid and negligent oversight on my part. I depended on Williams to be my contact. Now, I can only wait for Underwood to contact me.

Which is problematic. It will be hard to explain skipping out alone with Lance playing guard dog. I had hoped to meet with Williams yesterday or this morning before Lance got back to town.

Fuck. *Nothing* is ever easy.

With two hours to kill before noon, restlessness once again comes to roost on my shoulders like a leaden yoke. If I go to the office, I might at least have the distraction of a telephone call from a potential client. It doesn't take me long to decide anything—even work—is better than sitting around.

The office is closer to the airport, too, so more convenient when Lance calls that he's arrived. I leave a voice message on his cell letting him know where I'll be.

Mind made up, I'm on the road in five minutes.

IT'S ANOTHER POSTCARD-PERFECT DAY IN SUNNY SAN Diego. The water sparkles, the blue sky shimmers cloudless and bright, the harbor is so full of boats it looks like a floating traffic jam.

A day like this, it's a joy just to be near the water. I feel it even here on the deck outside our office.

Maybe I should buy a boat. No one can sneak up on you on a boat. Lance and I could anchor in the bay, stranding Underwood and his fortune-telling on shore. Maybe if I let the anniversary of my becoming vampire pass unnoticed, so would the prophecies. Let some other poor soul take on the mantle of the Chosen One.

Williams may be dead, but his goddamned legacy is as burdensome as Avery's. When I should be mournful that a two-hundred-year-old vampire just flamed out of existence, instead I can't let go of the animosity. If he'd been honest with me in the beginning, he wouldn't be dead.

"Williams, you fucker. It's all your fault."

"Talking to yourself now?"

The voice at my elbow startles me so much, the vampire reacts before the human. Teeth bare, a snarl erupts, and I have a neck in my hands in the time it takes my eyes to register to whom the voice belongs.

Lance. Here. Safe. My hands drop from the neck to the small of his back so I can pull him even closer.

"Damn, Lance, you scared me. I thought you were going to call when you got in."

He presses his body against mine. "It's only a ten-minute jog from the airport. It'd take you longer to get there by car."

His lips are so close, his body heat rising so quickly, it takes all my willpower not to pull his clothes off and fuck him senseless right here on the deck. Instead, exercising great restraint, I pull him into the office, sweep everything on David's side of the desk to the floor, and we fuck each other senseless inside.

THE SOUND OF APPROACHING FOOTSTEPS FROM OUTside clears our heads and startles us upright quicker than a splash of ice water on a sunburned back. Lance and I look at each other, then toward the door.

The door we hadn't bothered to lock.

This is a place of business.

Good thing we can move fast.

Giggling like school kids, we scramble into our clothes, put the desk back in order and stand looking innocently and expectantly toward the door.

The footsteps stop. There's a moment of silence.

Then an envelope drops through the mail slot.

Lance releases a breath. "Mailman."

He walks over and picks up the envelope and hands it to me.

I slip it on the blotter, drop into the chair on David's side of our partner's desk, motion Lance into my chair. We grin at each other, enjoying the afterglow of sex and adrenaline.

I ask, "How'd the shoot go?"

Lance waves the question aside with a flip of a hand. "Fine." He leans toward me, remembering what he'd intended to ask before desire trumped rational thought. "I want to know what the hell is going on here. I didn't see the headline about Williams until I landed."

The joy of the previous moment is erased by the concern on Lance's face. Carefully, I draw a curtain on my real thoughts and fill him in on the visitors I had this morning. First Harris and then Mrs. Williams.

"Jesus," he says when I finish. "You don't really think Williams committed suicide, do you? And what was he doing in the desert?"

Once again, I have to compose my thoughts. Lance has no idea Williams was with Underwood in Palm Springs. I shrug. "Maybe Frey was right when he said we were followed to Palm Springs. Whoever followed us may have reported to Williams and he was on his way to intercept us."

"Still doesn't explain how he ended up dead."

"No. It doesn't."

I've been toying with the envelope I'd thrown on the desk as I spin my tale. I reach into a drawer and pull out a letter opener, more a diversionary tactic than interest in the contents. When I slit it open, a single folded sheet of copy paper falls out.

Lance has picked up the thread of our conversation. "What's going to happen to Mrs. Williams now? I can't believe the bastard turned her and didn't teach her anything about being a vampire."

His words register in my head; I think I actually nod in reply. But my attention is caught by the four words printed in bold caps on the paper I hold in my hand:

TONIGHT. MIDNIGHT.
BE READY.

I'd been wondering when Underwood would get in touch. I have my answer.

Lance peers at me, eyes narrowed. "What's wrong?"

I shake my head, slip the paper into a desk drawer, toss the envelope into the wastebasket. "Nothing." I push my chair back, stand up. "Let's go to the cottage."

He stands, too, but gestures toward the drawer. "What was in the envelope?"

I take his arm and turn him toward the door. "Just a reminder from David. He's out of town, but we have a new partner and I'll be working with her for the first time tonight."

"New partner? When did that happen?"

I fill him in about Tracey. Most of what I tell him is the truth. Except, of course, the part about having a job tonight.

That's a lie.

CHAPTER 28

LANCE IS SHOWERING. I'M PACING. FOR ONCE, I WAS hoping Lance would say he had to go home tonight, to the beach house. It didn't happen. I should have known it wouldn't. He's still in protective mode.

We had a nice day. Took a walk on the boardwalk, had beers in a neighborhood bar. Watched a Padres game on the big screen. Did things that human couples do.

I might have enjoyed it more if I didn't have this appointment with Underwood looming. And if I didn't have to guard every thought that went through my head. Lance knows that my job entails midnight runs—he's just made it clear he intends to make this one with us.

How am I going to get out of this?

Lance comes downstairs wearing one of my robes. It's a big pink chenille job, and I laugh in spite of the heaviness I feel in my heart. "You look better in that thing than I do."

He raises an eyebrow. "I found it in the back of your closet. Did you really used to wear this thing?"

"I didn't have you around when I was human. I got cold in the winter."

He fingers the heavy material. "No wonder so many mortal women have dreary sex lives. This is about as appealing as a flannel nightgown."

"Good thing you didn't check the dresser. There are a few of those in there, too." I hook a finger in the belt and give a tug. "Besides, wearing it isn't the sexy part. Taking it off, that's the sexy part."

He bends his face close to mine. "We'll test that theory. Right after I fix us a drink."

He lets his lips brush mine, a tease, and steps away to head for the kitchen. "Hold that thought."

I start pacing again as soon as he's out of sight.

What am I going to do? I don't even have a sleeping pill in the house to drug him. Not that one pill would do it. Vampires have strong constitutions. It would take a half bottle to affect him. Nor can I bring myself to use physical force. I could knock him out but that would be painful. A headache is a headache no matter the species.

And when he came to, what then? He'd have every right to be furious with me. Caring for me has not exactly been easy. What if he wanted to stop seeing me? I'm not ready for that. I like having him around. I like the way he makes me feel. I like the way we *fit*.

Shit. The only thing I'm sure of is I can't tell him the truth. I won't risk his insisting on coming with me. Underwood has already shown how little regard he has for Lance. I won't risk another attempt on his life.

Lance is back with two glasses, an ice bucket, a plate of limes and an open bottle of tequila. "A penny for your thoughts."

"Funny expression for a vamp to use," I retort.

He fills the glasses with ice and booze and hands me one. "Not really. Not tonight." His expression is serious, his eyes veiled, a reflection of the barrier he's erected around his own thoughts. "You've spent most of the day locking me out of your head. Do you want to tell me why?"

He raises his glass and we touch rims and drink. His gaze never waivers from my face.

I'm the one who looks away first. I do it by pretending to spill some of my drink, by wiping at my mouth with a hand. "Jesus. I'm so clumsy. I'll get a napkin."

He takes my glass and I feel him watching as I leave for the kitchen.

This is going to be so much harder than I thought.

I stall as long as I can before rejoining Lance in the living room. He's taken a seat on the couch and refilled my glass. I still have no idea how I'm going to get away in—a surreptitious glance at my watch—an hour and a half.

Lance's mood has lightened. He smiles as he gives me back my glass. "I have an idea," he says. "Let's drink tonight. A lot. Let's forget the last few days and get roaring drunk. Drink until we pass out."

Now that's a plan I hadn't thought of. No drugs. No brute force. He's picked his own poison. All I have to do is pretend to drink as much as he does. Then distract him while I dispose of the liquor. There are enough plants around us here in the living room to take care of that.

Potted plants. Many soon-to-be *very* potted plants.

I grin at my own little joke.

"I like it." I tilt my head back and drain my glass. "Your turn."

Lance has already refilled our glasses. I put mine to my lips and take a long pull. I know how much liquor I can hold. I figure another glass or two, and then I'll stop drinking.

I don't know how Underwood plans to contact me at midnight but if Lance continues to drink at this rate, he should be too hammered to realize I'm gone. He's already started on a third drink.

I've been sitting close to him on the couch. He bends toward me to refill my glass and I peek into the gaping robe. "You have such great pecs."

It's what I'm thinking. In my head. What I hear coming out of my mouth is different. Slurred. My lips feel swollen and my tongue heavy. I look up into Lance's face and the room starts to spin. The glass falls from my hand.

"What the—?"

Lance takes me by the shoulders. He stands up so he can lower my body until I'm lying full length on the couch. He strokes my cheek.

"I'm sorry, Anna."

It's the last thing I hear before the darkness rises to swallow me up.

CHAPTER 29

I'M DREAMING.

I must be. My body is floating, rising on an invisible cushion of air.

No. Not on air. Hands lift me. Hands at my shoulders, my legs, someone cradling my head.

I open my eyes. Can't see. It's too dark. Odd. Vampires can see in the dark.

Why can't I?

Someone is singing in a clear, high voice. Pretty. Somber. A language I don't recognize. I like the sound. Comforting somehow.

I smell incense. A familiar scent. Floral, woodsy. Someone's cologne?

Can't remember.

I'm shivering. It's cold. Damp. Another smell underneath the incense. Musty. Stale. Like dirt.

Try to turn my head. Two strong hands prevent me. When I try to shake my head, to shake the hands off, the grip tightens.

"Don't try to fight, Anna."

Whose voice is that?

My mind struggles to penetrate the cloud shrouding my thoughts just as my body struggles to shake off the hands.

I accomplish neither.

Instead, those carrying me press closer, restrict my movements now with their bodies as well as their hands.

"She shouldn't be struggling," a voice nearby says. "She should be out. Did you do what I told you?"

"Yes. I gave her exactly the dose you prescribed." That same familiar voice at my head. "You underestimated her strength."

The feeling of fingers smoothing hair back from my forehead. "I don't want her hurt. You promised me she wouldn't be hurt."

I want to scream, "Then why the fuck did you do this?"

But I know I'm the only one who hears. The shriek echoes and bounces in the void as if entrapped in a vault.

Perhaps it's just as well.

I recognize the voice. Recognize the touch and smell of the hand on my forehead.

Bitter tears stream down my face.

The irony that one of my last thoughts before he drugged me was that I wanted to protect him.

Lance.

I stop struggling. I need a plan, need to gather strength.

The chanting grows louder. The procession comes to a halt. The hands lower me onto something cold and unyielding. My limbs are arranged, hands over my head and secured. Legs straightened.

Whatever I'm lying on is rough, where my back and legs rest there are uneven, jagged edges that bite into the skin. It's worse if I try to move.

So I don't.

Something is thrown over me. Something lightweight

that floats on my skin like silk. Its touch makes me aware that until now, I was naked, exposed not only to the hands but the eyes of whoever bore me to this place.

Revulsion roils in my gut, bile rises in my throat.

I'm going to be sick.

No.

Swallow it back down. Turn the disgust into anger. Taste the bile and savor it because it is fuel for the rage.

The chanting grows louder. Exhortations to a goddess. Mari.

How do I know that?

The name is sung over and over. The chorus swells. More voices. More phrases that I shouldn't be able to understand yet somehow, I do. Mari. The goddess of the earth. Protectress of those who rule in heaven, on earth, and below. Queen of the thunder and the wind and keeper of the storm. Beloved of her servants, those who surround her here, and her consort, Maju.

Maju?

The chant changes in tempo and pitch. It is Maju they call for now. Mari's husband. Her mate. It is time, the words proclaim, time to fulfill the prophecy. Time to make heaven tremble and the underworld quake. Time to bring Mari and Maju out of the dark and into the light. Time for them to take their rightful place as rulers over all.

Time to consummate their love anew so the reign of the Sorginak can begin. Time for the lovers to reunite after five hundred years.

Lovers?

A hand lifts the veil, pushes it up from my ankles, gathers it at my waist.

No.

Something sharp, clawlike, traces a path on the inside of my thighs. It tickles and burns at the same time.

I try to kick out. Hands grab my ankles. Thrust something under my buttocks so my back is arched.

No.

Another hand circles my waist, pulls me forward.

It's grown quiet around us—the chanting stopped. Now there are other sounds. Heavy breathing and lust-filled grunts. The smell of sex mingles with the incense. Those around us are pleasuring themselves as they watch.

Memories flood back. A year ago. In the backseat of a car. Donaldson hitting me until I blacked out. When I awoke . . .

A voice at my ear pulls me back.

"Don't fight, Anna. You are Mari. A goddess. Destined to rule beside me for all eternity. Give yourself to me. Willingly. You have nothing to lose and the world to gain. I will be good to you. I will give you all."

I force myself to grow still under his weight. Force myself to endure the feel of his hands as they push the veil higher to cup my breasts. Still, I force myself to endure the feel of him as he pushes against me, as he pries my legs open with his own to receive him. Force myself to wait until my mind is clear. Until I'm strong enough.

I couldn't fight Donaldson. Didn't understand the changes wrought by our exchange of blood.

This isn't Donaldson.

Concentrate. Gather strength. Feel as it coils inside me. Tighter and tighter.

He is trying to ram himself into me.

I tense muscles and squirm away.

He grows angry. He curses. His hands clutch at my hips, pull me back and up. He will not stop.

I will make him.

I call out.

First to Lance.

Only silence responds. A flickering ember of regret quickly extinguished.

Then to the vampire. To the animal inside me. I know she hears. She's struggling. Frantic. Full of rage.

It happens.

The vampire bursts free of her drug-induced chains. Her voice, my voice, unleashes its fury in a primal scream that reverberates in the cave like a roar of thunder. My eyes fly open. This time, I see.

I pull at the bindings at my wrists. They rip away.

A cry of alarm goes up around me.

When he raises his head, Underwood's eyes have only an instant to register surprise.

Only an instant before I've ripped out his throat.

Only an instant before I've drained him of every drop of his blood.

CHAPTER 30

SILENCE. UTTER AND COMPLETE.

I sit up, thrust away the leathery shell that was Julian Underwood.

My teeth are bared. My eyes sweep the shocked faces surrounding me. Twelve of them. Men and women. Stinking of sex and that cloying smell. Incense. Underwood's cologne. The same.

They are all naked, the women with potbellies and sagging breasts. The men with flabby arms and shrinking members. When their eyes meet mine, they step back, press against the wall of—

I look around. We're in a cave.

I look again.

Where is he?

"Lance!"

The name rips from the bowels of my belly, full of anger and the bitterness of betrayal.

There is no answer.

I jump from the rock bier on which I'd been tied. It is elevated, surrounded by candles—some sort of ritualistic altar upon which I was to be joined with Underwood.

For what purpose?

Is this the fate of the Chosen One? Is this what it means? My destiny was to be raped by a madman in front of a delusional sect of . . . I don't even know what they are.

There is a woman standing at the head of the altar. She is clutching a thurible, the kind used in churches, by its silver chain. Incense curls up from the bowl, polluting the air around us. When her eyes meet mine, the thurible crashes to the floor. The incense flares and burns out.

I grab her by the throat before she can flee. "What are you?"

She blinks at me as if not understanding the question.

I shake her. "What are you?"

She goes limp in my hands. When I release my grip, she falls to the floor, her neck at an odd angle.

I reach for the man next to her. He does not flinch or try to get away. He lowers his eyes and bows his head.

"Mother," he whispers. "Mari."

"No." I bark out the word. "No. Who the fuck are you people? Why did you bring me here?"

He looks puzzled at the question. "You are the goddess. We are your servants. We are Sorginak. Here to do your bidding. Here to serve."

He speaks accented English. The emphasis on the last syllable in each word produces a singsong effect that I recognize. It's a French accent.

I throw a scathing look toward Underwood's desiccated corpse. "And who is he?"

"He is—" A pause, a shudder. "He was Maju. Your husband. He—we—have waited five hundred years for your return."

The words of the chant fill my head. I realize now why

I was able to understand. Three years of high school and four of college French. It wasn't French, not the French I remember, but obviously a dialect.

I release the man. For he is a man. Nothing more. "How do you know of five hundred years? You are mortal."

He takes one step back, head still bowed. "Our line has served you since the beginning. We will serve you until the end." He gestures toward the body of the woman at his feet. "We are yours to do with as you will."

Rage still cuts through me, turning my thoughts red with the bloodlust. These pathetic, deluded creatures would have watched as Underwood raped me, watched while indulging their own sick fantasies. I want to tear at their throats, one after the other, and drink until there is nothing left but husk.

Instead, I turn my back to them. Pick up the coverlet of red silk that had been thrown over me and wind it around my body like a sarong.

When I face them again, the human has regained a tenuous hold. With the return of reason, comes something else.

The realization that it was Lance who delivered me to Underwood.

"Where is the other?" I ask.

"He has gone."

I close my eyes. Allow one moment of grief to wash over me.

Lance.

When I open them again, I grab the man nearest me and shove him forward. "Get me out of here."

Wordlessly, the procession moves through the cave. I follow behind. Watching. Probing the air with my senses. Underwood's blood feels thick, polluted in my veins. I've tasted evil. I will need an infusion of clean blood to rid myself of the poison.

I think of Lance. His scent hangs in the air. He passed this way recently.

Lance.

No. No sadness. Only bitterness. Only the desire for revenge.

His blood will do nicely.

When we come to the mouth of the cave, the man who has led us stops. Turns to me. He bows his head.

"I am Zuria, high priest in your service. Descendant of Maju. He has been the guide for five hundred years. With him gone, you must give us instructions. What do you want us to do, Goddess? We are powerless without direction."

I look around at the men and women gathered around me, their faces wreathed in shock and sadness. Wretched. Dismal creatures with sagging flesh and stooped shoulders.

I try to dredge up some feelings of compassion. Nothing stirs within me but contempt. They were willing to watch, hell, they were *participating*, in Underwood's assault.

I ignore the question. From our vantage point, I still cannot see anything outside the cave but darkness. I can hear something, though, the ocean. "Where are we?" I ask.

He points toward the cave entrance. "We are near the city of Biarritz. In the cliffs above the shoreline."

"Biarritz? In France?"

He nods. "Basque country. Home of the Sorginak."

Since my parents moved to France, I've spent more than a little time on the web teaching myself about a country that has become their home. I know the Basque region spans the border of Spain and France on the Atlantic coast. Something else floats to the surface of my mind, too.

Lance. Telling me that Underwood was born in Basque country. That he called Underwood's father a Sorginak witch.

How did they get me here? How long have I been out?

The little circle of humans has not moved. They stare at me with big eyes. Waiting.

I look away. Spy piles of clothes scattered amid the rocks. My jeans, T-shirt and tennis shoes among them. Without a word, I scoop them up, move behind a rock to get dressed. Awareness that hands belonging to the creatures outside no doubt stripped me of my clothes sparks another flare of anger. If I don't get away from them soon, I may not be able to wait to purge Underwood's blood. Even from behind the rock, the vampire inside senses the clean blood pounding through the veins of those standing a few feet away. She asks why we hesitate, and I don't have a good answer. The fact that they are human is not enough. They were one with Underwood.

When I step from behind the rock, the others are still there, too, but like me, have dressed. The women wear baggy, shapeless dresses of cotton, the men trousers and loose-fitting shirts.

Time to get some answers. I address the one who called himself Zuria.

"What do you call yourselves?"

"We are Sorginak."

"Are there many of you?"

He waves a hand. "This is the circle. The protectorate. There are not many who follow the old ways anymore. Even our children have no interest. Your coming was to be the spark."

"The spark?"

"The resurgence of traditional Basque ways."

I don't know what that means. I don't *want* to know what that means. I only want to go after Lance. Which calls up another question.

"How did I get here?"

He frowns as if I should know. "Maju. Brought you here across the sky on his chariot of fire. You and the younger man."

Chariot of fire? That this man really believes this shit in the twenty-first century trips another spasm of barely containable anger. The vampire within me writhes to be set free, to exact revenge. I have to close my eyes a moment to plea with vampire to be patient, to assure her that she will have an opportunity to vent her wrath soon.

When she is quieted, I face Zuria again. Even with the effort to suppress it, my voice shakes with frustration. "You didn't find it strange that I, your so-called goddess, came to you drugged? And that the man who called himself my husband had me bound to that altar and was about to rape me?"

He shows me the same blank expression as when I asked how I got here. "It is not up to us to question the ways of the gods. Maju told us what to do—how to prepare for the ceremony. We did as he asked."

There is no outrage. Not even a spark of confusion or doubt. This man believes he did nothing wrong.

Now what?

"How far are we from an airport?"

That question, at least, allows Zuria to respond like a rational human being. "Not far. There is an airport in Biarritz."

The impression lasts barely as long as it takes him to answer. A shadow darkens his face. "You are leaving? What are we to do?"

There are so many ways I want to answer that question—most involving various body parts. Instead, I take a moment to choose my words carefully.

"First, you are to take me to the airport. Then you will return to your homes and forget what happened here. The one you called Maju was a false prophet. Keep vigilant. When the time is right, I will be back with my true consort. Do you understand?"

Hope shines from Zuria's eyes. "You will not punish us for Maju?"

Hopefully the law will do that when they discover the body inside the cave. As for Underwood? Trying to explain his desiccated corpse will merely change the nature of the plea from murder to insanity.

I shake my head. "No. This man who pretended to be Maju was a powerful sorcerer. But you must heed my words. No more ceremonies. Live your lives quietly and in peace with the world. Wait. For my return."

The words are so much garbage. I expect someone in the group to challenge what I've said. Instead, the reaction is one of relief. They gather their personal belongings from the floor of the cave and prepare to go. They are chatting amongst themselves as if coming from a church social instead of having just participated in an ancient ritual that left their deity, Maju, not to mention one of their own, dead at the hands of a vampire.

I look around in bewilderment.

Unbelievable.

Unfuckingbelievable.

I'VE NEVER BEEN TO BIARRITZ.

When we exit the cave, we are looking down on a beach. Five-foot waves kiss a pearlescent shoreline. It is a clear, moonless night and a half dozen surfers take advantage of the well-formed breakers. The sight provokes a spasm of longing for home—for my cottage. A broad boardwalk is lined with people watching the surfers perform, and I remember another bit of web-generated trivia: Biarritz is an ocean town bordering the Atlantic, a well-known surfing beach.

Cafés and bistros sparkle under strings of twinkling lights. Music floats upward. I see all this from a vantage point that has us facing a lighthouse with a statue perched on a nearby rocky promontory.

Zuria follows my gaze. "That is you, Mari," he breathes with quiet reverence.

Somehow, I believe it is Mari only in his deluded mind. More likely a statue of a better-known protectorate. My defunct Catholic training stirs in my memory. The Virgin Mary.

The group scatters once we are out of the cave. Each one passes me with a bowed head and some kind of prayerful entreaty. Some try to take my hand. I step back out of reach.

Once just Zuria and I remain, I look around. We appear to be on a walking path whose direction takes us away from the shoreline. It must be close to the trailhead because I already hear car engines starting up.

"How far to the airport?"

Zuria motions me to follow him. I step in line with him and ask again. "How far to the airport?"

He seems reluctant to answer the question. "It would be a bad idea for you to play with me, Zuria. I want to go home. I'll only ask you nicely once more. How far are we from the airport?"

He wipes a hand across his mouth. "Not far, Goddess. But that is not the problem."

I raise an eyebrow. "Oh? What is the problem?"

He glances at his watch. "It is almost two in the morning. The airport doesn't open on Saturday until five thirty. I would be remiss in my duties if I didn't offer you the hospitality of my home until you could be accommodated."

I almost laugh at the suggestion. Spend time in this crazy bastard's home? I'd sooner sleep—

Then the implication of what he said hits me.

I glance at my wrist. Where my watch should be. The Rolex my family gave me last Christmas.

Another spasm of frustration and anger flares through me. My watch is gone.

Bad enough. But that's not what's triggering the reaction. Shock. Confusion.

If it's Saturday, the anniversary of my becoming is past.

I take mental inventory. I feel the same.

Flex muscles. Nothing.

Glance down. No wings have sprouted. I'm not glowing or shimmering. My body appears normal.

For a moment, I'm so relieved I almost forget where I am and how I got here. I throw back my head and laugh.

Zuria watches with a puzzled frown. "Goddess? Are you all right?"

Better than all right.

It's over.

Williams. Julian Underwood. Their crazy notion of a destiny.

The euphoric feeling that I am free lasts only as long as it takes vampire to push herself into my thoughts.

Not over.

Not yet.

Don't forget Lance.

CHAPTER 31

DESPITE ZURIA'S OBJECTIONS, I CONVINCE HIM TO drop me off at the airport. It is not lost on me that I have no money, no passport, not even a change of clothes. I need the time to figure out what the hell I'm going to do.

As I get out of his battered Citroën, Zuria reaches into the backseat and hands me a jacket.

My leather jacket.

"The young one left this for you," he says.

I take it. Wonder when Lance had time to think of a jacket? Was it before he drugged me or when he was stripping me naked for Underwood and his band of loonies?

Zuria's reluctance to go manifests itself in a drumming of fingertips on the steering wheel and an expression of sadness that borders on tearful. I finally have to turn away before he puts the car in gear.

"Come back to us soon, Goddess," he says.

Yeah. Don't hold your breath. I walk toward the terminal and, finally, hear the clutch engage as the car roars off.

The trailing noxious plume of burning motor oil tickles my nose and burns my eyes.

I shrug into the jacket, almost regretting it as soon as it settles over my shoulders. Lance's smell wafts up. He must have worn it. The urge to take it off and throw it away is powerful, but damn it, I *like* this jacket. I'll have it fumigated as soon as I get back home.

The building I'm facing is low-slung and utilitarian. Quiet. I can't see anyone moving around inside. It's not big as far as international airports go. There is a small grassy park in front of the terminal and I lower myself to sit cross-legged on the grass while I review my options.

The obvious first option would be to call my folks.

The drawbacks to that are just as obvious. How do I explain being in France with no money, no passport and no notice?

Shit.

If there's an American consulate somewhere in the vicinity, they may be able to help with money and an emergency visa so I can get out of here.

But I'll need a story. What story can I use? That I was mugged?

That could explain no wallet and no passport. But what about when they ask me where I've been staying? And if I notified the police?

Lance. This is all your fault.

What the hell were you thinking?

How did you get away? If the airport was closed, did you have a car stashed nearby?

For a moment, I'm awash in depression. Drowning in a pool of sorrow, a sense of loss.

The moment passes quickly. Anger swallows it up.

No time for angst.

In frustration, I shove my hands in the pockets of the jacket.

Freeze as my fingers close around—

From the right pocket, I pull my watch.

From the left, an envelope.

I slip the Rolex on my wrist, fasten it before looking at the envelope.

Lance's handwriting.

To Anna.

I don't want to feel what washes over me. Regret. Sadness. I want to feel only anger. The man who claimed he loved me delivered me to Underwood, then watched while he violated me. What excuse could he offer that would allow me to forgive such treachery?

Something shifts in the envelope. Curiosity makes me tear it open. I withdraw two folded sheets. When I open them, a small key falls to the grass. For the moment, I ignore the key, eyes drawn reluctantly to the familiar script.

Dear Anna,

If you're reading this, something has gone wrong. Julian will be dead. If I'm not, I know it's just a matter of time before I will be. Betrayal is the one thing you can never forgive.

The only thing I offer in my defense is that Julian said you wouldn't be hurt. The ceremony was to open the door. Your role was to be the conduit through which Julian gained his power. It would need to be done only once. You were drugged so you wouldn't remember. After, you and I would be free to live our lives. Together.

Empty words.

Lance Turner is no more. My affairs have been put in order. By the time you read this, my lawyers will have informed Adele of my death abroad. She will assume the property in Palm Springs. I ask only that you leave her in peace. She doesn't know anything about what happened. The Malibu property is yours to do with as you wish.

As for me, if you must come after me, I understand. You feel betrayed. You are so strong. It's hard for you to understand that not all of us are. I have always been weak. I thought after what Julian did to me, you would see the weakness and our relationship would change. That you would no longer look at me as a lover. That you would ask what kind of man lets himself get whipped like a slave. Julian did it as punishment because I told him I wouldn't go through with his plan. He did it because he could and because I let him. He did it because he thought you would leave me.

I should have ended our relationship myself. I didn't have the guts to do even that. When you didn't leave, I started to believe what Julian had been telling me since the day we met. That you and I were destined to be together once the prophecy was fulfilled. One night in exchange for a lifetime. It's when I stopped fighting. It's when I agreed to help.

More empty words, but I wanted you to know.

I did love you, Anna.

I always will.

Lance

My hand crushes the letter into a ball.

Love. My only consolation is that I never told the bastard that *I* loved *him*. A small, meaningless triumph but a satisfying one nonetheless.

I look around for the key that fell from the envelope when I withdrew the letter and pluck it from the grass. It's a slender, brass key with a numbers printed on the head.

A locker key.

For the first time since I awakened in the cave, I feel a

glimmer of hope. If this is what I think it is, Lance may have earned himself a quick death instead of a long, painful one.

AT FOUR THIRTY PEOPLE START FILTERING INTO THE airport. Uniformed pilots and flight attendants and security people, and then the less obvious cadre of reservationists and gate attendants and janitors in one-piece jumpsuits. At five thirty, promptly, the doors are opened to a small group of customers who, like me, are waiting to be on their way.

In my halting French, I ask one of the security guards where I can find the *casiers*. He points down a hall at the end of the ticket counter.

The number on the key is 118. When I find the locker, insert the key and see what's inside, a thrill of relief washes over me.

Wallet. Credit cards. Passport.

Another note.

We left your plane at the borne privée. Proceed through the VIP lounge and inquire at the concierge desk. They will put you in touch with a pilot.

Another grievance to add to the list. The bastard used my own plane to transport me here. What did they tell security when they manhandled me off? That I was incapacitated by what? Illness? Did they say I was infectious to avoid close scrutiny?

No matter now. I find the VIP lounge and enlist the help of a trim, sophisticated young woman who speaks perfect English. She assures me that she will have no trouble making the necessary arrangements to secure a crew and have my plane readied for the trip home. She hands me a manifest to look over and sign.

The cost is staggering. I could have flown round trip

commercially a dozen times in first class for far less. When I prepare to offer a credit card, however, she waves it aside.

"No, no, mademoiselle. Monsieur Turner took care of it. He paid in advance. I'm afraid it will take several hours, however, before all is ready. You are welcome to stay here. Food and drink are available in the bar. Spa facilities are through the door in back. You may shower and change if you wish."

I nod my thanks and turn away. A shower sounds good. You have no idea how dirty you can feel until a demon in a man suit rubs himself all over you.

I noticed a few shops on my way to the VIP lounge so I head there now. Like the airport in San Diego there aren't any clothing stores. No designer boutiques. Not even the equivalent of a Gap. I end up buying a little tangerine-colored beach cover-up that will have to do as a dress and a pair of sandals at a surf shop called Quiksilver.

Not exactly my style. When I hold it up, the dress hits mid-thigh.

At least it's clean.

IT TAKES A LITTLE OVER THREE HOURS BEFORE I'M finally allowed to board. The pilot and copilot are American.

"Good to see you looking so well," the pilot says to me, extending a hand. "Mr. Turner said he was bringing you here to recuperate from an illness. Obviously, you have."

He's young, early thirties, oily—his hair, his obsequious smile, his voice.

I smile back, though it feels more like a grimace. The lie is hard to swallow. What I want to do is beat my chest and ask how he could have been so stupid. Did I look like I was ill? Or did I look like I was drugged and being kidnapped?

Maybe that's not fair. Maybe he couldn't have known. Somehow, though, I think it more likely the money he was paid for the charter smoothed away any misgivings he may have harbored about the way I was brought on board.

He leaves for the cockpit. The copilot takes care of the door. He's a little older, forty maybe, and when he's through latching and securing, he joins me in the main cabin.

"Flying time is thirteen hours, Ms. Strong. We will put down once in Bangor, Maine, to refuel. We should be on the ground in San Diego about one o'clock, Pacific daylight time."

He doesn't smile. He doesn't display any of the sycophantic toadying of his coworker. He doesn't even look particularly happy to be here.

I like him.

I'M ASLEEP BEFORE THE PLANE GAINS CRUISING ALTITUDE. One moment I'm gazing out at the Basque countryside as we rocket down the runway.

The next, I'm not.

I WAKE UP TO THE WHIR AND PNEUMATIC CLICK OF the landing gear engaging. I stretch and yawn and check my watch. This must be the refueling stop.

The telephone on the console beside my seat buzzes. When I pick it up, the copilot's voice tells me I have a call. He disconnects and a familiar voice booms in my ear.

"My god, Anna. Where have you been?"

"Nice to hear your voice, too, Frey. What's the matter?"

"Everything. Williams' wife went crazy at Culebra's and killed a host. David is missing. Your new partner Tracey has been calling all over the place trying to locate you. She got halfway through the Fs before she found my number in your office Rolodex. I wouldn't have known to try the plane if Lance hadn't called. Where are you?"

His words are disjointed and rambling, launched at me through the phone with the speed of light in a burst of pent-up emotion that renders them almost incomprehensible.

Almost.

It takes me only a second to sort through the tirade and zero in on the one salient point in his rant.

"What do you mean David is missing?"

CHAPTER 32

BEFORE CONTINUING, FREY SUCKS IN A NOISY breath, as if the outburst forced all the air from his lungs. "Tracey said David was supposed to meet her at the office on Friday. In fact, she said *you* were supposed to meet her at the office on Friday, too. When neither of you showed up, she waited. While she was there, the phone rang. It was David's girlfriend. She wanted to know if you were all right. David got a call Thursday evening saying you had been in an accident. He left her in San Francisco and came right back. No one's seen him or heard from him since."

He runs out of air again, stopping abruptly to inhale. "Was there an accident? Are you all right?"

A click over the line and the pilot's voice interrupts. "Ms. Strong, we'll be on the ground about forty-five minutes. Bangor has cleared us for takeoff after fueling at oh six hundred hours. ETA for San Diego is thirteen hundred Pacific daylight time. Do you want to deplane at the fueling station?"

I press the intercom button. "No. I'll stay on board. Get us off the ground as soon as possible."

Frey cuts in as the pilot clicks off. "Bangor? As in Maine? What are you doing in Maine?"

I rub a hand across my eyes. "You don't want to know. I'll fill you in later. Right now, I'm more concerned about David. Christ, I don't even know what questions to ask. This could be a skip we turned in. Or a supernatural. Someone out to get me because of Williams." I sit up straight in the seat. "What did you say about Mrs. Williams? She killed a host?"

I can almost see him nodding as he says, "Drained her. Culebra was there, but she lost control. Swatted him away as if he were a fly on the wall. Knocked him cold. She's incredibly strong for a new vamp. Culebra should have been able to stop her."

Culebra *should* have been able to stop her. Did she get her strength from being sired by a two-hundred-year-old vamp? Or is it something else?

Concentrate on the problem at hand.

"What happened then?"

"She took off. When Culebra came to, she was gone. Along with another human, according to the barkeep. Carried him off. Culebra is beside himself with worry. She's behaving like a rogue, which puts the entire supernatural community in danger."

God.

Frey hesitates, as if waiting for me to say something. I don't know what to say. I'm trembling. For David. For the thoughts swirling around in my head.

If Mrs. Williams blames me for her husband's death, what better way to exact revenge than by taking David?

"Anna? Are you there?"

I rouse myself out of the miasma. "Frey, do you know where Avery lived?"

"Avery?" He repeats the name in a voice reflecting bewilderment and surprise. "What does Avery have to do with anything?"

"Maybe nothing. But Warren Williams and Avery were friends for two hundred years. He blamed me for Avery's death. Now Mrs. Williams blames me for her husband's death. I think there's a good chance she took David. And the logical place to take him would be where my connection to the three of them began."

Frey is silent for a moment. When he speaks, his words are reflective and deliberate. "You may be right. Do you want me to go out there, take a look around?"

"Not in your human form. She'll be looking for someone to come snooping. And she knows you're my friend."

"What about as panther?"

"During the day? How would you pull that off?"

I do the arithmetic. If we're in San Diego about one p.m., I'll have time to see Culebra and get back to meet Frey before dark. "Wait for me to call you. We can't do anything before dark. She's not going to hurt David until she makes sure I'm around to watch."

He's silent, and I know the idea of waiting for eight or nine hours is chafing. I know because I'm feeling the same thing.

"Don't try to go on your own, Frey," I warn. "Wait for me. You will wait for me, right?"

"Of course."

Too quick. But Frey is not stupid. He won't take unnecessary risks if David's life is in jeopardy.

I'm ready to thank him and hang up when something else he said bubbles to the surface of my consciousness. "You said Lance called? When?"

"Two hours ago. Said you were on your way home. Could be reached on the plane if I needed to get in touch with you. He sounded strange, Anna. Gave no reason for calling except for that. Rang off before I could ask how he knew I was trying to get in touch with you. Is there something going on? Did you two have a fight?"

Fight? I feel the bloodlust stir in anticipation.

No. Not yet. But it's certainly coming.

I thrust the vampire back into her box. "It's not important."

"Is that the reason you left town? Because you were fighting with Lance?"

"No. Let it go."

"Then was it to be away for the anniversary of your becoming? Because if it was, there's something else you should know."

I don't like the way that sounds. "What?"

A moment of silence, as if Frey is choosing his words carefully. "I've been doing some checking. We were wrong in thinking the anniversary date was the date you and Donaldson exchanged blood. It isn't. It's actually the first time you fed as a vampire. The ingesting of blood marked the conclusion of the physiological change. From that point on, you were no longer human but vampire. That is the true anniversary date of your becoming. And it is on that date that you will become what is destined to be."

For a moment, he sounds so much like Julian Underwood spouting his goddess of the Sorginak garbage that I'm tempted to laugh.

But what they wanted to do to me in that cave wasn't funny. What they *did* to me in that cave wasn't funny.

Why should I assume this would be any better?

I thought it was over—the craziness about being the Chosen One. Now I'm not so sure.

If Mrs. Williams intends to carry the banner for her husband, I'm right back where I started. She seemed clueless about vampire ways, but she must have spent hours listening to her husband talk about how he might win me to the cause. He might have mentioned David and how I fought Avery to save him. She may see David as the key to fulfilling her husband's mission.

I think back to the dark days of my becoming. I was attacked on a Friday night. I was in the hospital for what? One or two days. Then Avery came to my house and told me that I was no longer human. That I was vampire. Two days later, I fed from him. If what Frey says is true, four days after I was bitten would be Tuesday. When whatever is supposed to happen, will.

Unless I can stop it.

I ask Frey to do one more thing before we ring off. Well, two things actually. The first is to call David's girlfriend and tell her something—anything—to keep her from reporting David missing. Police involvement we don't need. The second is to call Tracey and do the same. Make up a story that David and I went out of town on a job. Assure them both the accident thing was a false alarm. That we'll be in touch with them by the end of the week.

In touch, I think ironically, or dead.

Either way, it won't matter.

After hanging up, I cross the cabin, head directly for the bar. Pour two drinks. Scotch, neat. One I down in a single gulp standing up at the teak counter, enjoying the burn as it scalds a trail down my throat and bursts with the impact of a fireball in my gut.

The other I take back with me to nurse in my seat.

The thing I have to figure out now is what Mrs. Williams is up to. She has David. There's not even a glimmer of doubt in my head about that. *Why* she has David is the question. Is it simply a way to get back at me for her husband's death? Or is there something more?

Warren Williams was adamant and vocal about my destiny. I'm sure he shared those feelings with his wife. As a mortal, she probably listened with bored indifference to his rants about me. How ignorant I was, how ineffectual as a vampire, how uninterested I was in learning the ways. She knows more about what being the "Chosen One" means than I do. Hell, I don't know anything about what it means and I seriously wish now I had taken the time to learn. My gut, however, says that power goes along with that title. It has to. Williams and Avery were all about power—having it, controlling it, hoarding it.

And that may be the problem.

As I see it, there are two possibilities. Either Mrs. Williams means to see that I fulfill that mysterious destiny and assume the crown as a tribute to her husband.

Or she means to wear that crown herself.

CHAPTER 33

IT'S A LITTLE BEFORE TWO WHEN WE LAND IN SAN Diego. Disconcerting since we left France at nine this morning and have been en route for thirteen hours. If what's happening isn't bad enough, the time difference will make this day hellishly long.

The pilot taxis from the runway to Jimsair, the private terminal. I wonder first how he would know to do that and then I realize how stupid that question is.

Of course he would know. It's where he picked me up, unconscious and with Lance as my companion.

When I deplane, a Jimsair employee is waiting. He and the pilot have a brief conversation before he turns to me.

"The same arrangements as always, Ms. Strong?"

Since I have no idea what that means, I just nod. Williams took care of the details before. When I went to France to visit my folks, I simply called the pilot I'd used before and told him when I wanted to leave. He took care of the rest. I suppose now I'd better take more interest.

That will be first thing on my to-do list after getting David back safely and killing Lance.

But right now . . . "I need to call a taxi. Can I do that inside?"

The guy nods and gestures toward the lounge. "Georgia at the desk will help you."

I thank him. I'll go straight home. Change out of this ridiculous outfit and go to Beso de la Muerte. There are questions I have for Culebra and, I imagine, questions he has for me.

I PUSH THROUGH THE OLD-FASHIONED DOUBLE swinging doors.

Culebra looks up, frowns and his greeting is a curt, "I've been wondering when you'd show up."

He's standing behind the bar, polishing glasses with a towel. He could be a Hispanic Clint Eastwood stand-in. Weather-beaten, tanned-leather face, slightly stoop-shouldered skinny frame, jeans and long-sleeved shirt faded from too much exposure to sun and soap.

Usually, you'd peg him as one of the good guys.

Today, however, his mood is black and dangerous. Today his shape-shifter name fits him. Rattlesnake.

I look around.

The bar is deserted.

Unusual for a Saturday afternoon.

He's in my head. *What did you expect? I lost two hosts. That crazy bitch killed one outright and took off with the other. His body was found yesterday in the desert. I thought Williams was a menace. His wife is worse.*

I'm sorry. I had no idea. I thought having her brought here was better than the alternative—sending her out to hunt on her own. The Revengers have left us alone for a while. She was frantic to feed and I didn't want to take the chance she'd do something to attract them.

The Revengers are a powerful human group sworn to exterminate the vampire race. They have been around since the time of the Crusades when vampires and heretics were hunted with the same fervor. There has been no activity lately to attract their unwanted and dangerous attention. My intention was to keep it that way.

Culebra throws the towel down, snarls, *Vampire hunters are the least of your worries. Once word gets around, how many hosts do you think will come back here? Or vampires looking to safely feed? Sanctuary has been violated. I'm not sure I can fix this. I'm not sure I want to.*

His words trigger a spasm of alarm. *Why not? This is your home. Your livelihood. What would you do?*

Retire. Sit on a beach. Think of myself for a change. Drink tequila all day and fuck all night. Sounds like a pretty good plan right now.

This is so unlike Culebra, I don't know how to react. Is he simply venting? He can't be serious. He's run this place for decades. It's where I come to feed. It's where I've come when I've needed help. It's where he saved David's life and where I saved Culebra's.

He must be kidding.

Do I look like I'm kidding?

He blames me for what happened. There is so much malice in his tone, the realization hits me like a physical blow. I wish it were physical. I wish he would hit me. Yell. Scream. Get it out of his system. No physical injury could be more painful than Culebra's hostility.

Don't be too sure, vampire. He leans toward me. His tone is dry, vibrates in the back of his throat like the warning sound of a rattler before it strikes.

The animal in me responds to the threat. I tense, take a wary step forward, two predators sniffing each other out.

No. This isn't the way it should be between us. I step back, shaking my head. *Why are you doing this? I thought we were friends.*

His laugh is merciless. *We are friends when you need something from me. I owe you for saving me from the witch Belinda Burke, but even that was not done without ulterior motives. You had your own score to settle. The drug lord Martinez wanted you dead. She sold you out to him. You lost Max because of what happened in Mexico. Admit it, Anna. You went after Burke as much for yourself as for me.*

And what if I did? He's beginning to seriously piss me off. All the shit I've been through in the last few days comes to a boil in my own caldron of rage. *What if everything you're saying is true? We had a pact, you and I, that we'd go after the witch together. Instead, you lie to me, take off on your own, serve me up to Williams and end up near death. Frey and I saved your miserable life, and I don't personally give a crap why you think we did it.*

His eyes narrow as he watches and listens. I don't care. I had a reason for coming here today and I fucking well plan to get what I came for.

"Williams is dead." My voice is shrill, my hands windmill around. The story erupts like a geyser. "I just get back from France where that maniac Lance and his crazy sire Julian Underwood attempted to use me in some stupid plan because they think I'm the reincarnation of a Basque goddess, and now I find out that Mrs. Williams has more than likely kidnapped David so she can use me to carry out a stupid plan of her own. I'm tired, scared, in need of counsel. It's why I came here. To see the wisest man I've ever known. I know he's here somewhere, Culebra. Under all that self-pitying, tortured, indulgent load of crap you've been spewing, I know he's still here. You can beat me up later, when we're all safe. Right now, I need my friend."

I run out of words and invective at the same time. Part of me feels relieved to have gotten the story out, part of me wonders if I've driven Culebra out of my life forever. Either way, I'm too weary to care.

Culebra is still staring, his body rigid as he peers at me with cold eyes. I don't try to get into his head. I can't take any more abuse.

The seconds tick by. I break the stalemate first. This is useless. I may as well go straight to Frey for a strategy session. I can't even remember now why I came here. I turn to go.

Culebra's words reach me at the door.

"Someone really thought *you* were a reincarnated Basque goddess? Now that's crazy."

CHAPTER 34

SARCASM. A VERY GOOD SIGN. I SNEAK A LOOK over my shoulder and Culebra is reaching under the counter. He pulls out a couple of Coronas and holds one out. I traipse back to the bar, sink onto a stool and take the proferred beer. We clink bottles and drink.

After a moment I venture a tentative, "What was all that stuff about retiring? You wouldn't really close this place down would you?"

He waves a hand. "There might not be anything left to close down. Look around. That Williams woman drove all my customers away, hosts and vampires. She was nuts. She killed a mortal without a shred of remorse and when I tried to stop her, she knocked me cold. I thought you said she was newly turned."

"She is. Williams turned her when he was in need of blood. Not more than six or eight weeks ago. About the time of Ortiz' funeral. Until now, she's never had to feed on her own. Williams must have been letting her feed from him."

I know how powerful that connection can be. It's the way Avery controlled me. She was Williams' wife. The bond of sex and blood is strong enough without adding love.

Love fucks up a lot of things. Maybe if I'd kept a clearer head about Lance—

Culebra is in my head before I realize those last thoughts were left unguarded.

"I'm sorry Lance betrayed you. Do you want to tell me what happened?"

"Why not?" I put the bottle down, rest my elbows on the bar.

"I was an idiot. Lance and his sire were part of some nutty Basque traditionalist group that believed their goddess, Mari, would return to earth and signal a resurgence of the old ways—whatever the hell they are. Julian Underwood convinced Lance I was Mari. Partly, I suppose, because of Williams' insistence that I was this *Chosen* One. Anyway, Underwood and Williams devised a plan. Long story short, they sent Lance to keep an eye on me. Williams told Lance to tell me that *you* sent him."

I lean forward, waiting for Culebra to make a comment on my gullibility.

To his credit, he doesn't. Not even in his head. I continue. "It worked. Lance and I became close. Williams made the mistake of trusting Underwood. He probably knew nothing about the Basque thing. Thought Underwood's goals were the same as his. He was wrong and ended up a pile of ash in a torched car."

"And what about Underwood and Lance?"

"Underwood is a corpse. Lance isn't. At least not yet."

Culebra is quiet for a moment when I finish. His dark gaze feels like a drill boring into my head.

When it gets too penetrating, I bark, "What?"

"You are awfully cavalier about Lance. You can't tell me this hasn't taken a toll on your emotions. You said yourself, you and he had gotten close."

I snort and resume drinking. Recounting the story has brought the vampire to the surface. I still have Underwood's blood inside, flowing like a river of acid. Deep down, I was hoping there would be a host here to dilute the poison. Right now, the only emotion I feel is disappointment.

"Maybe that's what you want to tell yourself," Culebra says, reading my thoughts. "But ridding yourself of Underwood's blood is not the only reason you came today."

No. But it's not what he thinks. I'm not here for therapy.

"David is missing. I believe Mrs. Williams took him. I think she intends to follow in her husband's footsteps and force me to accept the destiny he died protecting. You and I have never talked about it. So, I'm asking you now. Do you know what it means to be the Chosen One?"

Culebra's expression grows distant. I can't tell if he's searching his memory for the answer or if he knows it, and is burying it deep in his subconscious so it's hidden from me. He's locked me out and I can only wait, nursing my Corona, until he decides to come back.

At last, he does.

I can tell before he begins to speak, I'm not going to like what he has to say. His eyes tell me first. They are cold again, forged steel.

"These are things I can take no part in." His tone is formal and as cold as his eyes. "They are matters of the vampire. The supernatural community has long been divided as to its place in the world, but the one tenet always held dear is that when the Chosen One comes, it marks either the beginning or the end of what is to be for us all. I can't offer you counsel, Anna, because if it is true, if you are the Chosen One, the world as we know is yours to shape. Yours. Alone."

More existential bullshit. I clasp my hands together to keep from reaching across the bar to slap him. "This is Anna you're talking to," I whisper in a voice choked with anger. "I couldn't protect myself from my delusional boyfriend and his psychotic sire. How good do you think I'll be at changing the world?"

Culebra, *my* Culebra, smiles at that, a slow, sweet smile. He tilts his head and winks. "You will do what you always do when the time comes." He touches his chest with his fist.

Like the old Roman salute. "And what does that mean exactly?"

"You'll follow your instincts. Your heart. It's all that can be expected of anyone. Even a Chosen One."

I take the last pull and lay the empty bottle on the bar. "Not much in the way of practical advice."

He motions toward the bottle. "Want another?"

I glance at my watch. Still hours to go until it gets dark. "Why not?"

He's opened the cooler and is about to pull out a second Corona when the bar doors swing in. He looks up and I swivel on the barstool.

In walks Daniel Frey.

CHAPTER 35

I JUMP OFF THE STOOL TO GREET MY FRIEND, AND Culebra comes out from behind the bar. He and Frey trade man hugs.

Unusual display for Culebra. Seeing Frey must have triggered guilt over his little tantrum earlier.

When they step apart, I give Frey a real hug, then look him over.

He's dressed in pleated trousers, a cotton short-sleeved shirt with palm trees on a cream background and loafers. He's carrying a leather briefcase and wearing reflector sunglasses with big frames that are distinctly feminine—tortoise shell with opaque amber lenses and a fancy golden Dolce & Gabbana logo near the hinge.

"Let me guess," I say as he sweeps them off. "Layla's glasses."

He grins. "Damned if they don't work, too. I can drive with these things. I'll have to get a pair."

"You might want to rethink the frames," Culebra deadpans. "Want a beer?"

Frey parks his butt on a stool and lays the briefcase on the bar before nodding at Culebra and saying to me, "I figured this is where you'd be."

"I thought we weren't going to meet until tonight."

He accepts a Corona and we wait while he takes a first pull. "Got impatient," he says then. "Decided not to wait."

He looks around. "Place is pretty deserted for a Saturday. Fallout from what happened with Judith?"

"Judith? Is that her first name?"

Cuelbra and Frey both look surprised that I didn't know. I shrug. "We never were formally introduced."

Frey shakes his head. "Judith Williams. Pretty innocuous name for such a hellcat. I still can't believe the damage she did."

Culebra waves a hand. "And is still doing. I haven't had a customer since Thursday night." He motions us over to a table. "May as well get comfortable."

Once we're seated around the table I give voice to the question I know Culebra wants answered as much as I. "Why did you track me down?"

"I did a little more research," he says. "The good news is I don't believe David is in any real danger. At least not yet. I think you're right that she took him to assure your cooperation. In fact, I'm surprised you haven't heard from her yet."

"I checked my cell phone when I got home. Nothing. I haven't been to the office yet, though. Did you call Tracey and Miranda?"

"Both think you and David are out of town on a job. Tracey is pissed at you because you didn't tell her. Miranda is pissed at David because she thinks he lied. But it's bought us time—until the middle of the week at least."

Until the passing of *the* day. God, I hope it goes more smoothly than the fiasco in Biarritz.

I nod at Frey. "So tell us about your research."

He reaches for the briefcase he'd carried from the bar,

opens it and withdraws a file from inside. He spreads a dozen sheets of paper on the table. "This is some pretty interesting stuff," he says, excitement shining from his eyes. "I can't believe I hadn't come across the mythology before."

"Mythology?" The word sends a shock through me. Carries with it connotations of obsolete beliefs in long-defunct Basque goddesses. "Please tell me I'm not going to have to go through some archaic ritual." Particularly one that might involve ritual rape.

But Frey isn't fazed by my lack of enthusiasm. He doesn't notice. He's too caught up in his fervor to share what he's learned.

"The Chosen One is mentioned in ancient texts going back to the time when angels and demons walked the earth. But the references have always been obscure and subject to interpretation. Which is why it's been so hard to get specifics. Until now."

He reaches once more into the briefcase. This time he pulls out a worn leather tome about the size of a paperback. The cover and spine are cracked, and the pages so brittle, when he lays the book down, flakes of parchment and dust puff up and dissipate like pollen in the wind.

"What is that?"

Frey looks at the book with an expression of awe. He holds it up carefully and with great reverence. "This is the Grimoire."

Culebra and I exchange looks. His thoughts mirror my own. I speak them aloud. "What is a Grimoire?"

Frey places the book back on the table, resting one hand on it protectively as if afraid the book might sprout legs and run away.

For all we know, it might. Culebra's remark is in response to my own musings.

Frey catches the mocking tone of Culebra's comment and frowns. "You don't understand what this book represents. It is the accumulated wisdom of The First. It is an account of how a Chosen One came to be. And a written text not only for what followed historically, but for what is to come. You, Anna, are the descendant of The First. Only one vampire every two hundred years is marked for the change. It is quite an honor."

From his worshipful tone, I almost expect Frey to drop to one knee and kiss my hand. For the moment, I'm glad he can no longer read my thoughts.

Culebra, however, can and does. I expect him to be of one mind with me on this and even send him a private message to take it easy on Frey. He obviously believes the crap he's spouting.

The surprise is on me.

Culebra's eyes are shining when he turns his gaze on me. "Here is the counsel you were seeking."

I can't believe what I'm hearing. It takes me a moment to search Culebra's mind, to convince myself he isn't joking. Even then, I can't help blurting, "You're buying into this?"

"You were looking for the truth. I think Frey has found it."

For a dizzying moment, I feel like Alice down the rabbit hole. Culebra and Frey both stare at me. Their eyes reflect awe, as if recognizing something in me that was never there before. It's both disconcerting and ridiculous.

I slam my beer bottle down on the tabletop and they jump. Beer foams over the top and soaks the papers. Frey manages to grab the book before it gets soaked, too.

Now what I see in their eyes is something I'm used to—irritation—and that's a lot easier to deal with.

I lean toward Frey. "Earth to Frey. This is the twenty-first century. Angels and demons no longer walk the earth and I don't have a mark on me. I think you've either misread the prophecy or there is another vampire out there awaiting coronation. It's *not* me."

He's whisking beer off the table with the edge of one hand, holding the book aloft with the other. "I don't care whether you believe it or not," he says. "You are the Chosen One. Everything that's happened proves it. No newly made vampire has the strength and abilities you have. You're here for a reason. You are going to have to accept it."

"No. I don't."

He looks up and straight into my eyes. "Not even to save David?"

"That is so not fair."

Even to my own ears I sound like a nasal Valley girl and I want to cringe. But the sentiment is real. I start ticking off reasons why this idea that I'm some kind of vampiric prophet is beyond insane.

"Let's look at this logically. You said I'm the descendant of The First. How much sense does that make? Vampires don't choose to become. They are not born, they are made. Donaldson attacked me because I was trying to take him into custody. He didn't intend to turn me. He intended to kill me. I became vampire as the result of a *random act*. Nothing else. It was hardly destiny."

Frey lets me finish before he launches into a litany of his own. "Random? Let's see. Donaldson was in a parking lot that particular night because he'd gone out for a drink. Alone. To a bar he'd never gone to before on the night before he was to take off to Mexico. Did I get that right?"

He barely waits for my grudging nod. "You were there because you left a safe, secure job as a teacher to become a bounty hunter. In the grand scheme of things, makes as much sense as Donaldson risking his freedom to go out for a lousy drink. But let's get back to what happened. Donaldson turns out not to be the human skip you expect him to be but a vampire who does *not* kill you, but turns you because he is interrupted and has to flee before he can finish you off."

I don't like the direction this is heading. I open my mouth, but Frey barges ahead.

"You wake up in a hospital with no memory of what happened. You are being taken care of by a doctor who, coincidentally, just happens to be on duty the night you're brought in and even more coincidentally, happens to be a vampire himself."

"It is coincidence," I insist. "All of it."

"Really?" Frey asks. "Then why did Avery take such an interest in you? You've been vampire long enough to know vampires are not social creatures. They may feel responsible for ones they themselves have turned. Williams with Ortiz, for instance. But why did Avery go out of his way to mentor you if he hadn't seen that there was something different about you? Something special."

"It's called being horny, Frey. Avery wanted me for sex."

"I'm sure that played a part in it," he says dryly. "You do inspire that in men. But even when you met Williams for the first time, he called you 'the one.' He saw it, too. From the beginning."

Damn it. I know I hadn't told Frey all this. I wish now I'd bitten him sooner. He obviously had enough time to memorize every detail of my history before I broke our psychic connection.

I glance over at Culebra. He's so wrapped up in Frey's telling of the story, you'd think he was hearing it for the first time. I can't expect any help from that quarter.

"All right. Let's tackle this from another angle." I sit up straighter in the chair. "If I'm so all powerful, how come Lance was able to fool me? He hasn't been vampire that long and I didn't have an inkling who he was. I swallowed his story like a shark swallows chum. I wasn't even perceptive enough to *sense* that he was lying to me. He drugged me and dragged me off to France, for Christ's sake. I can't take care of myself. What idiot would want me to be responsible for the fate of the world?"

Finally, *finally*, I've rendered Frey speechless. He stares at me openmouthed. He didn't know what had happened with Lance. He thought we'd just had a fight.

Culebra is the one who speaks first. "Anna, what happened with Lance is no reflection on you. It's a reflection on him. He betrayed your love and your trust."

Frey finds his voice. "He *drugged* you? Did he hurt you?"

"Not nearly as much as I plan to hurt him."

"Why would he do it? What was he thinking?" He looks like he has a million other questions, none of which would make any more sense then the ones he just asked.

"Pretty much my reaction when I woke up. But I don't want to talk about Lance. My point is I think you're wrong about me. I'm not special and I'm not all-powerful and I don't want to be responsible for anyone other than myself."

"You're being too hard on yourself." This from Culebra. "And if Frey is right—" He sees me open my mouth to interrupt and forges ahead before I can. "If Frey is right, what you *want* isn't important, is it? You won't be the first leader to assume the burden of responsibility with reluctance and humility."

"Well, I can sure as hell *refuse* to assume that mantle of responsibility. Who's going to stop me?"

"If we've guessed right, Mrs. Williams."

Frey succeeds with that simple declaration in bringing the conversation back full circle. "She must have heard from her husband a million times how you were fighting the prophecies. How you clung to your family, to David and your human life. Your family was out of reach. David was not."

He's slipped the book back into the briefcase with a glance to me that says he's doing it to keep it out of harm's way . . . out of *my* way. Then he shuffles the beer-soaked papers into a soggy pile. "I made notes about what I believe will happen on the evening of your ascension."

"Ascension?" Another word that provokes a squeak of protest. "You can't be serious."

"As a heart attack," he says with an earnestness that borders on mania. "Now, do you want to hear what I've learned, or are you going to keep interrupting?"

Culebra lays his hands over mine on the table. "I want to hear it," he says. "Anna is through interrupting, aren't you?"

I shake my head. *For someone who may be addressing the Chosen One, you show remarkably little respect.*

He grins. *Come Tuesday, you might be able to smite me dead. Until then, this is my bar.* He lifts a chin in Frey's direction. "Go on. You have our attention."

CHAPTER 36

THE TEACHER IN FREY TAKES OVER. HE STANDS UP and assumes an at-a-podium kind of wide-legged stance, papers in one hand.

"You can't do this sitting down?" I grumble.

Culebra makes a shushing sound.

"Okay. Here's the deal. I've divided my research into two categories: the ceremony itself, what to expect after." He pauses, waiting, I suppose, for me to interrupt again.

What's the use? I'm going to hear this whether I want to or not. "Enlighten us."

"Okay." Another shuffling of paper. "From what I've been able to decipher, the ceremony will take place at midnight on Monday. It will be attended by a representative from each of the thirteen tribes."

Okay, my self-control doesn't last very long. Now I have to interrupt. "Tribes? What tribes?"

Frey doesn't look aggravated by the question. Instead he looks pleased. As if, for once, I asked the right one.

"The vampire community is divided into tribes—each representing a geographic area. They are North America; South America; Central America including Mexico and the West Indies; Australia and Oceania; Northern Africa; Central and South Africa; the Near East; the Middle East; Central Asia; Indonesia and the Philippines; China; Japan and Korea; Russia."

"So, I'm about to become the head honcho of the North American tribe?"

"No. You are about to become head honcho of the whole shebang."

No. Not going to happen. The impulse to run screaming from this ridiculous scenario is tempered only by the realization that Frey would track me down. He knows where I live. May as well let him finish spinning his fairy tale. I carefully modulate my expression and voice to reflect only curiosity when in reality what I'm feeling is panic. I think Frey is close to jumping off the sanity cliff, and Culebra is right there teetering on the brink with him.

"Why haven't I heard of these thirteen tribes before?" I congratulate myself for asking an intelligent question on an absurd subject.

Frey fixes me with the same kind of look that I used to get from Williams. I didn't like it then, I don't like it now. Still, I hold my tongue and wait for the answer.

"Williams would have gladly told you anything you wanted to know about your vampire heritage. You wouldn't give him a chance. Now you have no choice but to learn. Vampire society is somewhat decentralized. Each tribe governs itself. The thirteen only gather for a watershed event—like the coming of a Chosen One. It will mark your—" He hesitates, obviously suspecting how I'm going to react when he finishes the sentence. "Well, for lack of a better word, your coronation."

He suspects right. I'm on my feet before the last syllable of the word "coronation" has left his lips.

"This is beyond ridiculous. Frey, you and I have become good friends in a very short time. You've never let me down when I've come to you with a problem. I admire and respect you. But you have to know how crazy this sounds. I don't know how many ways I can say it. I don't want any part of this. There must be an escape clause. For argument's sake, tell me, what would happen if I don't show up?"

He counters with a quiet, "What about David?"

"We don't even know for sure if Judith Williams has him. You and I will check that out tonight. If what I suspect is true, and he's at Avery's, we'll get him out. In any case, there has to be a way I can refuse to go through with this. I'm not the one they want. I spend most of my time trying to forget what I've become. Surely, the leader of the world's vampires would be someone who doesn't spend the greater part of her life trying to be human. There has got to be a better candidate."

Frey lets me finish. He releases a breath, places both hands on the table, leans over it. "I wish I could tell you what you want to hear. Everything I read, though, is very specific. There is one chosen, he or she is marked, at the anniversary of that vampire's becoming, a change occurs. The Chosen One becomes the leader and the path for the next two hundred years is determined."

"Well, there you have it." I slam my fist on the table again for emphasis. "I have no mark."

Culebra has been silent during this exchange between Frey and me. "Are you sure?" he asks now. "When was the last time you looked at yourself in a mirror?"

The look I throw him is scathing. "Hello. Vampire. You know the answer to that. But I don't need a mirror to know whether or not I have some kind of magical mark."

Frey's expression turns introspective, as if searching his memory. "Maybe we're being too literal," he says then. "Or maybe I misinterpreted the meaning of the word 'mark.'"

He drops into his chair and shuffles through the beer-soaked pages. Then he dips into the briefcase and retrieves the book. He reads first from the book, then consults his papers, until he finds what he's looking for.

"I'll be damned," he says. "I think I *was* wrong. The word I translated as 'mark' may not be a physical characteristic at all. It could just as easily be interpreted as powers not ordinarily attributed to a vampire."

He grins at me, which is not at all comforting considering what follows. "Remember what happened in Palm Springs, Anna? You went into a burning garage to save Lance. And what about your evolving instinct to sense evil? Williams didn't know about that one, did he? How you reacted the first time you met Underwood?"

"I wish I'd told him. Maybe he'd still be alive."

Culebra turns a startled face my way. "What does Frey mean? What happened in Palm Springs?"

I give him a quick rundown, realizing by watching his reaction that he's now fully committed to the crazy idea that I am indeed who Frey believes me to be.

When I stop talking, he turns to Frey. "Why didn't I know any of this? Why didn't you tell me when you brought Judith Williams here?"

His harsh tone borders on accusatory, as if Frey betrayed his trust by not telling him what was happening with me.

Frey bristles, and I cut in.

"I didn't tell you, either, Culebra, because it had nothing to do with Mrs. Williams. As for the Underwood thing, I thought I'd taken care of it. Stupid assumption."

I switch my focus to Frey. He's staring at Culebra in tense silence, a growl rumbling in the back of his throat. I divert his attention with a hand on his arm. "Which proves my point. I wouldn't put much store in that so-called ability to sniff out evil. Lance fooled me completely. He turned out to be as much a bastard as Underwood."

Culebra says softly, "Lance's betrayal was a sign of weakness, not of evil."

I stare at him. Did he pick the details of Lance's letter out of my head?

No matter.

The thought of what went on in the cave at Biarritz produces a backlash of weariness that swamps my senses. "I don't want to talk anymore. I'm going back to the cottage."

That pushes Frey's resentment toward Culebra out of his head. He rounds on me. "I haven't finished. I have much more to tell you. You have preparations to make. There is protocol to learn. You can't pretend it isn't going to happen, Anna. And you must be prepared."

He is so earnest in his pleading, so accepting that what he found in that little book is the truth, that I haven't the will or strength to fight it anymore. I put a hand on his arm, sincerity in my voice. "You can tell me more tonight. When we go to Avery's."

He relaxes at that, gathers his papers and that stupid book and rustles them back into the briefcase. "I'll come over early," he says. "Well before dark so we have time."

Culebra is not so easily fooled. He is eyeing me the way a spider eyes a fly buzzing around a web. He sees the subtlety in my gesture, reads the intention behind the words. He guesses once we leave, the probability that Frey is going to get the chance to finish his tutorial is about as good as a fly's chance to escape if it touches that web.

I let him. I let him know he's right.

He cloaks his thoughts so Frey doesn't intercept. *Be careful, Anna. You are venturing into deep water. Don't make the mistake of thinking because you want something to be so, it will be. There are some things in this world over which you have no control.*

I meet his gaze, say nothing. So far as I can tell, since becoming vampire, I haven't had control over anything that's been done to me.

That stops.

Now.

I PUSH EVERY SINGLE WORD OF THIS AFTERNOON'S conversation out of my head on the drive home. I concentrate only on the mechanics of driving, on my weariness, on the bed I'm going to fall into the moment I get to the cottage. I've been up eighteen hours. A few hours' sleep and I'll be ready to face the only obstacle I intend to tonight. Judith Williams.

The cottage is cool and quiet, a haven from the bright, sand-reflected beach sun. I make sure the doors are locked, the drapes pulled, and let my head sink gratefully onto the pillow.

His smell hits me like a physical blow. It's in the bedclothes. Floats on the air. Floods my thoughts like a rising tide.

Damn you, Lance.

I toss the pillow across the room, snatch sheets and blankets and tear them off the bed.

I won't let him do this to me.

But the bare mattress still retains the scent of *us*. Of sex and blood and passion.

My hands curl into fists. I'll haul it down to the Dumpster tomorrow. After I have David back.

Right before I track the bastard down.

IT'S ONLY SIX WHEN I AWAKEN FROM A NAP THAT DID little to remedy a bad case of sleep deprivation. Vivid dreams of the cave in Biarritz were interspersed with equally vivid dreams of Lance—sexual images that my body responded to even as I slept.

When I open my eyes, my face is wet with tears and my body aching with loneliness.

I stumble into the bathroom, strip and force myself to step into a cold shower. The shock of the water is reviving. Sluggishness gives way to a sense of purpose, gloominess to renewed energy. I can't let despair make me forget what tonight is all about. Finding David.

I dress for a night operation. Black jeans, black long-sleeved T-shirt, black tennis shoes. As I prepare, my mind circles around one thought like a buzzard around a carcass. I'm assuming an awful lot. I'm assuming Mrs. Williams took David. I'm assuming she's taken him to Avery's. I'm assuming that she'll be expecting me. Valid assumptions from my perspective. She and her husband were friends with Avery. She knows our history as well as anyone.

If I'm wrong, then what?

I start over.

Once dressed, I'm antsy to get going. I wish now I hadn't asked Frey along. My thought that he'd have a better chance to prowl the ground unnoticed as a panther made sense at the time I suggested it. Now all I can think of is the baggage that goes along with his participation.

I'll have to listen to more of his bullshit about what he read in that stupid book.

It's just before seven when the doorbell rings. I grab keys and my handbag, and run down the stairs to the front door.

I'm expecting Frey.

I'm not expecting the frowning, angry woman who pushes her way into my home the minute I open the door.

Tracey Banker projects her fury like a bullet seeking a target. And right now, I'm the bull's-eye. She doesn't give me a chance to say anything before firing the shot.

"I know you weren't happy when David brought me on board. I don't expect us to become best buddies. But you have no right to lie to me. David is in trouble, and you better damn well let me help or I swear I'll go to the cops and tell them you knew about it all along."

She's yelling and waving a piece of paper in my face. I pry it out of her hands. The first thing I notice is that it's a copy of an email. An email addressed to me.

To me.

The second thing I notice is who it's from: Judith Williams.

What the hell?

I turn it around and shove it toward her. "You always read other people's mail?"

"Fucking good thing that I did." She's still yelling. "You had some guy call and tell me that you and David had gone out of town on a job. Wouldn't be back until Tuesday. That's not what this says. If I hadn't opened it, by Tuesday it would be all over. David would be dead."

There's no way I can explain that I wanted her out of harm's way. Or, more important, that this is none of her business. She's in no mood to listen. Instead, I turn my back on her and concentrate on the paper in my hand.

Anna. You and I have a date with destiny. David is along for the ride. Whether or not he survives is entirely up to you. I know if he hasn't already, your friend Daniel Frey will tell you what is expected of you. I also know your first impulse will be to find a way out. It's why I took David. I suggest you spend less energy trying to avoid what will happen on Tuesday and more on learning from the Grimoire. Who knows? You may yet find an escape clause in the teachings. It's the reason I arranged for Mr. Frey to find the book.

I have no desire to hurt your partner. He seems like a good man. A little confused right now. I had no idea he was unaware of your true nature. Trust me when I say he is being well cared for.

That can change, though. It's up to you.

Until Tuesday morning then—

Judith Williams

CHAPTER 37

BEHIND ME I SENSE TRACEY PACING LIKE A CAGED lioness. As soon as she sees my hand lower the page, she pounces.

"Who is she? What does she mean you two have a date with destiny? Why is she holding David hostage? What's that crap about your true nature?"

She grabs my arm and spins me toward her.

I let her. As long as she's venting, I can try to figure a way out of this mess. She doesn't recognize Judith Williams' name, which is a plus. But Tracey was a cop who worked for Chief Williams. It won't be long before something triggers a spark of recognition and she puts it together.

Crap. The only thing I can think to do is tie Tracey up and stick her in a closet. For three days? Not very practical.

Tracey still has her hand on my arm. She's staring at me. "Your skin is cold." She narrows her eyes. "The note said something about your true nature? What are you?"

The question catches me off guard. As does Tracey's reaction. She jumps back and away. The fight drains out of her. Her eyes no longer blaze anger, they blaze fear. I smell it on her, mingling with the stink of that perfume she seems to bathe in. Sickly sweet. "What are you?" she asks again.

I try for menacing. "What do you think I am?"

Her expression morphs from terror to confusion. "But is David—?" Her voice drops off before she completes the question.

This may be the opening I need. "Is David like me? No. I'm vampire. He's worse." Then I laugh. "Are you serious? You think this is for real? This is a game we play. Like Dungeons and Dragons. You weren't supposed to know about it. People tend to think it's a little strange when adults play role-playing games. But it's harmless. A way to blow off steam."

She's rubbing her hands together. "But you're *cold*."

"Poor circulation. Been a problem my whole life. It's hell on your sex life. Men don't like getting naked with an ice cube."

Tracey draws a breath. "Then this whole thing—"

"Is a game. I'm sorry you misunderstood. We only do this once or twice a year but authenticity is part of the fun. We stage mock kidnappings, arrange 'accidents.' David will be very embarrassed when he learns you found out."

I watch as she processes what I've told her. The fact that she reacted so violently to the idea that I might be something other than human is worrisome. But if I pursue that now, I risk destroying the illusion that the note is anything other than a game prop.

At last she relaxes. She looks uncomfortable as color floods her face. "I'm sorry I burst in here like a madwoman," she says. "First there was that call from David's girlfriend, then this note. You really should have let me know what you were doing. Maybe I can play sometime, too?"

I have a hand on the small of her back, ushering her

toward the door. "Maybe you can. But for now, this is our secret, all right?"

She nods. "I'll hold down the office until you guys get back on Wednesday. Then I expect to hear all about your adventures."

I smile and wave her out then lean back against the closed door. Is she for real? I thought *I* was gullible. Tracey not only bought the story, she wants to play with us next time.

This is why I hate taking on a new partner.

I peek out through the front window to make sure she's gone. Then I turn my attention to the note.

Being right about Judith Williams holding David brings no great sense of satisfaction. She's already killed two humans. She's fed, but what happens when the hunger strikes again?

The second impression is that she and David seem to be talking. Why does he think he's been taken? Did she really tell him I'm vampire? How did he react to *that* piece of news? She didn't say where she's holding him, either. I still believe I'm right about that one. Frey and I will check out Avery's as planned tonight.

Frey. He *found* the book? How? A little detail he didn't mention this afternoon. Of course, I didn't ask. He has a vast library of supernatural reference books. I assumed it was part of that library.

Which begs the next question. Where did Judith Williams get it? If the book does contain a way for me to get out of this ridiculous situation, why would Williams leave it laying around? He never gave *me* any indication that I had a choice. Just the opposite. According to him, my destiny was well—predestined.

I haven't moved from the door when there's another knock. I jump as if scalded, heart pounding, clutch the note to my chest like a life preserver.

Jesus. Get a grip.

Another peek out the window at Frey's familiar face and form. He stands looking straight at the door, still holding that briefcase and wearing those ridiculous glasses. He has a look of excited expectation. He's dressed in black jeans, too, with a linen shirt and a leather jacket. A square-jawed Indiana Jones about to embark on a great adventure. I wish I could share his enthusiasm.

As I swing open the door to let him in, I thrust the email toward him.

He places the briefcase at his feet, removes the glasses from his face and slips them into a jacket pocket before smoothing the paper to read what's written on it.

I give him a minute. "You *found* the book?"

He glances up at me, then back down at the paper. "Not *found*. Exactly. More like *discovered* in a box of books sent anonymously to me last week. Happens all the time. Witches, warlocks, all sorts of supernaturals will me their libraries when they pass on. They know I am a Keeper."

"Keeper?"

"Of the secrets. My father was one before me. My son will inherit the mantle when I pass on. It's tradition."

There is so much in that one simple declaration that demands clarification I scarcely know what to ask first. No, not true. I know exactly what to ask first. My voice torques up to screech.

"You have a son?"

He looks amused at the confusion reflected in my voice and the complete bewilderment that I'm sure is reflected in my expression. "Why do you sound so surprised?"

"Surprised? No. Surprised doesn't quite cover what I am. I'm dumbfounded. I'm fucking stupefied. You never mentioned a son. You never mentioned a family. Are you married?"

He shakes his head. "One does not have to be married to have children. I'm surprised you'd jump to that conclusion."

He's missing the point, evading my question. I have an overwhelming urge to shake him. I press the palms of my hands together to resist temptation. "Shape-shifter. Do. You. Have. A. Son?"

"Yes."

"How?"

Again, the look of amusement. "You know. Egg plus sperm equals conception. Bio 101. Has it been that long?"

He's enjoying this. Way too much. The growl starts deep in my throat. "You're fucking with me. Not a good idea. I'm tired, worried about David and trying really hard to resist the urge to slap that stupid expression off your face."

Frey relents with upturned hands and a sheepish smile. "You're right. I'm sorry. I shouldn't be making jokes. Not now. What do you want to know?"

The shock of being hit with this unexpected bit of information about a man I thought I knew leaves me weak in the knees. A condition that's becoming chronic. I want to sit down so I motion Frey over to the couch. When he's settled, I take the chair opposite him and lean forward. "For starters, you are a shape-shifter. They reproduce like humans?"

"We are human. With a genetic difference. And yes, we procreate in the usual way."

"How old is your son?"

"Four."

"Does he live here in San Diego?"

"No. He lives with his mother's people in Monument Valley."

"She's Native American?"

"Navajo, yes."

"Do you see him often?"

"No."

"Why not?"

"It is in his best interest."

These abbreviated answers are as irritating as they are devoid of useful information. Yet, there is an air of quiet resignation in Frey's manner that makes me refrain from pushing for more.

At least not now.

Later, though, when David is safe and my problem has been solved . . . That will be different. Then I intend to pursue this if I have to beat answers out of him. There is one other thing, though, that the bitch in me needs to know. Now.

"Does Layla know about your son?"

He looks at me and puffs out an impatient breath. He can't read my thoughts, but he knows me well enough to suspect why I'm asking. "No."

"Is that the truth?"

"You think I'm lying?"

I can tell by the defensive set of his shoulders that it's all I'm going to get. It's okay. The sense of satisfaction I'm experiencing over knowing something about her lover that Layla doesn't is childish but gratifying.

He puffs out another breath. "Can we get back to why I'm here?"

"Sure. Where did you say you got the book?"

Frey launches into the story. UPS delivered the books two days ago. He admits he paid no attention to the return name or address. He could have checked with the carrier to see where they came from if he'd wanted to. But it hadn't occurred to him to do so. Sometimes, he says, families are embarrassed when they find books on the occult in a deceased relative's possessions. Often, the box is already sealed and addressed, and even more often, the person to whom the books belonged mails them himself when he or she feels death is near.

He finishes with, "Happens two or three times a year so I no longer question it. I'm grateful because otherwise the written heritage of the supernatural community would be lost."

"But this didn't seem a little convenient to you?" I ask. "A book that just happens to be exactly what we were looking for? A book that details who the Chosen One is and what will happen on an appointed date? How do you know it's not a fake?"

"It isn't a fake." Frey's tone is adamant.

"If Judith Williams had anything to do with you getting that book, how can you be so sure?"

"I know, all right? I've been authenticating these books for thirty years. This is no fake. That it came from Williams should convince you if nothing else. He probably got the book from Avery. Avery had been vampire for four hundred years. It would make sense that he'd have such a book. Didn't you say he had a treasure trove of ancient artifacts in his basement?"

I press my palms against my eyes. That basement held more than artifacts. It became the repository of my worst nightmares—finding David near death and then later, watching a shape-shifter named Sandra battle the vengeful soul of Avery who had insinuated himself into her body in order to kill me.

Have we come full circle? Is David once again being held prisoner in that basement? I let two chances pass by and I didn't do it.

This time I will.

This time, I will burn that fucking house to the ground.

When I look up at Frey, he seems to know what I'm thinking and feeling.

"What?"

His expression is stern. "We can't go in there guns blazing."

"Is it that obvious? Or have you found a way to reconnect our broken link?"

He shakes his head. "I don't need to reconnect anything. I know you. It's not hard to figure out what you want to do. You have a habit of acting first, sorting out the damage later. Can't do that this time. There's an innocent involved."

He doesn't think I know that? I stand up. "We'd better get going."

"Wait." Frey stands, too, but doesn't take a step toward the door. "There is something else in the note. Have you forgotten? She mentioned an escape clause."

I had forgotten. I sit back down on the edge of the chair. "Go on."

Frey sits, too, reaches for the book. "She's right. The book does tell of a way for the Chosen to relinquish claim to the title."

But he pauses here, and it isn't until I snap, "Damn it, Frey, what is it?" that he continues.

Reluctantly.

"There is the challenge."

"Challenge?"

"Any one of the heads of the thirteen tribes can challenge the ascension of the Chosen One."

"Not that I want to give the impression that I believe all this crap, but what challenge? I thought the Chosen One was predestined. Had special powers."

Frey chooses to ignore sarcasm dripping thick and glutinous as honey from every word when he answers. "The identity of the Chosen One is predestined. But if there is a challenge and he or she is defeated, it is believed there was a flaw in the prophecy and the victor assumes the title."

I clap my hands. "Great. All we need is a challenger. I'll let that lucky vampire win the contest and we can both go on our merry ways."

"Not exactly."

"Well, then *what* exactly?"

Frey is not looking at me. He's looking down and around and everywhere except in my direction. The vampire loses patience and erupts with a snarl.

"Jesus, Frey. Do I have to reach down your throat and pull every fucking word out of your mouth?"

For a second, the panther flashes in Frey's eyes. This time the rumbling growl comes from him. "Watch it, Anna. You need me more than I need you right now."

He's right. I back down with a tight-lipped smile. "I'm sorry. I just want a straight answer. Something you seem reluctant to give."

"If I'm reluctant, it's because I care about you." Frey taps the cover of the book with an index finger. "I know how much you ridicule the idea of assuming responsibility for the vampire community. But the alternative is not one wins and one loses. It's one lives and one dies. It's a fight. To the death."

CHAPTER 38

A FIGHT TO THE DEATH.

Of course it is. What should provoke a startled reaction gets instead a resigned sigh. How could I expect anything less than a fight to the death when it involves the vampire community?

I meet Frey's anxious gaze. "That's why you didn't tell me about the challenge sooner? Because it's a fight to the death? Did you think that would scare me?"

Frey shakes his head. "No. I knew you wouldn't be scared. Judith Williams, though, doesn't know you as well. She would mention an escape clause for only one reason. She knows there will be a challenge."

No. I stand up and push the chair away with an impatient shove. "Pretty improbable, don't you think? When she came to us a few days ago, she didn't even know where to go to feed. Now she's organizing a challenge?"

"I can't explain it. But if she put it in the note, it means she expected you to ask me about it. Expected you to learn the truth. Maybe she thought it would scare you into doing something stupid."

"Like what?"

"Like not showing up for the ceremony."

"If we can get David out of there before Tuesday, why would that be such a bad idea?"

"Because, if you don't show up, you've declared yourself rogue. No ceremony. No challenge. The Chosen One's duty is to set the path for the next two hundred years. By ignoring what is written, you disrupt the balance. There must be a Chosen One. Only by your death can another be marked."

He doesn't say any more. He doesn't have to. It's obvious what follows. If I don't go through with this crazy ceremony, I'll be hunted down.

Great.

Just great. I'll spend the rest of my life looking over my shoulder. May as well stake myself now.

Still, David is out there somewhere. Whatever that crazy bitch tries to do to me, I can protect myself. David is defenseless. "Well, nothing you've said changes what we have to do now. We'll drive out to Avery's. If I'm wrong and the house is deserted, we'll decide the next step then."

He slips off his jacket and leaves it with the briefcase and book on my couch. We go out through the backyard and into the garage. Neither of us has much to say on the ride to La Jolla. While I'm still having a hard time accepting the notion that the fate of the vampire world rests on my shoulders, the sad truth is, there seem to be many out there who do. Including the two people whose opinion I've counted on most since becoming vampire—Frey and Culebra.

Maybe if I were smart, I'd stop fighting. There must be some vibe I send off that makes crazies like Underwood and not-so-crazies like Frey and Culebra see something in me that I do not. Maybe I should simply go to Judith Williams and tell her I'll do whatever she wants. Honor the crazy dreams of her crazy husband. Let her determine the course of my life for the next few hundred years. Become the Chosen One and rule from the ivory tower of her choice.

All I'll ask in return is David's safe release and a few weeks a year to visit with my family.

An offer she can hardly refuse.

If that is indeed what she wants.

I'm so deep in my own thoughts that the drive to Avery's is done on automatic pilot. Frey is quiet, too, probably afraid of setting me off again. It isn't until we're about a mile from the house on the top of Mount Soledad that I pull the Jag over and stop.

Frey turns toward me. "You want me to get out here and shift?"

"I think that's a good idea. There's lots of cover. Trees. Bushes."

It's dark on the road. Not many streetlights. There doesn't have to be. The homes on this street all have their own brightly lit security gates attached to high walls of brick or stone. The closer you get to the top of the mountain, the higher the fences, the more secure the gates.

Frey takes off his shoes, tosses them into the backseat. He unbuttons his shirt and shrugs it off and slips out of his slacks. No underwear. He catches me watching him.

"I think Layla would disapprove of the expression on your face."

"To the contrary, I think Layla would approve. Right before she scratched my eyes out. Anyway, get going. The sooner you find out how she's guarding David, the sooner we can make a plan to get him out."

I give Frey a description of the layout of the place—how the detached garage is at the back of the house, how there's a walk connecting the garage to the back door, how the back of the house is floor-to-ceiling windows overlooking the Pacific far below.

It's not easy talking logistics to a naked man. My eyes tend to wander. I'd forgotten what a nice body Frey has. He shifts slightly in the seat, giving me a better view. He knows exactly what he's doing, exactly what I'm doing. Probably the reason he undressed before we had this conversation instead of waiting until after.

At last he opens the door and steps out. He melts into the bushes without a backward glance. There's a rustle and a low catlike growl and the bushes beside the car no longer move.

I rest my head against the seat, close my eyes. I figure ten minutes for Frey to get to Avery's, thirty minutes max to check out the house, ten minutes back.

May as well take a nap. Otherwise all I'll do is stew.

A rap on the window brings me upright with a jerk. Frey is on the passenger side of the car, trying to keep out of sight. He's already shifted back from panther to human and from my low vantage point on the front seat I have an interesting view.

I glance at my watch. He's only been gone fifteen minutes. I hit unlock on the console and he slides into the seat.

"Did you get lost?"

He's reaching into the backseat for his clothes. "Of course not."

"Then why are you back so soon?"

"Panthers move fast." He pulls on his jeans, puts on the shirt, slips his feet back into his shoes.

"So what is it then? You couldn't have checked the place out in such a short time."

"Didn't need to." Frey drags his fingers through his hair. "We can do it together."

"Shit. The place is deserted?"

He smiles. "Just the opposite. I think Judith Williams is throwing a party."

A party? Frey is grinning at me and I realize immediately that we couldn't ask for a better scenario. I fire up the Jag and steer onto the road.

"Pretty ballsy on her part," Frey says. "Taking over Avery's house . . ." He shoots me a sideways glance, "*Your* house, actually, is one thing, but to openly throw a party is quite another. Who do you think she's invited?"

"No mystery there. I know who she's invited. Since the guest list for the ceremony on Tuesday includes the world's vamp royalty, I imagine they've already started arriving."

"She didn't invite you."

That provokes a laugh. "She didn't have to, did she? Because here we are. I have to admit, she's inherited her husband's ability to anticipate my every move right along with his ability to piss me off."

"She knew you'd come looking for David."

"And she knew I'd come looking here. She is a crafty bitch."

Frey's voice takes on a tone of warning. "Don't take any chances tonight. Keep close. Let me watch your back."

We've pulled up to Avery's gated entrance. The house is ablaze with lights. Music floats on the air, live music from the sound of it. A man approaches from the house side, opens the small gate set into the stone wall surrounding the place and comes to the car. He has a clipboard in his hand.

"This is a private party," he says.

"I believe I'm on the guest list. Anna Strong."

I follow his eyes as they scroll down the page, lips silently mouthing the names. After a moment he looks up. "No Anna Strong on the guest list. I'm afraid I'll have to ask you to leave."

He's human, big in a former pro-wrestler-gone-to-fat kind of way. His suit fits awkwardly across the chest, partly because he has too much chest and partly because of the not-very-well-concealed gun against his right shoulder.

"Well, here's the thing," I reply with my brightest good-girl smile. "I'm the owner of this house, and I didn't give permission for anyone to have a party."

That gives him a moment's pause. Long enough for me to shove the car door open. It slams into his gut and he goes down with a whoosh of expelled air. He struggles to get up. I jump out and clock him again with an elbow to the forehead. This time he's down for the count.

Frey is at my side. We each take a leg and drag him into the guardhouse. I take off his belt and use it to tie his hands, then shove his own handkerchief into his mouth. I wish we had something to secure his legs, but I can't find anything and neither Frey nor I are wearing belts. In his jacket, I find a set of keys, separate from the usual car and house keys most people carry. On a hunch and after a couple of misses, I find the one that will lock the guardhouse from the outside. After pulling down the shades, and locking the door, our rent-a-cop is tucked away for a nice, long nap.

Frey and I exchange glances. Obviously, I was wrong about Judith expecting me to show up. She didn't include my name on the guest list.

Frey says, "Front door or back?"

I think about it a minute. "Hell. Front. May as well shake things up."

I don't pull the car into the driveway but back it up and park it on the shoulder a few yards away from the gate. If we have to make a quick getaway, Frey and I can jump the fence and get to the car. Anyone following us will have to open the gate first.

Which gives me an idea. I bend close to see how the gate latches. "Think we can jam this?"

Frey gives it the once-over. "It's electronic." He looks up and around. "The sensor is up there on that post. If we broke it . . ." He starts looking around. "Here we go." He hefts a good-sized rock, balances it on his palm, aims and fires it straight at the little blinking light on the top of a ten-foot pole.

It shatters and goes dark.

"Good arm! I didn't know you had it in you."

"Three years of college ball."

For a brief sliver of time, Frey and I smile at each other like two kids pulling a Halloween prank instead of two adults breaking and entering.

The moment passes. "Better move," Frey says. "Someone may have heard the glass breaking."

We jog up the long driveway toward the front of the house. The music gets louder, the lights brighter. In the turnaround near the front door, half a dozen stretch limos sit empty. No drivers. I open one of the doors and sniff. Vampire and human.

No surprise there.

Frey touches my arm. "How do you want to handle this?"

I tug the hem of my T-shirt down and run a hand through my hair. "Let's party."

CHAPTER 39

I REMEMBER THE VERY FIRST MOMENT I REALIZED Avery was a monster. Remember the sick feeling of betrayal. Remember how hard it was to walk into this house and pretend nothing had changed so I could free David and plan my revenge.

I'm experiencing all those feelings again. Now.

The doorbell is answered by a young man in a tuxedo. If he's the help, he isn't very good. He looks me up and down before turning on his heels and walking away. No greeting. No invitation to come in.

I guess jeans and T-shirts aren't proper attire. I should tell him I didn't get the memo.

We follow him in. The guy's human and, by the smell of him, has had sex recently. Very recently. Like maybe moments before. Musk and testosterone ooze from his pores like sweat.

It makes my nose wrinkle and my hormones jump into overdrive. A restless shift in Frey's posture tells me he senses the same thing.

We watch as he crosses the slate floor toward the source of the music. The living room. Voices with accents rise above the music and the clink of glasses. The last time I was here, Avery had inhabited a werewolf's body to try to kill me. What will it be this time?

"Ms. Strong?"

A female voice—a familiar female voice—calls to me from a door to the right. The kitchen, as I remember. I turn toward the voice.

"Dena?"

A young Eurasian with straight black hair smiles at me as if the last time we saw each other she had merely been Avery's housekeeper instead of his blood slave. She's dressed in a black skirt and starched white blouse, a wide black ribbon around her throat. In her hands, she holds a silver tray with champagne flutes and an ice bucket.

"What are you doing here?" I ask.

"Working."

"For Mrs. Williams?"

She laughs. "For you, silly. I have been since Dr. Avery left. I've kept the house running. I thought you knew. I missed you when his friend was here a couple of months ago. My mom was sick. I'm glad to see you're back now."

Someone from the next room calls, "What happened to those glasses?"

She turns toward the voice. "Gotta go. Your room has been prepared. I look forward to serving you."

Frey looks as confused as I feel. "You know her?"

"She was Avery's housekeeper. And one of his hosts. I thought she would have left the moment he did. Go figure."

I don't know what Dena said when she left us but suddenly, the music, the voices, the clink of glasses stops as if a switch has been thrown. The living room plunged from party central to morgue central.

Frey goes tense and still beside me. I'm glad he's here.

A vampire and a panther. Should be able to cut a swath through whatever is thrown at us.

We wait. Count off ten, twenty, thirty seconds. Just when I'm ready to unleash the vampire and bring it to them, a familiar face appears in the doorway.

David.

He smiles when he sees me, would probably even give me a hug except that he has a big-breasted blonde hanging off each arm. "It's about time you got here. Judy said you might not make it until Tuesday. This is a helluva house, Anna. Why didn't you tell me you owned a mansion?"

David's got a goofy smile on his face and pupils the size of dinner plates. While his speech isn't slurred exactly, he speaks as if his tongue is too big and too heavy for his mouth.

Doesn't seem to be affecting his libido. His right hand has wandered down to grab the ass of the blonde on his right.

Got to hand it to Judy Williams, she treats her kidnap victims well. Don't know what David's on, but he's having fun.

David is a big guy—former pro football player, a bulky, muscular two-fifty on a six-foot-four frame. I carried him once, but he was unconscious and pliable. I have a feeling if I tried to deadlift him out of here now, he'd object.

Frey says, "What do we do now?"

David has moved things along from groping his playmates to kissing them—both, one after the other, with a lot of tongue action and deep-throated groans.

I wish I had a camera.

"Leave him. Let's go find our hostess."

Neither David nor the blondes notice when Frey and I walk around them and head toward the living room. It's still deathly quiet beyond the arched doorway. I have no idea what kind of reception to expect. We pause just out of the line of sight, then, like cops on a drug bust, take a quick step into the room. Frey goes to the left. I, to the right.

Judith Williams is standing in front of the fireplace. She smiles when she sees me and raises a glass in my direction. "Ladies and gentlemen, may I present Anna Strong. The one chosen to lead us for the next two hundred years."

There are seven vampires in the room. And ten humans. The humans have moved back to stand in a knot near the sliding wall of glass that separates the interior room from the outside deck. The young man who opened the door for us is among them. His expression isn't so contemptuous now that he realizes I'm not part of the kitchen staff. In fact, he has a decidedly nervous look about him. I meet his eyes, glare until he takes a fumbling step backward, then look away, hiding a smile.

May as well have some fun, too.

The wall is open to the night air, and the scent of the ocean mingles with the sweet smell of night-blooming jasmine. Under the natural scents, though is the smell of blood and earth. The smell of vampires.

Very old vampires.

The vampires raise their glasses in my direction.

"To Anna Strong." They say it in English, though the accents are varied. "And to the Year One."

CHAPTER 40

THE VAMPIRES DRINK THEIR CHAMPAGNE, BOW IN my direction and resume talking amongst themselves. We are forgotten. Frey and I exchange looks.

I feel like the unpopular guest of honor arriving late for her own birthday party to find her absence had gone unnoticed. Maybe until Tuesday I have no standing at all. No matter. Getting David out of here is the only reason I'd step foot in this house of horrors.

Judith Williams waves a manicured hand and the six-piece band in the corner begins to play. She fluffs her hair, composes her expression to reflect nothing but cordiality and walks over to us.

"What?" I ask, giving her the once-over. "No widow's weeds tonight?"

She smoothes a hand over the skirt of her bloodred silk dress. "I didn't expect to see you tonight, Anna, or I would have left your name at the gate." She tilts her head. "How did you manage to get by security?"

"The Chosen One, remember? Hiring a mortal to keep a vampire out is like carrying a rock to a gunfight."

She doesn't find the analogy amusing. "Is he dead?"

"I don't kill humans indiscriminately. That seems to be your thing. Do you realize how much damage you caused to the vampire community by killing those hosts in Beso de la Muerte?"

She sniffs. "If you'd gone with me, it might not have happened."

She looks at Frey. "He isn't welcome here." She gestures to the vampires behind us as if privy to some communication I am not. The vampires are no longer talking, but watching us.

No. Not us.

Frey. It's as if they've suddenly become aware he is neither vampire nor human.

I also realize she's learned a lot in a few days. Her thoughts are no longer easy pickings for me. But she's communicating with someone.

"Frey is with me."

"Then he must agree to the rules."

"Rules?"

"This party is for vampires and hosts only. Are you willing to share?"

I can see Frey's expression harden. I know what he's thinking. To stay with me, he'll agree. I speak up before he can. "No. Frey will wait for me outside."

He opens his mouth to object, and I close a steel hand around his arm. "Wait for me by the gate. I will be out with David in ten minutes."

Frey's anger burns through his eyes. "I thought we agreed to stay together."

I loosen my hold a little but not my resolve. "Ten minutes."

He's not happy. I don't care. There is something in the way the vampires are looking at him that makes me know it's not safe for him to stay. "Please, Frey. Don't argue."

There is another shift in the posture of the vampires, a subtle quiver of anticipation, like a cat gathering itself to pounce on an unsuspecting bird.

You must decide. He will stay or go. The others find it troubling that you would argue with a shape-shifter, an inferior being. They see it as a sign of weakness.

Judith's words are directed right at me. No mistaking it, she's mastered the art of psychic communication. I look from the vampires to Judith, tempted to challenge them, but it's Frey this time who touches *my* arm.

He was not privy to the message, but my reaction is obvious. "It's up to you."

"Go. I will be out in ten minutes."

I watch Frey make his way to the front door. I feel the others watch, too, with alarming intensity. *If anyone attempts to intercept him, you will learn how weak I am.*

I let the message carry over the music, over the resumed rumble of conversation. There is a heartbeat's hesitation as if consideration is being given to the sincerity of my threat. Consequences weighed against principle.

Evidently, principle isn't that important after all. Frey is allowed to leave unmolested.

Judith breathes an impatient sigh. "So much drama over one insignificant mortal. Anna, you are a puzzle to me."

Ten minutes. The clock is ticking.

"What did you give David?"

A smile. "Something wonderful. He's certainly a big one, isn't he? And so—enthusiastic."

My shoulders tense. "You seduced him?"

She laughs. "If you mean did I take advantage of him, the answer is most emphatically no. He needed very little persuasion to have sex."

I get a creepy feeling that there was more to it than sex. "Did you feed from him?"

The tip of her tongue glides over her upper lip. "Of course. Are you trying to tell me you haven't?"

She looks surprised, which gives way to a smug smile of satisfaction. "You haven't. You haven't fucked him, either. How long have you been partners? You sit across from as studly a piece of ass as I've ever seen, and you haven't fucked him."

I get an absurd flashback to the first time I saw this woman—here, in this very room, dressed in her tasteful little cocktail dress, diamonds flashing from ears and neck, looking adoringly at a man who has made my life miserable this last year. The contrast between that simpering woman and this bitch is beyond ridiculous.

She's been a vampire for less than three months. She thinks we are equals. She thinks this Chosen One thing is bullshit, even if the others seem to believe it, and she thinks if they insist on choosing anyone, she is infinitely more qualified to assume the position than I.

She lets these thoughts through because she is too stupid to realize that she is telegraphing her intentions.

In her head, Judith Williams has already assumed the role. That's the reason for the party. That's the reason I wasn't invited. That's the reason for my less-than-hearty reception. She's showing the vampire elite that she is in control. Since Warren Williams had been administrator for Avery's estate, she has access to the house and everything in it. The fact that it all belongs to me is of no importance because soon she'll fix that, too.

She had no intention of hurting David. She wanted to make sure I'd show up on Tuesday because all that's left now is the challenge. The challenge she's convinced I'll lose.

The fact that I haven't said anything, that I haven't reacted to the fact that she fed from David, that I've closed my thoughts so she can't read what's going through my mind begins to worry her.

Good.

"I'm leaving now, Judith," I say. "And I'm taking David."

I turn to go but can't resist another shot.

"Get these people out of my house. Unless I'm mistaken, this is my house, right? Your husband transferred all Avery's property into my name?"

Her mood turns sullen, dangerous.

I don't care. "You have one hour. Then I'm calling the police. You can explain being arrested for breaking and entering to the heads of the thirteen tribes. I'm sure you can make them understand.

"One more thing. Those hosts? They'd better be able to walk out of here on their own, unharmed and unassisted. I'm holding you personally responsible for their well-being. If you hurt them, or if I see you before Tuesday, you're dead."

CHAPTER 41

I CAN'T FIND DAVID.

He's no longer in the entryway so I try the kitchen. Dena is busy icing more champagne. I tell her she can go home because the party is about to break up. I encourage here to leave quickly, not telling her if she doesn't she'll likely get caught when the cops come.

She looks confused but takes off her apron and slips out the back door. I hope Frey knows a way to get that gate open. Breaking it doesn't seem such a bright idea now. Shortsighted if we end up having to haul David's ass over the top of it.

I make my way upstairs. I hate being here. Hate having to pass the door to Avery's bedroom. I wonder what Dena thought when she saw the damage I did to it the last time I was here and if she'd had it repaired. I don't open the door to find out.

There are six bedrooms on the second floor. I stop at the head of the stairs. Listen.

Heavy breathing. Grunts. Giggles.

Shit.

I find the playroom door and hope what I'm hearing isn't indicative of what's going on.

At least let them still have some clothes on.

The door opens quietly as a whisper. David is sitting at the end of the bed. From my vantage point, all I see of the girls are the tops of their bobbing heads.

"Jesus, David. What are you doing?"

One stupid question deserves another. David turns around to look at me, big eyes still glazed. He has something in his hand.

"What do you think I'm doing?"

The girls pop up, allowing me to see the low television console behind them. They have something in their hands, too.

Game controllers.

David is grinning at me. "What did you think we were doing, Anna?"

He sounds like a six-year-old. Whatever he's on, I hope it wears off soon.

"Come on. It's time for us to go."

"Not yet. We just started."

I reach across the bed and pluck the controller from his hand. "It's time for you girls to leave now, too. Do you have a way home?"

Reluctantly, the girls stand up. One of them says, "We came with Mrs. Williams. She said she'd take care of us."

Despite my threat, I know what Judith Williams is capable of. I seriously doubt if taking care of these two involves seeing the girls safely home. I crook a finger. "Come with us. My friend and I will take you home."

David is delighted. "They can come home with me."

Yeah. Right.

I open the door and step into the hall first. Quiet. No footsteps pounding up the steps to try to stop us from leaving. I shepherd the three downstairs and into the foyer.

Still, nothing. The only noise is the hum of conversation from the living room. I hope Judith Williams isn't dumb enough to think I was bluffing about calling the cops. She should be rustling her crowd out the door, too.

David and the Bobbsey Twins giggle their way across the foyer and out the front door. I try to get them to hurry, but it's like wrangling chickens. I've never seen David so loopy. I wonder if he's going to remember any of this when he sobers up.

I wonder if Judith Williams really told him that I was a vampire.

It's a long way down the winding driveway, the gate hidden until we're almost on top of it. Dena is sitting in her car in front of it, window rolled down, jabbing without success at the remote. When she sees us approach, she jumps out of her car.

"I don't know what's wrong. The gate won't open."

Frey pulls up then, at the other side of the gate. I don't remember giving him my car key, but at this moment, it hardly matters. He's still on one side of the gate and we're on the other.

I motion David and the girls off to the side. If I were alone, I'd jump the fence. I take a look at the gate. It's eight feet of wrought iron with an iron lock. I still have the guard's keys in my pocket. If I can get the lock open, I should be able to push the gate open.

Frey watches as I fish the keys from my pocket. There are about twenty, all about the same size and configuration. I start to jab them into the lock, one after the other.

"Give them to me," Frey says after a minute. "Let me try." He bends over, examines the lock, shuffles the keys until he finds one that to my eye is indistinguishable from the other nineteen on the ring. That's the one he slips into the lock and gives a turn.

The lock opens with a metallic snick.

"How did you do that?"

He grins. "It's the Y chromosome."

He worked his magic. It's my turn to work mine. I put my shoulder against the gate and heave.

The gate flies apart.

David says, "Way to go, Anna."

The girls giggle and clap their hands.

Frey holds open the car door. "That extra X chromosome ain't no slouch, either."

David and the girls crowd into the backseat of the Jag. Dena pulls out of the gate. I consider trying to blockade it in some way but what's the point? We'll all be back here in forty-eight hours and between now and then, I really don't care what goes on in the house.

The girls turn out to be college students, with an apartment up on Montezuma near the San Diego State campus. David is disappointed I won't let them go home with him. They part with kisses and an exchange of telephone numbers. When David isn't paying attention, I slip the girls' numbers out of his shirt pocket. The less he remembers about the last couple of days the better.

When we're back on the road, David slumps down on the backseat and falls asleep.

Frey says, "Shall we take David to your house?"

I give it a moment's thought. "No. Let's take him to his condo. If he wakes up in my place, he'll start looking around for food. We've already gone through that once."

Frey gives me one of those oh-what-does-that-mean quirks of an eyebrow.

"Not what you're thinking. I brought him home to sleep off a drunk. He slept on the couch."

I glance into the backseat. "What do you think she gave him?"

He raises a shoulder in a half shrug. "Hallucinogenic? Meth or ecstasy? A cocktail of all of the above? Hard to say. The good news is he hasn't been exposed that long. Hopefully, he'll sleep it off."

When we get to his place, we're able to rouse David to his feet and into the elevator. He doesn't appear to have keys on him, but I have a set on my key ring so at least this is one door we don't have to break into or down.

David looks surprised to find himself at home. "What happened to the girls?"

Frey and I steer him into the bedroom, strip him down to his tighty whities and bundle him into bed. David smiles up at me and holds up a corner of the sheet.

"Aren't you going to join me?"

Frey clears his throat. "I think I'll make some coffee."

He leaves for the kitchen and I take a seat on the edge of the bed. David's eyes have already closed.

I brush a lock of hair off his forehead. "David?"

"Hmmmm?"

"Did she hurt you?"

A snort. "You mean Judy? If anything, I probably hurt her."

Okay. Too much information. "Did Judy say anything strange to you while you were—uh—having sex?"

One sleepy eye pops open. "You mean did Judy tell me that you're both vampires?"

"What did you think when she told you that?"

"I thought"—he pulls the sheet up to his chin and rolls on his side—"that it explained a lot."

FREY IS STANDING IN FRONT OF THE PICTURE WINDOW in the living room staring out at the downtown skyline. The morning sun blankets the city with crimson rays of molten silk. When he hears me coming up behind him, he says, "This is quite a place. Must have cost David a bundle. The fugitive apprehension business must be more lucrative than I imagined."

He's holding a mug of coffee in each hand and holds one out to me.

"Business is good," I say after taking a sip. "But not this good. He bought the condo when he was still playing football."

Physically, it looks like Frey is focusing on the view but I can tell his mind is elsewhere. Probably thinking of what he might be doing now. At home with Layla. Or at school. Anywhere except here dealing with another of my crises.

"Frey?"

He half turns toward me.

"I'm sorry."

His brow wrinkles. "For what?"

"For dragging you into yet another drama. You should go home now. I'll stay with David. Then when I know he's okay, I'll go back to the cottage and take a look at your notes."

He places his mug down on the coffee table. "I will go home," he says. "To shower and change. Then I'll go by the cottage and get the book. I'll be back in an hour."

"What about school? How many days have you missed now?"

He holds up a hand. "Two words. Student. Teacher. She has lesson plans and an attitude. She'll do fine without me."

I walk him to the door. "Let me give you my keys. Take the Jag."

"I have a set of your keys. Remember, I drove tonight when we left Avery's?"

Yeah. That's right. "When did I give you a set of keys?"

"You didn't. I managed to abscond with the extra set you keep—make that kept—in the sugar bowl on the kitchen counter."

"Very resourceful."

"We cats are."

He pulls the door open. "You're not mad?"

How could I be mad? "I should have thought to give you a set myself."

He leaves with one last admonition. "Lock up. We don't know how pissed off Judith Williams is, but there's no sense taking chances. A locked door won't keep her out, but it'll slow her down."

I close the door behind him and turn the deadbolt. Then I head for the kitchen and a phone.

I hope Judith was smart enough to get her new best friends out of Avery's house. Time for her to know I don't make empty threats.

It's time for me call the cops.

CHAPTER 42

DAVID IS STILL ASLEEP. IT'S BEEN ALMOST TWELVE hours and I'm beginning to get worried. I peek in at him, but his breathing is deep and regular and he doesn't seem to be in any distress. I close the bedroom door and rejoin Frey.

Frey and I have made ourselves at home in the condo. David is as much a carnivore as Frey so food isn't an issue. We alternate lessons from the book with bouts in the kitchen. I'd forgotten how good bacon smells when it's cooking or the way a rare steak oozes when it's cut into. Which is what Frey is doing now. I take a seat on a barstool and watch.

Frey watches me watching him.

"Want a bite?"

I have another flashback. Retching into the sink after a mouthful of lasagna. "How do you feel about projectile vomiting?"

"Nice image."

I rest my elbows on the counter, lean forward. "How long do you think David will be out?"

"As long as it takes. No way to judge since we don't know what she gave him."

Frey is sopping up meat juices with a piece of bread.

"Are you going to lick the plate next?"

"How do you clean up after yourself?"

He's right. Vampires lick puncture wounds to heal them. "We have a lot in common."

When Frey finishes up, however, he doesn't lick his plate. Rather he takes it to the kitchen sink, rinses it, sticks it into the dishwasher. Very civilized. More civilized than the average vampire, though most hosts would probably object to being stuffed into a dishwasher.

He's bending now to look through the glass door of an under-the-counter wine cooler. "How about a glass of wine? David has some nice reds here."

I nod and he chooses one, a bottle with a black label and a gold crown. He uncorks it, swirls a little into a wide-mouthed wineglass and hands it to me.

"No. You taste. You have a much more sophisticated palate than I do. It's all I can do to distinguish type O from type A."

He laughs, completes the ritual, proclaims it drinkable and pours out two glasses.

We drink in silence for a few minutes. I sense that Frey has something he wants to say. He keeps looking at me but when my eyes meet his, he looks away. I let it go on through the first glass of wine but bring it to an end after we've started on the second.

"Spill it. And I don't mean the wine."

"Ha. Ha. Very clever."

I lay my hand over his. "Come on. You have something on your mind. God knows I unload on you all the time."

"This isn't about me." He comes from around the back of the counter to stand next to me. "I know you must be concerned about what's going to happen tomorrow. Do you want to talk about it?"

"Isn't that all we've done since I got back?"

He swirls the wine in his glass. He doesn't answer; he doesn't have to. We both know the ceremony is not what he's referring to.

I take a good, long drink, almost drain my glass, before reaching for the bottle for a refill. I have to wait for the liquor to spread its warmth before answering. I want to be honest this time. No more bullshit. No more posturing.

I look up into Frey's wonderful, thoughtful, concerned face and unexpectedly feel the sting of tears.

Stupid. Not me.

I jump up, try to turn away.

He grabs my arm and doesn't let me.

I fall against his chest, heart pounding, to feel his own heart racing, too.

His arms close around me. "Tell me."

I don't know where to begin. Don't know why after all that's happened, I'm more afraid at this moment then I've ever been. I've lost too much. I can't lose any more. Emotions swamp my senses like a tidal wave.

"Tell me." Frey says it again.

I squeeze my eyes shut for courage. Let my arms encircle his waist, hold on so he can't see the hopelessness on my face.

"I'm afraid."

"Go on."

"I've spent a year denying the possibility that I have some kind of mystical destiny. Yet here I am. Hours away from a supernatural showdown. What if I'm not who everyone thinks I am? I'm going to be killed for something I didn't ask for. Something I don't want. It's not fair. I try every day to exist as a human. If I die no one will remember that I was here. My parents won't even be able to give me a funeral. David will think I've deserted him again. I will have ceased to exist. No one will know."

Frey's words reach out to me, soft as a baby's breath. "You assume too much. You assume you are going to lose. I know you, Anna. Anyone who challenges you is a fool. You don't give in and you don't give up. It's what I love about you."

He raises a hand to stroke my hair. "I believe in destiny. Yours. Even if you do not. And I believe you will win and that you will become a force for good in the world. You have it in you, Anna."

His voice has taken on a gruffness that reflects more than concern. It's startling. Confusing. I don't dare move, don't dare raise my head to see if I'm misinterpreting a friend's attempt to comfort for something else.

His arms are still tight around me.

If I did raise my head, what would happen?

The voice of reason answers.

This is Frey. *Layla's* Frey.

Nothing will happen.

I draw in a breath and push against his arms. "Sorry. I don't know where that came from."

He doesn't let go right away. He doesn't let go until the rapid pounding of his heart slows. The rhythm of his blood—and mine—tempers and cools. For a moment, I'm able to suppress the fear.

The moment passes. He steps back. "Shall we get back to it?"

The book. The damned book.

"May as well."

FREY REVERTS QUICKLY TO BUSINESS AS USUAL. We've gotten through the *how* and *why* of the ceremony.

Viewed from the perspective of the twenty-first century much of the book is difficult, if not impossible, to understand. Some of the book contains tidbits of history not relevant but interesting. Animal sacrifice to the gods was actually prohibited before the draining of a human host. Animals were a valuable commodity. Humans were fodder.

Frey is reading a passage he's translated. The pages in his hand are clean, free of beer stains. He must have printed out a new copy when he went home to change.

I rest my chin on a cupped palm. "How did you translate this, Frey? Did you find a vampire Rosetta stone?"

He taps a finger against his temple. "All here. Part of the Keeper tradition. The ability to see meaning behind words, no matter what language they're written in."

"So, it's not like the other books in your library?"

"No. This is not a book I'd loan out. This book is irreplaceable. The others belong as much to the supernatural community as they do to me. Any supernatural can read a book in my library. The secrets of this book are revealed only to a Keeper."

It's a new side of Frey I never knew before. His being a Keeper. Along with having a son. Things I hope I'm alive to pursue when this is over.

I push gloomy thoughts of the alternative out of my head to listen. Frey has moved along to who is likely to be in attendance.

"We can assume there will be a representative from each of the thirteen tribes and more than likely they will each bring an ambassador or two. Judith Williams and her entourage."

A thought occurs to me that I can't believe I hadn't entertained before. "Is Judith the North American representative?"

Frey laughs. "Hardly. She obviously likes to think she has an important role to play because of her husband's involvement. She's no more than an invited guest."

And more than likely sponsor of the challenger. Frey

doesn't say it, but he doesn't have to. We both suspect as unlikely as it might be, if there is a challenge, she'll be behind it.

"Then who will be representing the North American vampires?"

It sounds more like a summit meeting of world leaders than convocation of vampire bigwigs. If I weren't so personally involved, I'd find the whole idea absurd.

Frey consults his notes. "Joshua Turnbull from Denver."

The name snaps me to attention. "Are you sure?"

Frey looks again. "Yep. Why?"

"Because he's the vamp who helped me when I was looking for Sophie Deveraux."

It's Frey's turn to look surprised. Sophie Deveraux was the witch who helped save his life when he was under the spell of the black witch Belinda Burke—her sister.

I nod. "And he was a good friend of Avery and of Warren Williams. Which, it's safe to assume, means he's no friend of mine. While we parted on amicable terms, Turnbull was happy to see me go."

I pause, remembering. "He never mentioned who he was. In fact, he made it a point to talk about the importance of vampires keeping a low profile in their communities."

Frey shrugs. "And I'm sure he does. No one in the supernatural community, especially those in power, would want to draw attention to himself."

"But don't they want some kind of tribute? What's the point of being king if your subjects don't know it?"

He laughs at the analogy. "Vampires, especially old ones, don't need tribute. Chances are, he knew who you were, though. Sensed it just like Williams and Avery. Don't forget, when this is over, he'll be answering to you."

He sounds so confident. I'm not so sure. I've assumed Judith Williams will be the one arranging the challenge. I know now that there's at least one other vampire who lost a friend by my hand. Joshua Turnbull.

"Okay, assuming I survive tomorrow night's festivities, what happens then?"

"There'll be an induction ceremony. Then anyone who has a grievance or a petition will present it. You'll listen to their arguments. You'll make a judgment. Then it will be over and everyone will go home."

It sounds too easy. Even the way Frey *isn't* looking at me as he recites the innocuous schedule of events makes the hair rustle on the back of my neck.

"After I make the choice, right?"

"You were paying attention in Palm Springs."

I press fingers against my eyes. "And the choice I make is the one the vampire community must live with for the next two hundred years."

"Not just the vampire community," Frey says. "The mortal community ascended to its place in society because the last Chosen One relegated vampires to a position of subservience. If you change that, the positions reverse."

He pauses. "Vampires rise to rule the world."

A moment passes while we absorb the implication. It's not as disturbing to me as it should be because I know there's no fucking way *I'd* ever make a decision like that. Frey knows it, too. But we both also know if there's a challenge, it might not be up to me.

After another minute, Frey rises, stretches, reaches for a small leather suitcase at the end of the couch.

"I'm going to take a shower. When I get out, maybe you should go to the cottage for a change of clothes. I'll stay here with David."

Just what does one wear to a coronation? Especially when the opening act is a fight to the death.

I watch Frey walk back toward the bathroom, wondering again what would have happened a few minutes ago if I'd let him kiss me.

He would have kissed me. I know it, Layla or no. I've never listened to a voice of *reason*. Why did I this time?

The water in the shower comes on with a rush. I picture Frey naked and wet. I could test my theory. Join him right now.

So what's stopping me?

Sex is sex.

We've done it before.

I've done it too many times to count.

Why would this be different? It's scratching an itch. A biological urge.

It means nothing.

Lance proved that.

Still, I can't rouse myself from the couch, can't take that first step.

I need Frey in my life. I don't want to give him a reason to feel guilty when he goes back to his real life. He will have a real life to go back to even if I may not. And Layla is a part of it.

My thinking is remarkably mature. Am I actually letting my head and not hormones dictate my actions?

Scary.

I'm staring at the doorway through which Frey disappeared moments before. I'm so focused, I don't realize until he opens his mouth that David has come into the living room.

"What are you doing here?" David asks. "And who's in my shower?"

CHAPTER 43

DAVID IS BARE-CHESTED, BUT HE'S PULLED ON A pair of sweatpants and has flip-flops on his feet. His eyes are clear, his expression puzzled but not vacuous.

"What's going on?" he asks again.

"How do you feel?"

He rubs fingers against his forehead and shifts. "I'm sore. In strange places. Was I in an accident?"

"What do you remember?"

He narrows his eyes, expression morphing to irritation. "Are you going to answer every question with a question?"

"Are you?"

He turns his back on me with a grunt and heads for the kitchen. I jump up from the couch and follow him.

He has his head buried in the refrigerator. "I'm starved. What happened to the steaks I had in here?" He pulls out a bottle of water and turns around. The empty bottle of wine on the counter grabs his attention. "Hey.

That's a bottle of Cavallina." He eyes me. "Anna, did we . . . ?"

Just then Frey pads out on bare feet. He has one towel wrapped around his waist and is rubbing his hair with the other. He stops when he sees David and me.

David stares. "Do I know you?"

Frey addresses himself to me. "I was coming out to tell you you could leave now. Looks like I'm the one who'll be leaving."

He backtracks into the bathroom.

David's irritation is blossoming. He rounds on me. "Do I know him? I don't think I do. So what's he doing taking a shower in my bathroom? Anna, what the hell is going on?"

I pat his arm. "Humor me and I'll tell you. But first, what's the last thing you remember?"

He scrunches his face, looking again like the kid with the computer games and the two buxom playmates. "Thursday. I think. Thursday night. I was with Miranda and I got a call that you were in an accident." He narrows his eyes. "You don't look like you were in an accident."

I wave a hand at him to go on. "Anything else?"

"I caught a shuttle back, went to the cottage . . ." He stops. "That's it." He looks disappointed. "That's the last thing I remember. Except—"

I cringe inwardly.

"I had some really crazy dreams. I was having sex. There were a couple of girls. And an older woman." He closes his eyes as if trying to remember. "I think she told me something about you."

Can't wait to tell Judith about the "older woman" remark, but I temper my enthusiasm and say, "Sex with a couple of girls and an older woman. Sounds like getting a bump on the head worked out pretty well for you."

He rubs his forehead again. "Can't remember anything else. It's gone."

I steer him back to the living room. "Sit down and I'll fill you in." Sort of.

He sits, noticing newspapers splayed over the coffee table. "What day is this?"

"Monday."

"Monday? I've been out three days?"

In a manner of speaking. "You have a concussion. Mild. Nothing to worry about." Unless those blondes aren't as squeaky clean as they looked. "My friend and I have been taking care of you."

"How did I get a concussion?"

"It's the damndest thing. You fell. At the airport. At the hospital they found my contact number in your wallet and called. My friend and I have been taking care of you since you were released."

"But what about the call I got? Someone said *you'd* been in an accident."

"A mistake. It was a woman named Hannah Strong, not Anna. Weird, huh?"

"My god. Miranda. She must be frantic. I told her I'd call her when I got back."

"Not to worry. I took care of it. She wanted to cut her business trip short, but I assured her there was no need. She'll be back in town on Friday."

Still, he lunges to his feet, heads for the phone.

I intercept him at the kitchen door. "You need to rest a couple more days, David. Miranda understands. Concussions are nothing to fool around with."

"I feel fine now. Just need some food."

But he's not. He's swaying, and his face has gone pale. Evidently the drug is not completely out of his system. A bit of well-timed luck.

"No. You're not all right. Get back to bed and I'll fix you a plate of scrambled eggs."

"Will you call Miranda for me?"

"Of course."

Frey emerges dressed now. He raises an eyebrow as I shuffle David back to the bedroom. "How about you fix David a plate of eggs?"

He heads into the kitchen, and I tuck David in once more.

"You just stay here another day and you'll be fine."

David takes my hand. "You are a good friend, Anna. I don't tell you that enough."

I have the grace to blush.

Too bad there isn't an Olympic event for lying.

FREY TAKES KITCHEN DUTY WHILE I MAKE A RUN TO the cottage. Shower and change into yet another pair of jeans and a cotton sweater. It may not be proper coronation attire, but I need clothes I can fight in.

When I get back to the condo, Frey is straightening the kitchen.

"Is David asleep?"

"Out like a baby. Again."

He motions to the couch. "Why don't you stretch out? You haven't slept in two days."

"I'm not sure I can."

He gives the counter a final swipe with a towel and comes around to join me. He takes my hand and leads me over to the couch. "Try."

I sink down, let him lift my feet and slip off my shoes. He sits on the edge of the couch beside me.

"When did you feed last?"

He asks it matter-of-factly, like asking if I take cream with my coffee. I have to think a minute before it comes rushing back. Underwood. In France. I still have his blood in my system. I haven't had a chance to purge it.

I don't want Frey to see the excitement that floods my body at the thought that he might be offering himself. Offering his good, clean blood. I can't ask him. I won't. I turn my face away.

He lies down beside me, smoothes a tangle of hair away from my face.

"It's all right. Take what you need."

He's opened the collar of his shirt, fits himself next to me so that his neck is exposed and close. So close. I don't want to do this, but my body is reacting as if separate from my head and heart. It is thrumming with need, burning with the hunger. Frey's blood calls to me and my body answers because it has no choice.

I nuzzle his neck, pull him against me. He yields with a sigh. He smells of soap and shaving cream, clean, good. Just under the surface, the panther sleeps, wild, strong, contained. We lay cupped together, one of my hands around his waist, one of my legs entangled with his. He is quiet except for the beating of his heart, still except for the rushing of his blood.

He lifts his chin, allowing better access. He wants me to do this. I need to do this. When I break through, when the heady rush of his blood fills my mouth, I experience something I haven't for a long time.

Peace.

We lay together when it's done. Frey is quiet beside me. I stroke his arm, his hair. I can't remember the last time I fed without having sex. Ironically, I also can't remember feeling as calm and tranquil as I do at this very moment, even despite the fact that tonight may be the end of my life as I know it.

Does Frey feel this sense of peace, too?

It seems selfish to have taken and given nothing in return. I let my hand move along his arm, down his abdomen. "Do you want me to . . . ?"

He stops my hand, raises it to his lips. "Yes. No. Later, maybe. All I want you to do now is sleep."

I'm not the only one wrestling with head-over-hormone issues. For some reason, I find it comforting. Having sex isn't the best response to confusion.

Frey changes positions on the couch so we are facing each other. He is now holding me. His arms cradle my head against his chest. I close my eyes and drift away, soothed by the strong, steady beat of his heart.

CHAPTER 44

FREY'S BODY JERKS BESIDE ME AND I'M INSTANTLY awake.

David is standing over us. "Hey. It's ten o'clock. Why don't you two get a room?"

Frey pulls his arm out from under my head, and we stumble to our feet.

David has gotten dressed. He has a jacket over his arm and keys in his hand.

"Where do you think you're going?" I ask. "You can't drive in your condition."

He frowns. "I feel fine. I'm going out for a drink. And I'm walking. Stop acting like my mother."

I look at Frey. If David talks with Tracey or Miranda, our story is blown. After tonight it may not matter, but I can only deal with one crisis at a time. Frey studies me, reads my expression like he used to read my thoughts. He straightens his shirt, draws his fingers through his hair, turns to David. "Would you like some company?"

I expect it; still his words produce a flare of panic. I

wanted Frey with me. But he's not part of the vampire community. His presence would not be tolerated at best, met with violence at worst.

Once again, Frey is there to help me. He only needs to keep David occupied another few hours. After that, I'll deal with the fallout. If I'm still around.

David doesn't look thrilled with the idea. "I don't need a babysitter."

"Actually, I thought maybe you could tell me a little about Broncos' number four and that last trip to the Super Bowl."

David's brows lift. "You were a fan?"

"Never missed a game. Started following you when you played for Notre Dame."

Frey is not only resourceful, but smart. He couldn't have played David better. Mentioning his alma mater melts David's resistance like butter on a hot griddle.

"There's a great little sports bar about a block from here. Even has an old jersey of mine on the wall. Owner played for the Broncos the same time I did. I'll give him a call and have him come down to meet us."

He pulls his cell phone from a pocket and moves a few feet away to make the call. Gives Frey a chance to bend his face close to my ear.

"You'll be all right. Just remember what we talked about. You are the Chosen One. You are strong and fast. You have a good mind and a good heart. I'll be waiting for you at the cottage."

I don't want him to leave. I don't want either of us to leave the safe cocoon this place has become. I want to hold on to him with every ounce of strength. I want to stay in his arms until midnight is past. I want time to explore the possibilities.

My eyes must betray how desperately I want him to stay. His arms encircle me. He presses his body against mine.

"Show them who you are. They'll follow you once they know. We'll have time."

David's voice breaks the spell. "What do you think Lance would say if he walked in right now?"

Frey and I step apart. If Lance walked in right now, he'd be dead before he could say anything. "It's not what you think."

David claps Frey on the back. "Frankly, I'm glad she's seeing someone else. I never liked that scrawny model." He turns to me. "Ready to go?"

"You two go. I've been here for three days. I think I'm ready to sleep in my own bed."

David looks surprised but only for a moment. He's already ushering his new best friend out, chatting like they've known each other forever.

He does remember to pause and throw a "Lock up when you leave, okay?" back over his shoulder.

If I didn't have to preserve my energy for what's coming, the brush-off might be insulting.

THIS TIME WHEN I PULL INTO AVERY'S DRIVEWAY, THE gate is open. The guard who steps out to greet me is vampire. He doesn't ask my name, bows his head slightly and says, "Ms. Strong. They are waiting for you in the library."

Once again, the house is staged for a party. Every window blazes light. More limos than before line the turnaround. This time, a uniformed driver stands beside each car. When they see the Jag, they come to attention. Waiting for the guest of honor, no doubt. One of them separates from the pack, approaches the car, opens my door and extends a hand. He, too, is vampire.

I let him park the Jag and head for the house. Another vampire opens the door before I can ring or knock. Like the host who admitted Frey and me last night, he is in a tuxedo. Unlike the host, he is smiling and sycophantic in the way he bows and ushers me inside.

It's an effort to keep fear out of my thoughts. When I open my mind, I hear the murmur of a dozen voices rustling like leaves in a gale. Some speak in English, others in languages I don't recognize. I *understand*, though. It's a part of a vampire's genetic makeup, the ability to communicate across language barriers.

Like Frey and his book.

I wish he were here.

The conversation is banal. Talk of the trip over or musings about how pricey real estate is in Southern California. I could be eavesdropping on a group of CEOs called to headquarters for a board meeting.

The library is off to the left of the living room. There are people in the living room, too. Guests of those who await me now. They see me pass and grow quiet.

It is with some trepidation that I approach the closed doors. This was Avery's sanctuary and the first place I fed as a vampire. The voices I hear come from this room.

The door opens before I put a hand to it. It is Judith Williams. She is dressed in a long robe of black silk. Her hair is pulled back from her face. She does not look as smug today or as confident. Perhaps she has been reprimanded for what happened after the party the other evening.

She motions with a sweeping hand. "They are ready."

"They," not "we." I smile as she passes by.

I'm not sure what to expect. A few days ago, my thoughts had been on David and getting him safely away. I hardly noticed the vampires in attendance. What I do remember was a fleeting glance at vampires in costumes of varied colors and styles. A colorful blanketed figure that reminded me of an African tribal dancer, a vampire in an

Arabian burnoose, a high-necked coat of white linen on a vampire of Chinese descent.

Here, the dress reflects the tenor of their conversation—the heads of the thirteen tribes have donned business attire. Well-tailored suits representing the very best of the world's couturiers. I am suddenly self-conscious in my jeans. I chose what I am wearing because if I must fight, I need to be wearing what I am most comfortable in. I had not meant to trivialize the situation. The eyes that are watching seem to acknowledge my intention. There is no judgment in the way they look at me.

The thirteen stood when I came in. Now they take chairs around the big desk that was once Avery's. We are alone. Judith Williams has not returned. It makes me a little less anxious to know that she has not been granted equal status with the others.

There is one empty chair. The one behind Avery's desk. His chair. One of the tribal heads stands again and motions that I should take it.

When I am seated, the same vampire begins the introductions. He is Amardad from Persia, the ancient name for Iran. Then he presents each of the others in turn. They stand, bow slightly, touch their hands to their chest in greeting much as Culebra did a few days before. I listen and watch, opening my thoughts only in acknowledgment. These are the very oldest of the vampires from around the world. They have exotic names like Alexi and Cheng-Li and Dhakwan, Dato and Naruaki and Melisizwe and Bayani and Chael. Names that suggest power.

And less exotic names like Miguel and Joshua Turnbull, the vampire from Denver, the only one to allow a smile to touch his lips. There are two women among them. A beautiful West Indian whose name, Rani, I'm told, means queen and Brianna, an Australian.

The faces behind the names are ageless and old. They

are devoid of expression as they look at me, allowing not a glimmer of thought or emotion to escape. The history of the world could be concealed behind those perfect, empty faces.

When introductions are concluded, Joshua Turnbull takes over. He rises, bows his head in my direction. His attitude here is far more deferential than when we were together in Denver.

He begins to speak, telepathically, so all can understand.

This is the Council of Thirteen. Gathered together as we have since the beginning to anoint the Chosen One. We come from all parts of the world. Some of you have made the journey before. Some of us are newly appointed to our positions, the result of having lost one of our own to the second death.

He pauses, points to the woman Brianna. *This one lost her friend and mentor, the ancient one we called Aiden, by the hand of a Revenger. We mourn his passing.*

He looks at me. *I lost a friend, as well. Avery, in whose house we gather today. Some would say he brought about his own destruction by a careless and unnecessary act of violence against a human who bore him no harm. Still, he is gone and deserving of our respect. We take a moment to honor our fallen comrades.*

Turnbull's eyes are on me as the circle pays final respects. I hadn't known before this moment that Avery had been one of the thirteen. It suddenly becomes more likely that Turnbull will be the one to make the challenge. If Judith has convinced him that I am responsible for Williams' death as well, it is more than likely.

Turnbull waits until the others raise their heads and look to him to continue.

As it is written in the Grimoire, we meet on this occasion to determine the future of the vampire community. We place this terrible burden on the shoulders of one. One who is marked as Chosen. A vampire of particular cunning and strength. A vampire who possesses extraordinary abilities.

Anna Strong was so marked. She is unharmed by fire. She is canny in ways we are not. She has strength and courage. Avery saw it from the first moment. He was not wise in the way he chose to teach her our ways. He paid for that mistake. But he brought her to our attention, and we are here today because of him.

The vampire known as Chael stands. He is slight of stature, dark-skinned, with eyes that are hard and black as flint.

Is it true that she is responsible for Avery's death? And also that of our friend Warren Williams?

I stand, too, to defend myself.

Turnbull stops me with a message sent solely to me. *You will not speak. I am appointed to defend you. You may have an opportunity later. But I will answer for you now. This is the way.*

His eyes narrow, as if asking me to acquiesce to his request. He is somber and respectful and despite my natural inclination to forge ahead, I do give in. I am out of my element here. I can always revert to the impulsive, imprudent and immature side of my nature later.

I sit back down.

He addresses Chael. *Avery was my good friend. I loved him as a brother. But he had a flaw. He felt it necessary to exercise complete control over everyone within his sphere of influence. He attempted to control Anna Strong. He kidnapped her human partner, bled him almost to the point of death. He burned her home. He committed acts that could have brought unwanted and harmful attention to the vampire community. Anna Strong staked him in defense of her life. The act, while regrettable, was justifiable.*

I'm surprised to hear him defending me. And surprised

that he knew the story. Well, most of it. He didn't mention how Avery came back and attempted to kill me a second time. It's possible he doesn't know. Where did he get his information? From Warren Williams?

Warren Williams.

It's not over yet.

Chael accepts Turnbull's pronouncement. About Avery. *And what of Warren Williams? Our newly turned sister, his widow, tells us their relationship was contentious. She tells us Anna Strong was the last to see him alive.*

I wait, tension bunching my shoulders. Turnbull isn't jumping to my defense this time. When at last he speaks, it is quietly and with great sorrow.

Warren Williams was a man who was able to navigate both the human and vampire worlds and be a friend to both. He defended the human community in his role as law officer—and did so for two hundred years. As a vampire, he worked tirelessly as head of the Watchers.

We may never know how he met his end. It is true, Anna Strong was with him shortly before his death. I can say no more than that. There are no witnesses and no evidence to prove guilt or innocence.

Chael's dead eyes flash. *How is it then that she is allowed to stand unchallenged as the Chosen?*

Turnbull turns to face me. *She is not. A challenge has been issued. She is called to defend her innocence in the way proscribed in the Grimoire. Anna Strong, do you accept the challenge?*

My thoughts whip out to him. *Don't I get the chance to defend myself against the charges first? I had nothing to do with Williams' death. It was at the hand of another.*

Is this other a vampire?

A sorcerer.

Do you have proof? Witnesses?

I shake my head. *I killed the one responsible.* I think of Lance, of his betrayal. *There is one other who knows the truth. But I don't know where he is. Give me time to find him.*

Turnbull shakes his head. *This must be decided on the day of the becoming. It is written.*

Fuck it is written. I lean toward him, fists clenched. *I am not guilty.*

Then you will survive the challenge. That, too, is written.

I knew this was coming. I tried to prepare. But reality crushes me under the sudden weight of fear.

Because of some ancient book and two thousand years of vampire folklore, I may be dead before dawn.

CHAPTER 45

I'M FACING THIRTEEN PAIRS OF STARING EYES. WAITing for my reaction, no doubt. They heard my exchange with Turnbull.

They don't care.

For the first time, they allow emotion to show on their faces. Some are thoughtful, some are indifferent. Some, like Chael, are excited, aroused. He is looking forward to the fight. He expects me to lose.

He made the challenge.

I face him. *Why?*

A smile as cold as his eyes. *You have no right to be here. You are too new. One of us should have been allowed to assume the mantle. The time of the vampire is at hand. You stand in the way of what should be.*

He speaks as if I've already lost. *And what of the Grimoire? Of the Chosen One?*

Superstition. We have lived under the mortal yoke too long. It's time to assume our rightful place. We are gods among men and it is time they acknowledge it. It is time the world acknowledges it.

I think I know that speech. You borrow Hitler's play-book?

A shadow passes over his features. *You prove my point, Anna Strong. When I was told of Avery, of Williams, I knew you could not be allowed to ascend. You place human life above all else. You choose man over your own kind. You are unworthy.*

I glance around to see how the others are reacting to our exchange. No outrage. No objection. No indignation. The heads of the thirteen tribes are like sheep under the spell of a wolf.

And why shouldn't they be? Nothing that happens today will alter their lives. Not really. If I win, it's business as usual. If Chael wins, they assume dominance in every part of the world.

Frey's words come back to me. Show them who you are.

Time to swallow the fear and show them who I am.

Chael waits with the patience of a sphinx. Power emanates from him, the power of a thousand years. He is calm. Confident.

I allow the beast to spring forth. *Let's get this party started.*

When he understands what I'm saying, he laughs. *You think I will fight you? I would not sully my hands with your worthless life. You will fight another.*

He waves a hand. From behind me comes the sound of a door scraping open. I turn to see a section of a bookcase swing inward on a rusty track.

Light shines from the room, illuminating what looks like an amphitheater. It's not very big, maybe twenty square feet, with bench seats around the perimeter. All that's missing is a crowd chanting "Caesar."

Or "Chael."

I turn to him. *You're kidding. An arena? Am I fighting a vampire or a lion?*

Oh, you're fighting a vampire. He calls out to someone inside the room. *Bring him in.*

A familiar scent.

My body recognizes it before my mind. Muscles tense. Blood turns hot with fury.

He steps into the light. *I'm sorry, Anna.*

Lance.

I don't know whether to howl with eagerness or dismay. I see the logic behind Chael's choice. He thinks I will be at a disadvantage because Lance was my lover. He thinks I cannot kill a lover.

He thinks wrong.

Chael doesn't know what Underwood did to me. He doesn't know the connection between Lance and Williams and Underwood.

Otherwise, he would have chosen another. He would have known that I have sworn to kill Lance.

I let Chael see the glimmer of satisfaction on my face. *You have made a grave mistake. You may have had a thousand years to acquire wisdom, but your arrogance has clouded your judgment.*

For the first time, he looks into my face, really looks into my face, and the realization that he may have made an error cracks his smug mask of confidence. Admitting it, however, will never happen. He steps back, waves his hand. *Let us begin.*

Us? Is that a joke? The euphemism sparks a short bark of mirthless laughter. *Why don't you and I have a go at it first?*

Turnbull steps between us, forcing Chael to take another step back. He places a hand on my arm and ushers me into the room. A room I never knew existed. It's cold inside and smells of dirt and neglect. There is another scent, too. Blood. A shudder runs through me. What did Avery use it for? It's another reminder of how good Avery was at hiding things from me. I can't believe I let that monster touch me. I can't believe I thought I loved him.

All these thoughts go through my head because I don't want to think about the one standing, waiting, in the center of the room.

Another monster I thought I loved.

Lance does not move, does not try to communicate with me. He's stripped to his shorts, his feet are bare. In his hand is a pointed stake.

Turnbull whispers to me, "Do you wish to change?"

"Into what? Or is titillation one of the perks of this freak show?"

He lets a smile touch his mouth. "I like you, Anna Strong. You cut through the crap. But I don't make the rules. Like you, I'm new to the fraternity. How you wish to fight is up to you."

His head is bowed close to my ear. He's talking in sotto voce and in English. I'm guessing it's to prevent the foreign delegates from understanding the exchange. He's drawn a cloak around his thoughts for the same reason.

Chael sees it and is not pleased. He says again, *It is time to begin.*

The benches are all occupied. The heads of the tribes are seated close enough to catch any drop of blood that might spray their way, to get maximum enjoyment from the pain we will inflict on each other. I am disgusted by the eagerness shining from their faces, by the taste of their excitement as they anticipate what is to come. I am disgusted to think that when I win, I will have to be one of them.

When I win.

I must be channeling Frey.

The thought of him brings a smile to my lips.

Lance's quiet voice reaches to me. "I do not want this. I have no choice."

When I turn to face him, I'm struck once more by his

beauty. His face and body gleam in the light. He might be Jupiter or Apollo stripped for battle. Instead, he's Janus, treacherous, a betrayer. "You have a choice. You had a choice before. You chose Underwood."

"You lied to me."

"What?"

"You didn't trust me enough to let me know what you had done. That you had gone to Julian and made a bargain. If you had trusted me, none of it would have happened."

I have to swallow down the anger before I can speak again. "Don't you dare suggest what happened in Biarritz was my fault. You drugged me and turned me over to that freak. You stood by while he attempted to rape me. Then you ran like a dog when it didn't go the way you planned. What I did, I did to protect you. What you did, you did to protect yourself."

The tribal heads are growing restless. Most don't understand what is passing between Lance and me. The few that do, don't care. They want the blood sport to begin. I feel their impatience grow.

"I don't want to fight you," Lance whispers. "But I don't want to die, either."

There is a fleeting moment when I wonder what would happen if I proclaimed to the gathering that the one who can corroborate my story about Williams is here. Would Lance lie? It doesn't matter. One way or the other, justice must be done. "You should have thought of that before you let Underwood touch me."

Turnbull comes up behind me, hands me a stake similar to the one in Lance's hand. *Are you ready?*

I nod. Lance straightens, tightens his grip on the stake.

Begin.

Lance moves first. He lunges toward me, but it's a clumsy move and I only have to sidestep to avoid the stake he holds in front of him like a dagger. I follow with a side kick to the small of his back and he goes down to his knees in the dirt.

He doesn't know how to fight. His boyish good looks and the protection of a five-hundred-year-old vampire have atrophied the animal instinct. He stumbles to his feet, whirls to face me. For the first time, he lets anger unleash the beast.

Anger isn't enough. As a human, I learned how to protect myself. It was and is part of my job as a bounty hunter. The second time Lance comes at me, I grab his hand and twist his arm back until I feel the shoulder pop.

He yelps and pushes back against me to lessen the pain.

I could stake him now. Thrust his own weapon through his back and into his heart. End this charade.

Those watching know it, too. They are furious that the fight may be over so soon, frustrated that their bloodlust will not be satisfied. They want one of us to lie bleeding in the dirt, to beg for mercy. They want to taste the fear and experience the pain.

Lance cries out. "Please, Anna. I love you."

For a moment, I'm torn—not with sympathy for Lance. He doesn't deserve sympathy. But with wondering if I want the same thing. Am I no better than the beasts watching us? Do I want to toy with Lance a little longer? Break his bones and make him beg for death?

The fight has been so one-sided, the vampire in me has yet to emerge. But now, holding Lance against me, I'm suddenly aware of the pulsing of his blood just a kiss away. It calls to the vampire and she springs forth with a growl and a gnashing of teeth. This is the way. Leave something for Adele and his family to mourn over.

I drop the stake, take a firmer grip on his squirming body. His strength is no match for mine. I pull his head back, his body arching and straining against me. With a snarl, I bury my face in his neck, tear at the jugular until I feel the skin snap. Find the artery.

And drink.

CHAPTER 46

IT GROWS DEATHLY QUIET AROUND US. I CAN ALmost taste the excitement. This is the spectacle they came to see.

Lance fights at first, tries to break away. I am stronger. There's a breathless rush when his blood pours into my mouth and it seems I cannot swallow fast enough. Then, as his heartbeat slows, I take my time. He is losing himself in the pleasure of surrender. His knees buckle and I lower him to the ground, folding myself around him so he is like a doll in my arms. His thoughts are neither fevered nor bitter, his blood as sweet as I remember.

And I remember.

I remember the first time I saw him—at Glory's, a face like an angel. I remember the first time we made love. It was frenzied, passionate, our desire so intense, the bloodlust so high, we barely made it out of our clothes. I remember other times when we went slow, making love the way humans do. Enjoying our bodies and letting simple tactile senses, touch, smell, drive us to the edge. We gave each other so much pleasure. I am glad ending it this way spares him pain.

I wonder what he is remembering. His thoughts are cloaked in shadow, growing dimmer. When I try to reach him, I catch a flash of unfamiliar faces. His parents, perhaps, and his sister and brother the way they must have been the last time he saw them. So long ago.

And then even the shadows are gone. I don't stop until I feel the last flutter of his heart, savor the last drop of his blood as it flows out of his body into mine. I know it is the last because of the texture and taste. Lifeblood is mead and tastes of the earth and life. This is water and tastes of tears and death.

I, the human Anna, hold him for a long moment when it is over. I wish I felt sorrow. A part of me is devastated at what I am capable of. At what I've done. A part of me knows this is my nature. I can't fight it. I'm not sure I want to anymore.

Turnbull approaches me first. He offers his hand to help me to my feet. At this moment, I will accept nothing from him, not even the simplest act of courtesy. I close Lance's eyes, already filmed and cloudy, and stand up and away.

When I look back down, it is no longer the Lance I knew, but the husk of an elderly man. His skin sags, his hair thins to long, silver tufts. His face morphs into a gaunt mirror reflecting the rictus of death. Was it only a week ago when we were in Palm Springs and he told me his story? It was 1925. He was born in South Africa in 1925.

I turn to face Turnbull. "I want his body shipped to his family in South Africa. There is a woman in Palm Springs who will know how to reach them. I will see you get the information. Will you take care of it?"

"Yes."

He is uncomfortable, as if unprepared for this outcome. When I look around at the others, the same expression of incredulity is mirrored on the faces staring back at me.

They all expected me to lose. Even Turnbull.

"Don't I get a big gold belt? Or at least a trophy?" Sarcasm is the only way I have to give vent to my outrage. It's either that or tear Turnbull's head off.

Chael is the first to speak. *This was an unfair pairing. You obviously had history with this one.*

The vampire had retreated at Lance's death, now she's back. And thirsty again for a taste of this one's blood. *Wasn't that the point, Chael?*

I step up to him. *Lance wasn't a good enough fighter? Then let's you and I have a rematch. I have no history with you.*

There is a stirring among the others, a collective gasp. No one has ever challenged one of the thirteen. The surprise quickly turns to a thrill of anticipation. Lance was disposed of too quickly. There is still bloodlust to be satisfied.

Chael feels the group's enthusiasm swirling around him like sand in blowing wind. They want him to accept the challenge. Put this upstart in her place.

He also feels the depth of my fury.

He addresses them like a teacher admonishing unruly students. *There is no contingency in the Grimoire for a second challenge. We are bound by the outcome of the first. It is so written.*

He says it like he is disappointed but can do nothing but abide by the rules. Rules he, moments before, called "superstition." The smell of him tells me something different. It is acrid and sharp. The smell of a coward.

At that moment, I know. As old and revered among vampires as these thirteen are, they are jealous of their lives and not quick to put them in danger.

In that respect, they are no different than humans.

CHAPTER 47

I DON'T KNOW WHAT IS GOING TO HAPPEN NEXT. Frey said there would be some kind of induction ceremony. I wonder if it will involve secret handshakes and funny hats.

I want to go home. I want to see Frey.

I want to forget what I just did.

Lance is still in my heart and in my head. I did what I swore to do after Biarritz. I wish I felt more a sense of satisfaction. Instead there's emptiness and sorrow.

At least his family will know that he is gone. They can bury him, and he will have something to show for having lived—even it's only a piece of marble.

The fastest way to get out of here is to move this freak show along.

"Turnbull, what happens now?"

He is talking with two humans who appeared a moment ago. Summoned, I suppose, to take care of clean up. They have a gurney upon which they place Lance's body. They cover it with a shroud of black velvet.

Turnbull sees me watch as they wheel it out. He says, "As soon as we have the necessary information, we will see that his body is returned to his family."

"I'll call you tomorrow." At least Adele will be spared the shock of hearing about Lance's death for the first time from a stranger. She already knows. It was part of his escape plan.

Turnbull takes my elbow. "We will adjourn to the library. There the ceremony will continue."

The others must have been waiting for me to lead them from this chamber of horror. As soon as Turnbull and I pass through the door, they follow. Quiet. Subdued. Still not over the shock that the fate of the world for the next two hundred years is in the hands of someone so inexperienced. My question is of a different nature. How did they plan to control Lance? Had he won, he would have been the one making the decisions.

I think about his relationship with Underwood and have my answer. The only difference is that this time it would have been Chael pulling the strings, I'm sure.

Lance was weak. Chael made the mistake of thinking because Lance had been a vampire longer than me, he had more cunning, more guile. I wonder what they promised Lance to get him to face me. Or what they threatened him with. I watch Chael as he takes his place once more among the tribal heads. He should have paid more attention. Learned from history.

Avery and Underwood underestimated me, too.

Turnbull assumes emcee duties, his words pulling me out of my own thoughts.

The challenge has been executed. The Tribe of Thirteen hereby bestows on Anna Strong the true and worthy title of the Chosen One. The decisions she makes bind us all. The fate of the vampire community rests in the hands of the Chosen One now as it has since the beginning. We swear allegiance and loyalty.

He bows toward me. Then, one by one, the others follow suit. Some bow stiffly, a small display of resistance. Some bow deeply, not caring one way or the other who is leading them. Chael inclines his head but not his body. He's the one likely to present the petition Frey warned me about.

He's the one likely to continue to cause trouble.

I acknowledge his pretentiousness with a nod of my own. He may be a thousand years old, but he refused to fight me. My confidence is undaunted by this posturing.

Turnbull waits for the circle to be complete. Then he waves a hand toward the door. *We will adjourn for an hour.* He glances at his watch. *We will meet back here at one a.m., when petitions will be heard. Refreshments are available in the living room.*

He waits until the exodus is complete and closes the door behind him so we have privacy.

"Refreshments?" I raise an eyebrow at him.

"These old-time vampires don't go anywhere without a blood host along. I'm sure there are extras if you'd care to partake."

I flash on this evening—Frey and then Lance. "I'm fine, thanks." It sounds as though I'm turning down a glass of wine or a martini instead of human blood from a live host. When did I become so jaded?

I've come around from behind the desk, and he and I take seats in the circle. He draws a breath, exhales slowly and with deliberation. "I know this wasn't easy for you. I told Chael what he did was despicable—bringing in a challenger with whom you had personal history. He even knew you two had had a falling out. He still thought Lance could beat you."

He seems to have something else on his mind. I can guess what it is.

"I was telling the truth about Williams. I had nothing to do with his death."

He meets my eyes, taking measure, considering the person he sees here and the person he helped in Denver. "I believe you. You may be hotheaded and arbitrary, but you tell the truth."

I smile. "That again? You still believe what Warren Williams told you about me?"

He laughs. "More than ever. You challenged one of the thirteen. I've seen it firsthand."

There's something different about Turnbull. Something I hadn't noticed before for obvious reasons. I was facing a fight to the death. Now, however, I know exactly what it is. When I saw him in Denver, his hair was darker and his build was different—thicker through the middle. A disguise technique he used so he could stay in his home in Durango. A new look for each generation.

"Hey, you've lost weight!"

He laughs. "Didn't need the body padding here. It's a relief to be rid of it for a while."

We lapse into silence. I wonder if I should try to reach Frey on his cell. Let him know I'm still among the living—so to speak. The evening isn't over yet, though. Maybe I'd better wait until it is.

Turnbull sits with me. At first, we don't speak. Neither of us opens our thoughts to the other, but I'm not uncomfortable with it. After a few minutes, though, my mind turns back to a familiar theme, and it occurs to me that Turnbull may be the only one willing or able to answer the hundred questions I have about what just happened.

I'm not sure how to begin, but asking, "Turnbull, what exactly am I?" seems as good a place as any.

He raises his eyebrows. "What do you mean?"

"The Chosen One. How did it come to be? Who chose me? Why? Before becoming vampire, I was a single woman from an upper-middle-class background. I had—have—a loving family. I work an unconventional job, sure, but what qualities elevated me to the head of a tribunal of the most powerful creatures on earth? Everyone is sure of *what* I am, no one can tell me *why*."

Turnbull shakes his head, and I have the sinking feeling he's not going to be any more help than Frey.

"You don't know, either, do you?"

"I'm sorry, Anna," he says. "There isn't much I can tell you. It's like any belief passed down from one generation to the next. There are forces at work beyond the realm of our understanding. I suppose the *reason* there is a Chosen One is pretty obvious. If vampires were allowed to run roughshod over humanity, the world would erupt in chaos. I have to believe that whoever or whatever is behind the grand design recognized this. It placed the burden of decision making on the shoulders of one. How that one is determined is a mystery. But that *you* are the one was recognized by Avery immediately. And by many others who came in contact with you before this gathering made it official."

"How are the tribal heads picked then? How were you picked?"

He smiles. "At last a question I can answer. There is a right of succession. Avery picked me as his successor just as he was picked centuries ago. It's the first duty of a tribal head, to pick one to come after him."

"And have you? Picked a successor?"

"Not yet. It would have been Warren Williams." A shadow passes over his face. "You never told me who is responsible for his second death."

"It was a sorcerer. Julian Underwood. He has paid. He is dead."

Turnbull releases a breath.

We are silent for a few moments before I ask, "What happened to the last Chosen One?"

I expect the answer to be obvious. Staked or beheaded. Turnbull raises his shoulders. "I don't know. I didn't think to ask. This is my first gathering, too. Would you like me to find out? Among these old souls, I'm sure someone has the answer."

"No." There's no hesitation in my reply. "I think I'd rather not know what fate has in store for me."

CHAPTER 48

WHEN THE DOORS OPEN AGAIN AND THE TWELVE file in to take their seats, it's obvious how they spent their hour. The smell, the heat radiating from vampire bodies only warmed by feeding and sex fills the room like some exotic incense. I have a mental image of the human hosts in the other room lying sated and replete, the detritus of a Roman orgy.

Turnbull asks petitioners to rise and present their requests. There are only two. Chael and Brianna, the female from Australia. Chael waves Brianna to go first.

Brianna is a small woman, compactly built, with a ruddy complexion and curly red hair. She looks to be in her thirties, which is to say, she was in her thirties when she was turned. I have no idea how long she has been vampire. She has handed her petition to Turnbull, who in turn passes it to me.

I don't bother to look at it. *Tell me,* I say.

She glances to Turnbull. *As he mentioned at the beginning of this gathering, I am here because of the death of the one before me, Aiden. He was in the six hundred fortieth year of the second life. He was a benevolent man, well loved by those in our community. He should not have been taken from us.*

Her thoughts falter as she is caught in a wave of emotion.

By the hand of a Revenger, was it not? I prompt gently.

I want to move things along. I want to go home. Weariness has been a constant companion for the last few days, and it threatens to swamp me now. Both physically and mentally, I am exhausted. I'm not sure how much longer I can keep my thoughts hidden from the constant prying of thirteen powerful, probing and inquisitive onlookers.

Still, I wait for Brianna to gather herself and continue. At last, she does, with a small bow. *My apologies. Aiden was more than a friend and mentor to me. We were lovers, sealed for the last two hundred years. So it is of particular importance to me that I be allowed to avenge his death.*

I sit up a little straighter. *It is a dangerous thing to mount an attack against a Revenger. It risks unleashing consequences far more disastrous to the community at large than what might be gained by punishing one responsible for the death of a loved one.*

I agree. You are correct. It is not against a Revenger, though I would not hesitate to kill Aiden's murderer if the opportunity arose. No, it is against a werewolf. The Alpha Male of a group that hunts in the forest near my home in Brisbane. He is the one who told the Revengers that Aiden walked daily in the forest. He is the one who orchestrated the ambush.

And you have proof?

He brags about it. He was angry because Aiden was protective of the forest and forbade his pack to hunt there. Now he does so with impunity because he thinks there will be no consequence. We who have been long on the earth need to protect what is here from those who have no respect for nature. This Alpha would kill every living creature for sport.

I'm as much impressed by her vehement defense of the forest as I am by her passion for her lost love. I wonder if I will ever form that kind of attachment.

But I can't base my decision on her declaration of love. Love is too often deceptive and illusory.

What does this Alpha do when he is not in wolf form?

Brianna looks confused by the question. *What does he do?*

Is he a teacher? Does he have a family? Is he known as a good man in the community?

Does that matter? Her voice takes on a hard edge. *He killed one of us. Aiden cries out for retribution. I demand it.*

Brianna's façade of bereaved lover slips a little as her anger surfaces. It allows me a moment to penetrate her mental barrier, see the truth that flares and is suppressed in the time it takes for our hearts to beat once, twice.

I block out everyone else and send her a message. *It was not the werewolf who betrayed Aiden. I saw the truth in your heart. It was you. I don't know why. I don't know why you came before us today with this story. I can only imagine you have some grievance against the wolf. Or you wish to make him a scapegoat. Withdraw your petition, and I will let your deception go unpunished. Pursue it, and I will make sure the others know that you are responsible for the death of an ancient.*

Brianna's eyes lock with mine. She wants to argue, test me. She glances away, toward Chael, perhaps sharing with him what I said to her. It doesn't matter. For the moment at least, I am the one in control.

At last her shoulders relax, her expression softens. Her communication is open to all.

Perhaps I have been too hasty. That the wolf bragged

about his part in Aiden's death was told to me second-hand. I will withdraw my petition until I have proof.

She steps back and returns to her seat.

I release a breath and sit back a little in mine.

Too easy. Was this some kind of test of my psychic powers? A demonstration to warn the next petitioner to guard his thoughts more closely? Did I make a mistake in keeping Brianna's deception private? Was the concession interpreted as weakness rather than compassion?

Fuck.

There is so much I don't understand.

Chael's eyes watch, his lips pressed in a grim smile. He is savoring my confusion, and I know the farce with Brianna was orchestrated. He sees me as gullible and weak.

And he is next.

CHAPTER 49

CHAEL WASTES NO TIME GETTING TO HIS FEET. He has no written petition. He faces me squarely, feet apart, hands at his side. His face is composed. He must have been in his early twenties when he was turned, his Middle Eastern ancestry evident in his dusky complexion and angular features. He is powerful, of that I have no doubt, but I remind myself that he is also a coward. He refused to face me when I challenged him.

He searches my face, trying to find vulnerability. I wave a hand at him to begin.

The decision you made barring Brianna from avenging the death of Aiden shows us how inappropriate it is that you have assumed this position of power. You continue to place the welfare of lesser beings above those of your own kind. For centuries, we have been relegated to the shadows. Like the First who walked the earth, we are still creatures of the night.

He pauses, as if waiting for me to argue. I have no intention of debating him. *Do you have a point you wish to make?*

A spark of temper blazes hot and fierce before he smothers it. He smoothes the anger from his face and continues. *My point is that we are the most powerful creatures on earth. We are stronger than any mortal. We will be here long after man has destroyed himself. But if mankind is allowed to rule and ultimately destroys itself, our food source is gone and we perish as well. We should be guardians, protectors of the earth from those like Brianna's wolf and from those mortals who threaten the future because they cannot see past the puny span of their lives.*

A pretty speech. What is it you are proposing?

I am proposing what is our right. It is time we seize control.

I see. And how would you do that?

He gestures to the circle. *We represent every corner of the globe. Thousands of vampires exist in our communities. We have already assumed positions of power in many places. We can form alliances to increase our control. We can become what we are destined to be—rulers over all.*

Excitement shines from his face and eyes. His body trembles with the zeal of a religious fanatic at an old-time revival. He is serious.

I glance at the others. Some are caught up in Chael's passion. They flash teeth and fist.

Others are hesitant, watching me, waiting to see my reaction before revealing their own.

I shake my head, slowly, deliberately.

Yes, Chael, you are correct when you say I am new to the vampire existence. However, no matter how long I exist on this earth, I will never agree to a plan that relegates mortals to nothing more than a link in the food chain. Even if such a thing were possible, which I seriously doubt considering there are seven billion people on earth, an in-

surrection such as you propose would do nothing except incite violence against us.

I pause a moment, thinking of Frey. *I have a good friend who is a Keeper of the accumulated knowledge of otherworldly creatures. There have been attempts made to eradicate us many times in history. I do not want to see a new crusade launched against us.*

Chael listens, his body tense, his expression black. *What has happened before has no relevance now. We would strike first at the Revengers and any others organized against us. We would wipe out the opposition, ruthlessly, make them examples for the rest. I tell you, mankind will fall easily because most are weak and cowardly. We will turn those who are strong and add them to our ranks. When it is done, humans will live in compounds to service our needs—both as food and as servants. They will be treated humanely. More humanely than they treat each other, and the earth we all inhabit will thrive as it did in the garden.*

Wow. He does know how to make a point. My immediate response comes from the human, the practical Anna. Chael failed in his attempt to orchestrate an attack on me, whom he finds so easy to belittle. How does he think he can wage war against humans, who outnumber us by billions, in the open, with all the technology of war at their disposal?

The idea of my family being relegated to a gulag is loathsome. When I look at the faces gathered round me, I realize I am the only vampire with relatives still living. The only one with strong ties to the human community.

For the first time, a glimmer of understanding.

Maybe that's why I'm the one sitting in this chair.

I gather my thoughts, knowing now how to answer him.

I agree we need to preserve the earth. We will be here long after present generations have passed to dust. But we need to do it as guardians of humanity, not wardens.

We are integrating into society. We must continue on that path, working with mortals. There may come a day when we need no longer hide our true nature. But it's not today.

Chael bares his teeth and shakes a fist at me. *You think me arrogant. I say, it is you who are arrogant. A new vampire who has barely seen thirty mortal years. You have no knowledge of what has come before. You are not worthy to tell those of us gathered here what is in our best interest. We could strike you down and be done with it.*

A gasp goes up from those gathered around us. Even those who grudgingly acknowledged my position after the challenge shrink back into their seats as if distancing themselves from Chael. He sees it. The tradition of the Chosen One is sacrosanct, and he has crossed a dangerous line.

Turnbull rises. *You are out of order, Chael.*

I wave Turnbull back to his seat. *I will answer Chael. He is right that I do not have centuries of experience to draw upon. But listening to you makes me understand why I may have been chosen to sit in this chair. I have not forgotten the urgency of a limited, mortal life. I still sense among mortals the basic urge to seek wisdom and do good. I look around and see what man has achieved. They have built the cities we vampires merely inhabit. They have created engineering marvels, split the atom and explored the heavens. And still you give them no credit.*

What have vampires created? Our unbounded lives seem to have made us shallow and hedonistic. We lack the wisdom of mortals because we lack the urgency to create and innovate that burns in mortals because of their "puny life spans." Mortals don't need us. We need them. You forget that we are the parasites. Herd them into pens like cattle and you will destroy their spirit. Then the world will be a dull gray place and we will suffer for it.

You have made it clear that in spite of your age, you have not gained wisdom. You have not said one thing to convince me that unbounded life has made you anything but conceited and contemptuous of those you consider beneath you. You would not make a good ruler, Chael. And that is reason enough for me to reject your petition.

There is a moment when the stillness in the room becomes tangible. One can taste it on the back of the throat like the pungent smoke of a cheap cigar.

All eyes are on Chael. He is a storm cloud threatening to unleash his fury with a roar of thunder.

His eyes are on me. He locks on, boring into my head, trying to penetrate my defenses. A mind game to save face. He wants to inflict pain, make me suffer, force me to acknowledge that while I may be the Chosen One, he is the stronger.

I have faced his kind before. Learned to resist attacks on my mind as I have attacks on my body. Avery, Williams and Underwood. The witch Belinda Burke. I learned painfully from the best.

I stand up so our eyes are level. I hurl his own power back at him. He is surprised, first, then determined. He has had centuries to perfect the technique, he reaches deep into himself, gathering strength, preparing for the final assault.

He means to bring me to my knees because he knows he has no argument to match my own.

But his attempt is broken, not by me, by Turnbull.

He steps between us, turns a snarling face on Chael.

You overstep, Chael. As one of the thirteen, you are sworn to abide by the decisions of the Chosen One.

But she is ignorant, a female too young to understand.

A female who survived the challenge. Survived your challenger, in point of fact. She has proven herself worthy to lead, and she has made her decision.

I cannot accept—

You refuse, and you are banished from the council, stripped of your title. Another will be appointed to take your place. Is that what you want?

Chael drops his eyes. *What I want I cannot have. I will accept the decision. But I invoke another right. The right to reconvene the council. Later. When all have had a chance to reconsider.*

He looks at me when he says the last words. I read the true meaning in his eyes. Chael will reconvene the council when I am no longer a part of it. When he has killed me.

Or tried.

CHAPTER 50

WONDERFUL. I HAVE MADE YET ANOTHER ENemy.

Chael returns to his place in the circle. Turnbull waits for the tension to dissipate. It does, to be replaced by disappointment. Disappointment that Chael and I will not do battle. Disappointment that there will be no more bloodshed, at least not here and not now.

But there is something else, as well. The eyes on me have a new respect. Not that I don't doubt battle lines may still be drawn, alliances forged. There is discreet acknowledgment passing one to the other that the subject is not closed just as there is acknowledgment that I am a force to be reckoned with.

Turnbull allows a moment to pass, then asks, "Are there any other petitioners?"

A murmur of negative replies, a shaking of heads.

"Then I declare this convocation closed." He moves deliberately to the library door and holds it open.

The tribal heads file out. All approach and offer their

hands to me. They bow, a symbol of respect, bound by a centuries-old tradition they are not ready to challenge. Had Chael been triumphant, I have no doubt it would have been to him they'd be offering their allegiance.

At last, Turnbull and I find ourselves alone once more in the library.

"Was that as much of a disaster as I think?" I ask.

"You didn't win them all over. But you won their respect. You presented a thoughtful and intelligent argument. Very un-Anna-like."

He sounds surprised. I feel myself smiling.

"Thoughtful and intelligent? Not words I hear very often ascribed to me. Hotheaded and arbitrary. Now that's more the norm."

He laughs. "I did say that, didn't I?"

"Just a little while ago."

I sit down in one of the chairs, motion Turnbull to join me. He does.

"To be frank, I don't know where those words came from, Turnbull. It's as if there was something—a spirit—speaking through me."

He lifts a hand. "Maybe there was. Maybe that's what makes you the Chosen One. You see the world as it is as well as what it can be."

I smile again. "You know, I like you more now than when we met in Denver."

"Different set of circumstances. Frankly, I was concerned about the purpose of your visit. I was afraid I'd be cleaning up your mess long after you left."

"Fair enough. I had no idea how things would work out, either. Do you ever see Sophie Deveraux?"

I ask the question casually. When I killed her sister, the lines of communication between us were cut.

Turnbull is shaking his head. "No. She doesn't leave the estate very often. She has a group of vampires living with her. The rumor is they don't possess true vampiric powers. It's a strange story."

And a true one. The vampires were created by her sister for one purpose—their blood. The image of how I found them still makes me shudder.

I don't share the story with Turnbull. It's one best left between Sophie and me. Nor do I tell him that Sophie has another secret—she shares her body with a vampire. She accidentally absorbed his essence when an experiment using immolated vampire ash went bad. Now they coexist if not easily, at least comfortably. His name was Jonathan Deveraux, and I suspect Turnbull would have known him. He may even have been at the party where the "accident" took place.

"Well, if you do see her, tell her I send my best. I'm very grateful for the help she gave me."

I let a moment pass before asking, "So. What happens now?"

Turnbull shrugs. "You're done here. Unless you want to join the party in the living room."

"Is it necessary that I do?"

"No. In fact, it may be better if you don't. Without your presence, Chael may let his guard down and tell us what he has up his sleeve."

"I thought my ruling was final. Can he really bring us back together again?" I say "us" knowing full well he doesn't intend I be a part of a new council.

Turnbull seems to know it, too. "It is his right. Especially if the makeup of the group changes in any significant way."

No subtlety there.

"So this thing about meeting once every two hundred years . . . ?"

A shrug. "In the last thousand years, the council has only convened five times as prescribed by ancient law. But in the last two hundred years, circumstances in the world have changed drastically. Most now believe two hundred years is too long between councils. The Grimoire provides for any tribal member to convene a council if the circumstances warrant."

He continues. "That's why I believe it wise for you to leave, Anna. Alone, I am in a better position to learn the truth. And to alert you of their plans."

I press fingertips against my weary eyes. "Then I will go. There is one other piece of business, though. Will you please give Judith Williams a message? I would like all files pertaining to Avery's estate sent to me. I never wanted anything to do with it, but I'll be damned if I let her take over. I want to sever all ties between the Williams' family and myself."

Turnbull nods his understanding. "It will be done."

He walks me to the front door. One last glance into the living room before I leave imprints an image I'm sure will prove to be a portent of things to come.

Judith Williams and Chael. Huddled together alone near the fireplace, their heads bent in conversation, their backs to the room.

Why do I have the feeling my troubles have just begun?

AFTERWORD

I COULDN'T GO TO THE BAR WHEN I LEFT THE HOUSE. I called Frey, gave him the all-clear signal, some sketchy details about what had transpired. I know he has a million questions, but something in my voice must have betrayed my weariness because he didn't press. I asked him to call Culebra, tell him I survived, and he said he would.

The next day, I met with Tracey. I told her David would be in but asked that she not repeat our conversation. I admitted there was no "game," that I wasn't in a position to explain and that the situation was complicated. A nice catchphrase.

Instead of challenging me, she looked me straight in the eye. "Okay. For now. But I know you aren't what you seem. I can be patient. You need to trust me. You will."

Somehow, I believe it.

David came in, still sore, still wondering what happened during his "blackout." He told Tracey about his "accident," and she listened to him with wide-eyed attention and said she was glad he wasn't hurt more seriously. She didn't even wink at me.

She lies almost as well as I do.

We had a skip to trace, so we got to it.

I felt back in my element for the first time in a while.

This is where I want to be. This is where I belong. I know I haven't begun to realize the ramifications of being the Chosen One. But for now, I've survived. My first year as a vampire. My first challenge from the council. My family is safe. My friends close.

Not a bad way to start a new year.